If the
BOOT FITS

By Rebekah Weatherspoon

If the Boot Fits

A Cowboy to Remember

If the
BOOT FITS

**REBEKAH
WEATHERSPOON**

Kensington Publishing Corp.
www.kensingtonbooks.com

DAFINA BOOKS are published by

Kensington Publishing Corp.
119 West 40th Street
New York, NY 10018

All Kensington Titles, Imprints, and Distributed Lines are available at special quantity discounts for bulk purchases for sales promotions, premiums, fund-raising, and educational or institutional use. Special book excerpts or customized printings can also be created to fit specific needs. For details, write or phone the office of the Kensington special sales manager: Kensington Publishing Corp., 119 West 40th Street, New York, NY 10018, attn: Special Sales Department, Phone: 1-800-221-2647.

Dafina and the Dafina logo Reg. U.S. Pat. & TM Off.

ISBN-13: 978-1-4967-2541-7
ISBN-10: 1-4967-2541-7
First Kensington Mass Market Edition: November 2020

ISBN-13: 978-1-4967-2544-8 (ebook)
ISBN-10: 1-4967-2544-1 (ebook)

10 9 8 7 6 5 4 3 2 1

Printed in the United States of America

If the
BOOT FITS

Chapter 1

Amanda McQueen opened her eyes and immediately closed them again.

The night before must have been a dream. There was no way her friend and rising A-list actress Helene Sawyer had scored her an invite to the Vanity Fair Oscar party. There's no way she'd let her tag along to Kata and Rina's A-list after-party. There was absolutely no freaking way she'd run into Samuel Pleasant at both events, and surely you'd be joking if you told her that sometime in the night she and Sam had completely hit it off. And that somehow he'd asked her back to his hotel room. She'd call you a bold-faced liar—to your face—if you even hinted at the idea that Amanda and Sam had slept together and that the sex had been top tier, mind-blowing even.

No. There was no way any of that had happened.

But then how did Amanda explain to herself how she'd woken up, still very naked and aroused, tangled in high-thread-count hotel sheets with now Oscar-winning actor Sam Pleasant? If she wasn't afraid of making any sudden movements she'd pinch herself. His arm was still draped over her, his fingers resting on her breast. Slowly she turned her head and looked over at him, the dim light coming from the small part in the blackout curtains making it just bright enough to see. Sam was still very much asleep, snoring softly, his dark brown cheek pressed against the white pillow.

His skin was amazing, Amanda thought as she took in the dark lashes brushing those cheeks. She could spend all day looking at him and another night as well. Too bad she had to be at work in exactly ninety minutes. She didn't need to look at her phone to see what time it was. Amanda woke up every single morning twenty minutes before her alarm. Call it peak readiness. She took pride in her work and the lessons both her parents had taught her. On time was late. And now, she was definitely going to be late.

Okay. First thing, extract yourself from the bed without waking Sam up. Then flee from his hotel room before you have a chance to exchange another word. They'd agreed, no names. As if she didn't know who he was, but when he'd asked her name in the middle of her enthusiastic rendition of the cha-cha slide, she'd played it cool.

"Sorry, I can't hear you. I'm dancing," she'd said. He'd laughed. They'd danced some more and more, until it was time to go their separate ways. Or so she'd thought. It wasn't until she'd gotten off the elevator and found him waiting right where he said he'd be, right outside of room 1020, that she'd realized this thing between them was actually happening. No, it wasn't until he'd asked if it was okay if he kissed her, that he'd been wanting to all night, ever since she'd made that crack about doing the breaststroke through a chocolate fountain. (Listen, it was her first night out in almost six months and some very nice woman named Lisa had done a great job on her makeup. She was feeling a little peppy and loose.)

That kiss though, the soft slowness of it that had somehow managed to work its way through the pulsing excitement of the night and of Sam's Oscar win, she'd felt something in that kiss. It had been the only reason she'd shimmied out of the sparkling gold and silver romper that she'd scored from the Forever 21 plus-size section. The only reason she'd been glad she was still carrying the emergency condoms she always did on her boss's behalf. That kiss had only been proof that Sam Pleasant knew exactly how to treat a woman. He wasn't too bad at the sex part either.

But none of that mattered now, because she had to be standing at the foot of her boss's bed in exactly eighty-seven minutes.

Amanda glanced toward the floor and calculated just how loud of a thud she'd make if she rolled off the bed. Her mental math told her that would be the quickest way to wake Sam up. Slow and easy would be the way to go.

Carefully, oh so carefully, she eased to the side, pointing her foot toward the ground. When her toes made contact with the carpet, she gently lifted Sam's hand and eased out from under his arm. She set his fingers in the warm spot she'd left behind, then quietly sat up and stood before pulling the covers back over his shoulders. She froze when he sniffed a bit, then rubbed his nose. Her heart started beating again when he rolled over and settled deeper into the sheets.

She quickly but quietly began to search the room for her things. Her jeans and shirt were back at Helene's house up in the Hills. She'd have to worry about that later. She grabbed her sequin jumpsuit and her silver strappy sandals, then slipped into the bathroom, dressing in record time. Her bladder was screaming, but there was no way she could risk flushing the toilet. And she sure as hell wasn't going to be the nasty ass who peed in Sam Pleasant's hotel room and didn't flush. She telegraphed the message to her bladder, *just wait five more minutes*, then she checked her face in the mirror. Thank God her makeup was barely smudged.

Normally she was good at being invisible. Every Hollywood assistant had mastered the skill—ever present, but never seen, never heard, and definitely never photographed. She hoped being Black, a size twenty, and not at all famous would reduce the chances of anyone noticing her walk of shame. Or should she say, strut of triumph? She'd definitely had sex with Sam Pleasant and that was worth celebrating. In any event, smudged makeup would attract someone's attention. For now she was just your average Oscar night partygoer on their way home. With eighty-five minutes to spare before she had to be at work.

She crept back into the room and grabbed her clutch off the hotel desk, then grabbed the swag bag she'd received from the only post-award-show gifting suite Helene had managed to sneak her into. No way Amanda was leaving that behind. She'd investigate the full extent of her spoils once she got home. She did one final visual sweep of the room, then fled into the morning.

In the elevator she called for a Lyft. Jerod was five minutes away.

In the lobby things were still quiet. No one but people like Amanda woke up this early, the first-shifters who got other people's days started for them. Amanda would be lying if she said she didn't find a little thrill in it. Yeah, the work was thankless, but often she was the first to witness so many things. Things she couldn't talk about, but still, she was always in the know.

She used the restroom, then stepped out into the predawn morning just as Jerod pulled up to the curb in front of the W Hotel.

"Fun night?" he asked as she buckled her seat belt,

"It was a great night. Thank you."

"Well, let's get you home."

Fifteen minutes later, they pulled up to her place in Beverly Hills. Technically it was Beverly Hills, but not the rich, fancy, big mansion part most people thought of when they pictured the famous zip code, and the adorable cottage facing the street definitely wasn't hers. She lived in the back. She tipped Jerod in the app, then hurried inside. She had just enough time to shower and shovel down a quick breakfast before she got on with her day.

She threw a frozen breakfast burrito in the microwave, fixed her triangle braids up in a high topknot, then hopped under the hot spray, where she scrubbed the night off her face. Quick lotion up and wardrobe change and she was almost ready to go.

She flopped down on her bed to pull on her Converse and accidentally knocked her after-party gift bag to the floor. It landed with a sickening thud that she was sure had dented the old hardwood floors. She picked up the bag and glanced inside, just to make sure her brand-new bits of expensive swag were okay.

And that's when she realized her mistake.

She'd grabbed the wrong bag.

There was an iPhone in its crisp white box. Beside it was another box and beside *that* was a pristine Oscar statue.

"No, no, no, no, noooo." Amanda carefully pulled the beautiful golden knight out of the bag and examined the envelope that had been lying beneath it.

Best Performance by an Actor
in a Supporting Role,
Samuel Pleasant, *The Sky Beneath Our Feet*

"Oh my gosh. No!" This was not the time to panic, but of course she was panicking. She had to get the award back to Sam or Sam's team, and she had to do it now.

Amanda fell back on the bed and googled frantically, looking for the name of Sam's agent. She knew everyone who represented everyone in prime-time TV, but film stars were not her area of expertise. Not while her boss Dru Anastasia was still employed in the world of teen paranormal dramas. It took a few clicks and swipes, but she managed to find it. John Coffey at TCA. He shared an agency with Helene. Great. She swiped over to JackRabbit, the courier app she used at least twice a day, and scheduled a pickup for right outside Dru's apartment building on Sunset. Hopefully, Sam was a late sleeper and the missing statue would be back in the right hands before he wondered where she'd gone.

With the pickup confirmed, she packed her bag for the day, making sure she didn't forget Sam's swag bag or his award, and hurried out to her midsize SUV parked out on the street.

Traffic and the parking gods were on her side. She made it to Delightly, Dru's favorite restaurant, and found an empty meter right in front. She ducked in and grabbed Dru's breakfast, then booked it over to her apartment building on the west end of the Sunset Strip. She had to park two blocks away, but if she power walked at just the right speed she would be two minutes early. Dru didn't like to see her sweat.

She made it to the front door just as the JackRabbit driver pulled up. She handed off the heavy swag bag as soon as he rolled down the window of the white Prius.

"Please, please, please. Get this to the receptionist and tell her it's for John Coffey. Samuel Pleasant's Oscar statue is in there. He lost it last night. He *needs* to get it back," she said, giving him a meaningful look. There was no room for error in this delivery or both their heads would roll.

"Oh shit," he said, his eyes popping wide with horror. "Okay, got it. I'll make sure I walk it right into her. Don't worry. I'll make sure she gets it."

"Thank you."

A smile forced her panic away as she watched him buckle the bag into the passenger seat beside him. He nodded to her with a little salute of his fingers and then pulled a U-turn back on to the street. She sent up a prayer for a safe delivery, then snapped back into work mode.

She headed to the front door and waved at the handsome face she saw through the thick glass doors. Francesco, the doorman, buzzed her in.

"Good morning, my Amanda," he said with his warm accent as she nudged her way inside with her elbow. He was from New Jersey and his real name was Eric, but the tenants didn't need to know that. The Italian lie seemed fancier. His secret was safe with her though.

"Good morning, my love. What's the news?" she asked as she walked to the elevator. It was their little game. Fake headlines by Francesco.

"Hollywood starlet plummets to her death after heated affair ends in tragedy."

"Oh no!" Amanda said dramatically. "Give me something more upbeat tomorrow."

"I'm sorry, my dear. Only sunshine for you from now on."

Amanda winked at him just as the elevator chimed. Five stories above, she quietly let herself into Dru Anastasia's apartment. As she made her way into the kitchen, Gus, Dru's woefully neglected Ragdoll cat, emerged from behind the island and wove his way between her feet.

"Hello, my precious. I didn't forget about you." She grabbed a can of wet food from under the counter and fed the sweet creature whose body mass was 90 percent fur.

When Amanda moved to LA five years ago she was determined to make it as a screenwriter, but that's the thing about dreams. They rarely work out the way you want them to. She tried to work her way into a writers' room, but something was always off. A job promised suddenly taken away, a project canceled. She'd gotten work as a production assistant and after a particularly bad day on set had her reconsidering her whole West Coast adventure, she'd met Kaidence Kener. She'd remembered her vaguely from her own brief run on the nineties beach drama *Bay Guards*. Her acting days were long behind her, but her daughter Dru was just getting started and Dru needed an assistant.

Amanda had told herself the job would just be temporary, a paycheck to keep a roof over her head and food in her stomach. She made a promise to herself that she wouldn't give up on her writing. And she hadn't. She stole whatever moments she could, jotting down bits and pieces on her phone and on her tablet. She'd finished two more screenplays in that time, but this gig, it had turned out to be anything but temporary. Somehow, she'd become Dru's

Girl Monday thru Saturday and definitely on Sundays if they were traveling. Kaidence put her to work whenever she felt Amanda was idle, organizing her closet or researching new avenues for Dru to explore on social media.

The money was good and it covered her health insurance, but it wasn't her dream. One day she'd move on. She just wasn't sure when or how.

Her phone vibrated as she set Dru's breakfast out on her favorite bamboo serving tray. She pulled it out of her pocket and looked at the text from Helene.

> I know you're working but text me as soon as you can. Ignacio said you he thinks you left with someone. I need deets!

Helene added an eggplant, a water-squirting, and a peach emoji, in that order. Amanda covered her snort, then slipped her phone back into her pocket. She grabbed the tray, then carried it into Dru's darkened room.

"Nnhgggg," Dru groaned as she covered her head with her pillow.

"Good morning."

Dru sat up and tossed her pillow across the room. There were still a dozen more on the bed to keep her comfortable. "What's so good about it?" she snapped.

"Oh, you sound so much better."

"And you're too fucking cheery. Dial it back like five notches, will you." Dru rubbed her eyes, then grabbed the remote for her curtains. Sunlight flooded the room.

"Happiness keeps you healthy and I need to be healthy for you," Amanda said. She was absolutely joking, but she knew her sickly sweet personality drove Dru crazy. Killing her slowly with kindness was part of her retirement plan.

She set down the tray on Dru's wide night table. "Here's your breakfast when you're ready. If you're feeling up to it, Sage will meet you at the yoga studio in thirty minutes or I can call her and cancel."

"No. I need to go. I've been in bed too long. My muscles are going to atropy."

"Atrophy."

"Whatever, you knew what I meant."

"And I think it takes a little longer than a weekend for that to happen. I'll text her and let her know you're on your way."

"Gee thanks, you're the best, Mandy," Dru said sarcastically, knowing full well how much she hated that nickname. Amanda let the insult slide off her back because she knew what came next. Dru pulled her soft purple blanket up to the bottom of her chin. "Tell the whole truth. Do I look that bad?"

"You look beautiful," Amanda replied, and it was the truth. Dru's stunning natural beauty was the thing that landed her on three successful television dramas back-to-back, a nearly unfathomable feat for a young Black actress in Hollywood, even if she was light skinned with green eyes. Currently she played an intergalactic vampire queen on the show *Andromeda*. Her character, Kalexa, was known throughout more than one universe for her stunning gaze and luscious lips. This morning, however, Her Majesty looked a little rough. Whatever bug had knocked her on her ass had done a number on her. Her edges could use a little control and her lips were dry, but most people would kill to look like Dru Anastasia even with a few bags under their eyes.

"I'd brush my teeth and throw in some lip gloss before I posted any selfies, but you're still a ten."

"Thanks. Please get out of my room."

"Sure."

Amanda grabbed the pile of dirty clothes off the floor and carried them down to the laundry room before she went to hop on her morning call with Kaidence. Sam's laugh popped into her head as she made her way down to the other end of the apartment. She smiled to herself, thinking about the way he'd kissed her, the way he'd felt on top of her.

Today it didn't matter how nasty Dru was or how many absurd tasks Kaidence threw her way. For one night, she'd gotten to be *that girl,* not just a D-list actress's lowly assistant. The night she'd spent with Sam Pleasant might carry her to the end of the year. Or at least until the Teen Choice Awards.

Chapter 2

Sam Pleasant couldn't remember the last time he'd woken up with a smile on his face. Today his mood before he even opened his eyes could only be described as good as fuck. He could still hear the sound of her laugh over the thumping music, feel her soft skin as his fingers trailed down her wrist. He stretched with a sigh, then rolled over to see if he could interest his new lady friend in some room service and possibly round two before they both started their day.

But of course she was gone. What did he expect from a post-award-show one-night hookup? Not that there was anything wrong with the one and done, but he'd had such a good time with her—even before they'd made it back to the hotel—he'd already made up his mind that he wanted to see her again.

Disappointment flooded through him as he looked at the empty side of the bed, now cold like he hadn't spent the night with one of the most beautiful girls he'd ever laid eyes on. He glanced around the room, hoping to spot a note or something, but all he saw was his Gucci suit placed over the hotel room chair. He smiled again, knowing full well who had set it there. He had vivid memories of dropping it on the floor piece by piece as he and Cha-Cha made their way to the bed.

He'd called her Cha-Cha in his head all night. But now he wished he'd gotten her real name. And her number. It didn't have to be a *thing*, but . . . he didn't want it to be over just yet.

Apparently, she didn't feel the same way. Sam tried to shake off the rejection as he stood and made his way to the bathroom. He found his boxer briefs under the cover at the foot of the bed, then checked his phone. It flooded with texts and calls. He let out a deep breath and scrubbed a hand over his face as he scrolled to the text messages from his assistant, Walls.

I'm up. You have a key?

Walls responded right away.

Yup got a key. I'll be right over.
I have your clothes and shit.

Bet. Thanks.

He switched back over to his text inbox. Looking over the congratulations and well wishes from friends and colleagues and castmates and a few unknown numbers, he still couldn't fucking believe it. He was now Oscar-winning actor Samuel Pleasant. He couldn't put the way he felt into words. He had another two years before he saw his thirtieth birthday, but he'd been working toward that golden statue his whole life.

When his agent had brought the script for *The Sky Beneath Our Feet* to him, Sam had had his doubts. The story of the first recorded slave revolt needed to be told. It was a part of America's history, his history, but like many other young Black actors, Sam was torn about telling another painful story of the Black experience. The part they wanted him for wasn't the lead, and the true event had also involved white indentured servants. Sam hadn't been sure if this was the right move for him.

He'd talked to his family about it, and had several long conversations with his older brothers Jesse and Zach, but the opinions that mattered to him the most were his father's and his grandmother's. His father had left their family business, Big Rock Ranch, in the capable hands of Sam's brothers to pursue his own acting career. His grandmother was the one and only, the incomparable Miss Leona Lovell. His grandma had nearly hit that EGOT before Sam was born and if anyone was equipped to give him career advice, it was her. They'd talked about the pros and cons, the timing, the money, and in the end he knew *The Sky Beneath* was the type of film that would generate some awards season buzz if not some actual nominations.

Either way, once he'd signed on the dotted line, he'd poured himself into the role of Josiah. He'd mentally prepared himself for how draining the work would be, trying to fully comprehend the horrors of chattel slavery and how hard this country tried to forget it. After they'd wrapped he'd gone back to Big Rock for months, just to get his mind right again. He'd never been more grateful for how hard his grandparents had worked to give their family everything, including a lucrative business that gave Sam the financial freedom to chase his passion.

The reviews were mixed. There were things audiences

and critics loved, but the main criticism was that it was just another white savior film. The box office numbers were good, but the nominations were even better. Acting, directing, and cinematography from every nominating body in the industry. Walking down the red carpet into the Dolby Theatre with his grandmother and his cousin Corie by his side had been more than memorable. Walking out of the theater with the golden statue? No way, man. No way that had been real. He still couldn't believe it. During the presser he thought he'd done a pretty good job of answering all the questions thoroughly and thoughtfully, but in the back of his mind he was still in disbelief. As the night had gone on and they'd moved from photo op to photo op and then on to the after-parties, he'd started to feel off. He'd won. He'd gotten exactly what he wanted, and yet . . .

Maybe the weight of his accomplishments hadn't sunk in yet. He was sure sometime soon, maybe later in the week, he'd finally understand that he'd knocked one hell of an item off his bucket list. For now though, it didn't feel the way he'd expected. When he'd rehearsed his acceptance speech, he'd thought sheer joy would be the main emotion to take over, but that hadn't happened at all. From the moment he'd heard his name fill the theater he'd been dealing with a low-grade panic attack. He hadn't had a chance to consider what the hell that was all about before he'd been whisked off to perform the rest of his duties as an award winner.

The pressure on his chest had lifted a little when he and Walls had ended up back in the limo. Walls had been determined to make him celebrate his win. Sam couldn't fight his infectiously boisterous demeanor. He'd snapped himself out of the strange haze that had come over him and focused on the night of partying before him. He hadn't realized he'd been going through the motions until he'd spotted *her* dancing, laughing, and smiling with her friends. Sam wasn't into that hotep shit, but there had been something about that girl's energy. In a room full of people trying to get close to him and the other winners, the other important names, it had been clear that she'd just come to have a good time.

When Sam had seen her again at Kata and Rina's afterparty, he'd known he had to say something. He hadn't been sure what the fuck he was gonna say when he'd crossed the room, but as soon as he opened his mouth, she'd solved that problem for him. Cha-Cha hadn't wanted to talk. She'd just wanted to dance. So they'd danced until it became clear that whatever had been happening between them needed to continue somewhere else. He'd seen the doubt in her eyes when he'd suggested she join him back at his hotel, but just as quickly the hesitation vanished and she'd taken over the plan as they made their way toward the exit: He should leave first and then she'd follow. Man, he'd been glad when she'd actually shown up instead of leaving him standing in the hotel hallway looking like a fool.

And then she'd dipped out sometime in the morning, never to be seen again.

Nah, Hollywood was a small town. He'd probably see her again, it was just a matter of when. He was pretty sure he'd seen her hanging around with Helene Sawyer, his costar from his breakout film, *Inferno*. *Wait until after her wedding*, he reminded himself. Helene was getting married at the ranch that upcoming weekend. He knew she had much more to worry about than his sex life.

He'd ask her after the reception.

Which reminded him. He dug back through his texts and found the messages his brothers had sent him during the ceremony. He'd called them quickly in the limo, but they didn't get to talk long.

Zach: CHECK OUT YA BOY!
WINNING OSCARS AND SHIT. WHAT
DID I TELL YOU!

Jesse: So proud of you. And you know granddad
would be over the moon.

Another wave of strange emotions crashed over him as he tried to think of a heartfelt response. He couldn't do it. Not over text. So he settled for their signature greeting.

It's the rock!

Zach: Yeah, mane!
We're throwing a big party for you as soon as
you get home.
So proud, man. So proud.

Thanks man.
I still can't believe it.

Jesse: Well believe it cause it's true.
You got your statue.

Sam sank down on the bed and let his head hang between his shoulders. His brain just wasn't processing. He'd really done it. He'd won an Academy Award.

A moment later, he heard the keycard lock engage and Walls came striding into the room.

"What's up, man? How you feeling? I got your breakfast."

Walls set a travel cup of coffee and a small pastry bag down on the table. Sam's ritual was always to eat whatever the fuck he wanted *after* a big event. He'd put in his order with Walls over a week ago. The biggest almond croissant he could find. At the moment though, he had no appetite.

"Pretty good, pretty good. I can't complain." Sam forced a smile and straightened up as Walls crossed his arms over his skinny chest.

"I'm real happy for you. For real. But I do have one question."

"Yeah? What's that?"

"You lose something last night?"

"No, I don't think so. Why?" Sam glanced down like he wasn't sitting there in his boxer briefs, then quickly glanced around the room. His suit, the phone, and his swag bag were all there. "What are you talking about?"

"A JackRabbit runner dropped off your statue over at TCA a few hours ago. Coffey's assistant has it."

"What?" Sam jumped up and crossed the room. He opened the swag bag that was still on the floor near the door. He searched through it and sure enough his Oscar statue wasn't in there. But there was a small, see-through makeup bag with some mints, lip gloss, and the extra condoms they hadn't used the night before.

"Shit. She must have taken it by accident."

"Who?"

"Uh—no one. Just—"

Walls slapped the table, then pointed right at Sam's chest. "I knew you went home with that chick last night!"

"What chick? I don't know what you're talking about?"

"Uh, the thick girl with the braids, all up like this," Walls said, gesturing above his head in a swirling motion. "Sparkly jumpsuit thing. I saw you watch her Milly Rock back from the bathroom."

"Oh, her! It wasn't like that."

"What was it like?"

"Listen. She's an old friend. We just wanted to catch up and it was loud in there. Couldn't hear my own damn thoughts."

"Old friend, huh? From Charming."

"Yeah, sure. That sounds about right."

"You're a dog, man. I hope you wrapped it up."

"I did. She came prepared." Sam's dates for the evening had been his elderly grandmother and his bi-flexible cousin. The last thing that had been on his mind was whether he would end the night with someone in his bed. Lesson learned. Always come prepared, no matter what.

"But for real, who was she?" Walls said as he walked toward the bed. He looked at the sheets for a moment, then headed for the love seat on the other side of the room. "I saw her talking to Kata for a sec, but the rest of the night she was crushing it on the dance floor. Big girl had moves," he laughed. He wasn't lying either. His mystery woman had some serious moves and some serious curves. Sam almost got hard thinking about it. Instead he cringed.

"I didn't get her name."

"Man, what?!"

"Yeah, yeah, I know." It wasn't like Sam to pull off the anonymous run-in. He was in his prime, but he'd always been a relationship guy. He wasn't ashamed of that fact. He was also fiercely private. He never stopped Walls from doing his thing, but his buddy knew when he joked about going out and using the Pleasant name to pick up girls, Sam wasn't really into it. He wasn't shy like Jesse, and he wasn't the former lady killer his brother Zach pretended not to be before he finally got back with his childhood sweetheart. He fell somewhere in the middle. He needed to get to know someone, establish a little something before he fell into bed with her. Also, falling into bed with random people in his line of work wasn't the best idea.

The way he'd broken his own rules and on such a public and important night was just proof of how off he'd been. But the more he thought about it he couldn't bring himself to regret it. He'd do his night with Cha-Cha all over again if he could just find her.

"You see who she came with?" he asked Walls. It wasn't a subtle question.

"No. I mostly saw her on the dance floor, then in the corner with you. But forget about her," Walls said. Sam knew that tone. Walls was scheming.

"Just say it."

"I'm just saying. There are plenty of other fish in the sea. And your DMs."

"Nah, I told you—"

"I know what you told me and I know you don't roll with randoms, but that was before you won an Oscar. You have some A-list talent hitting you up."

"Don't talk like that," Sam said, frowning. Not that it made him special or unique, but Sam's grandmother raised him to treat women a certain way and calling them names like *talent* didn't sit right with him. They were human beings with feelings and they deserved to be respected. Even if they had slid into his DMs looking to hook up.

"My bad. A few nice young ladies have made inquiries as to your relationship status," Walls said. "Think of it like this. You've been fucking sulking since you ended things with Natalie. Maybe now—"

"The fuck I have!"

"Oh, I'm sorry. You poured yourself back into your work. My bad, my bad."

"That's right." Okay, there had been sulking. He'd also met his ex Natalie Burke on the set of *Inferno*. Sam had hoped that over time things would progress, but after only two months she'd told her parents she was basically ready to get engaged, and Sam knew he had to end things. It wasn't that commitment wasn't on the table. He was pretty damn committed. It was the way she'd said it, over Christmas dinner, in front of most of her family, all while giving Sam this look like he had between then and New Year's to get his ass to Jared or he would be in big trouble. They hadn't even talked about marriage or what they wanted from a life together in the long term. So he'd ended it. Still it had taken him a while to get over her.

But no one else needed to know that.

"What's your point and don't be a pig about it."

"I was just saying, since you're in the big leagues now, and you clearly miss having a girlfriend, you should know that some interesting people have popped up in your DMs in the last twenty-four hours."

Sam rolled his eyes and flopped back onto the bed. He caught the faint hint of Cha-Cha's perfume as the sheets bounced around him. The way his stomach tightened made him think he should at least entertain Walls's stupid suggestion. "Like who?"

"Gemma Lopez for one."

"Try again."

"What?!" Walls laughed.

"She's like twelve."

"She's twenty-one."

"No. What else you got?"

"Dru Anastasia."

Sam sat up. "Hmmm."

"See?"

"But nah," Sam said, flopping back down again.

"What's wrong with her? She's fine as hell. And she's working working. *Andromeda* just got renewed. I love that show."

"I do too, but nah. She seems intense." Sam had only run into the young starlet once, but he remembered a brief interaction between her and her mom. It wasn't cute.

"Tanica Parry."

Sam had to pause there. "What she say?" Tanica Parry was a gorgeous action star on the rise. She was in the running for a *Charlie's Angels* reboot with Helene. And she was fine as fuck.

"I thought you didn't care."

"Listen. I just want to know the facts."

Walls snorted. "Are you going to call Tanica Parry?"

That made Sam pause, 'cause he knew the answer. "No."

"You're still thinking about ol' girl from last night."

"I am." Sam scrubbed a hand over his face again. "I can't believe I didn't get her name."

"If you want to get with her that badly, I'll ask around."

"You don't have to. I'll ask Helene this week."

"Imma snoop around anyway. You know I like to snoop."

"I do."

"In the meantime, maybe we should reunite you with your Oscar."

"Oh shit. Yeah."

"See, I know you're sprung on this girl. If I were you, I'd have taken that thing to bed with me. It wouldn't have left my sight."

Sam knew he should have felt the same way, but he

didn't. He'd posed for pictures kissing his award. Carried it around for photo ops, but as soon as he could he'd tucked it away in his bag. Still he knew he had to get it back because a week or maybe a month from now it would actually hit him that last night hadn't been a dream or some cruel joke, and he'd actually want to hold the thing. For now, he was still off his game, still out of sorts.

What the hell was he supposed to do next?

And why did finding this mystery girl suddenly feel more important?

Chapter 3

Amanda walked a little faster toward the makeup trailer, her bright orange umbrella patterned with tiny flamingos shielding her from the rain. A little less than a week had gone by and Amanda had fully settled back into her life as lowly servant, far from the glitz and glamour of award season. She stopped just near the steps, then reached up to grab the door latch just as Dru and Henrik, the production assistant holding the black umbrella over her head, made their way across the parking lot. Amanda loved the rain, especially in LA. It cleared the air, refreshed the earth. Made it a little easier to breathe, if only for a few hours. It was much better than filming in Atlanta, where Dru's last show had been on location. Amanda understood the producers had chosen Georgia for the tax breaks, but she did not miss the humidity.

"We'll see you on Monday," Henrik said as Dru stepped under Amanda's umbrella and up the stairs. Dru didn't respond.

"Thanks, Henrik," Amanda said.

"Hurry up," Dru grumbled.

"Oh, sorry." Amanda opened the door and followed her

inside where Dru's attitude immediately changed. She couldn't muster a single word for the production assistants, but Tally and Patience had been hired just to keep Dru happy. The wig the previous hair person had slapped on her had been dragged up and down the Internet for weeks, and Dru's mom had quietly raised hell until they brought in a Black woman who knew how to build and install a proper lace front. Tally was one of the best in the industry, and the studio learned pretty quickly that hiring her had been the right move. Everyone on the show was now sporting a sleeker head of hair, wig or natural. Since Kaidence got her way, Dru figured why not push for a makeup artist who understood how the camera picked up Dru's light brown skin tone without making her look oddly washed out.

Yes, Dru was playing a space vampire, but that was all the more reason for her to look amazing. Vampires in the next galaxy did not let their looks go. Tally and Patience made Dru look sexy as hell, and she was too smart to get on their bad side.

"Hi," Dru said bashfully as she shuffled toward Patience. Tally was busy taking down Dru's costar Webber's elaborate updo at the far end of the trailer.

"Hey, doll. You killed it out there today," Patience said, and she pulled Dru into a light hug.

"Thank you. It's not every day you have to banish your most loyal servants to a deserted outpost. It was a very emotional day."

"I bet it was. Have a seat and let's get you out of here."

Amanda brought over fresh bottled water and set it down at the station, then took the empty seat near the door. She had to finalize Dru's schedule for the next few days before she left for Helene's wedding.

She checked her email again, half paying attention as Webber started talking.

"It's so weird seeing people like that out in the wild. She's that glamorous. No makeup, nothing. She was an absolute ten."

"Who are we talking about?" Dru asked just as she popped her fake fangs out of her mouth. Amanda didn't miss the hint of jealousy in her voice.

"Helene Sawyer. I saw her last night grabbing takeout from Lux. It was a real Celebs Are Just Like Us moment."

"Oh, yeah," Dru said. It was a struggle for her to sound gracious. Even with years of professional training. "She is so beautiful. Great actress too."

"Head-to-toe athleisure wear and she looked like she'd just come off the runway."

"Oh that reminds me," Tally piped up. "You will never guess who I saw the other day, walking down Melrose."

"Who?" Webber replied.

"Sam Pleasant."

Amanda froze, glancing up from her phone. It wasn't strange to hear people talk about her best friend. Helene was a huge star now and she was gorgeous. People talked about her all the time.

They talked about Sam Pleasant all the time too, and a week ago, Amanda wouldn't have batted an eyelash at the mention of his name. But that was before the mind-blowing night they'd spent together. Since then, Sam Pleasant had done nothing but invade her thoughts. She was mature enough to handle a one-night stand, but that didn't stop every detail of their time together from playing over and over again in her mind. Hadn't stopped her from conjuring thoughts of Sam's body moving over hers before she slipped her hand between her legs every night since it happened.

The whole thing had been a fluke, and she knew in a few months the memories would fade, leaving her with her own You'll Never Guess Who I Slept With a Hundred Years Ago story to blurt out in front of her grandkids one day. In the meantime, Amanda was desperately in need of a real vacation, and Sam Pleasant had made her realize how much sex had been missing from her life too. That's all this bizarre infatuation was. Exhaustion and sex deprivation. She'd get over both eventually. Eventually. For now though . . .

Amanda fixed her face and looked back down at her phone, ignoring the way her ears had suddenly gotten hot.

"He is so fine," Patience went on.

"Helene's wedding is this weekend and I heard the top-secret location is Sam Pleasant's ranch. Well, his family's ranch," Webber said. A knot gripped Amanda's belly. She knew the wedding was going to be held at Big Rock Ranch in Charming, California, about two and a half hours away from the city if traffic was on your side. She'd heard in passing that it was Black-owned, but she had no clue the ranch was owned by Sam's family.

She almost started beating herself up for not researching the ranch more, but why would she? All Helene needed her to do was show up and be emotionally supportive and happy for the lovely couple. She wasn't working and she wasn't in the wedding party. What wedding guest researched the owners of any venue? And what person researched a person's family before they had a spontaneous one-night stand with them? She swallowed and pretended to focus back on her phone.

"Not so top-secret then," Tally laughed in reply.

"It'll all be in *People* next week. Who cares?" Dru said with her own chuckle.

"I care," Tally replied. "I want to see what she's wearing."

"Enough about her though," Webber said. "Back to Sam Pleasant. What did he smell like?"

Laughter came sputtering out of Tally. Amanda would have laughed quietly too if she didn't already know the answer to that question. Amanda was currently in hell.

"Sorry, hun. I didn't *smell* him, but he just—ugh—godly up close. Great skin."

"I'm so glad he won," Patience said. "That movie was brutal, but he acted his ass off. He deserves that award."

"I may have slid into his DMs the other day," Dru announced. Amanda looked up then. Luckily, Dru was looking in the mirror as Patience removed the foam latex ridges from her cheek. She didn't catch the wide-eyed horror on Amanda's face.

"What did he say?" Tally asked. "What did *you* say?"

"I just told him he should ask me out for a drink some time. He hasn't responded yet, but I'm sure his DMs are flooded. He pretty much announced that he was single and looking in that *GQ* article. I'll give him some time to sort through the riff-raff before he gets back to me." She winked at Webber in the mirror before she looked back down at her phone. Amanda pretended to stretch her neck and let out a quiet, but deep breath. Dru said a lot of things. Maybe she was just lying about messaging Sam. Not that it mattered. Sam was a nonentity in Amanda's life.

If Dru wanted to shoot her shot, she was welcome to. Amanda had bigger problems. Like what the hell she was going to do if she ran into Sam at this wedding. Maybe she should tell Helene what actually happened after Kata and Rina's party, that she hadn't gone straight home to get

some much-needed sleep. She could totally trust Helene
with the dirty details of that night, but Amanda wasn't one
to kiss and tell. Especially when there wasn't much to tell
beyond the intimate bits she wanted to keep to herself.
That she'd really spent the night in Sam Pleasant's arms.

No. It was Helene's wedding weekend. She was not
going to bother her with her petty problems. If she ran into
Sam and he mentioned their night together, she would
simply remind him why they were both there. For Helene
and Ignacio's special day. Not to rehash the interesting
things Sam could do with his thumb. Forcing herself to
shake the thoughts off, she opened the email at the top of
her inbox. Valentina's assistant had finally replied, con-
firming Dru's Met Gala fitting for the following afternoon.

She idly listened as they moved on to less interesting
gossip. By the time Dru was back to her normal human
self, Amanda had caught up on all her emails. She thanked
Tally and Patience, then followed Dru back out into the
rain.

"Have you talked to my mom?" she asked, her tone
cold again.

"She's still in Malibu, but she said she'll get back in
time to meet you for breakfast tomorrow."

"No she won't."

Amanda fell silent until their short walk brought them
back to Dru's car in its reserved parking space. She held
the umbrella until Dru was behind the wheel of the matte
red G-Wagon she'd bought herself at the end of the last
season. She never let Amanda drive, which suited her just
fine. Freed up her hands to do more admin work as they
made their way back to Dru's apartment.

Amanda buckled her seat belt and waited until they left
the studio lot before she went on.

"Your mom is going to meet you after your workout tomorrow at ten for breakfast and then at one you have your audition for the Spright holiday movie."

"Ugh."

"Remember," Amanda said carefully. "This was the one you wanted. You were so excited when you heard they were interested in talking to you." Yes, that had been six months ago, but that didn't change the fact that Dru had not so secretly been dreaming of starring in a made-for-TV holiday romance since she was twelve.

"Do you think Sam Pleasant would date a TV movie actor?" she asked wistfully.

"I'm not sure what kind of woman he dates," Amanda replied, which was the truth. Though she did know some more personal things about him now. Like how he looked when he was sleeping soundly.

Dru glanced over as they slowed to a stop at the next red light. She scoffed, then looked back toward the road. "I don't know why I'm asking you. When was the last time you went on a date?"

"Well, it's tricky to date when you're trying to keep up with the hottest actress in a paranormal prime-time TV show."

"Whatever, don't blame me. Mom made me give you weekends off. Surely there's some single personal assistants' meetup you could go to. Or like a janitor or something that's looking for a low-rent sugar baby."

"I'm not sure which part of that to find more offensive and just wrong, but what if I get lucky and leave you? How will you go on without me?"

"You won't. You'll be with me forever and then you'll watch my children. The children I have with Sam Pleasant."

Amanda's eye nearly twitched. "Did you really DM him?"

"Sure did," Dru said, the bravado back in her voice. "This show has two more seasons before it goes stale. I need to be ready to upgrade and what better way to upgrade than on the arm of someone like Sam Pleasant? Just not sure I can do that if I downgrade to TV movies."

The horrible and somewhat gross idea of using Sam aside, Amanda didn't like to hear Dru disparaging other mediums that way, especially when this type of role was something she wanted. Dru was a difficult person, but there was a sensitive romantic deep inside. It was one of the first things they'd bonded over. Their mutual love of all things love. Amanda didn't want her to pass the opportunity up just because it wasn't a role that would put her in the running for her own Oscar.

Plus she was right about one thing: She had three years max left on *Andromeda*. Who knew what was in store for her down the road? A TV movie meant a paycheck and though Dru was biracial, she still read as Black. Being offered roles was a blessing in this industry, no matter how unfair and racist that truth was. Developing a relationship with the folks at Spright absolutely wouldn't hurt. But Amanda kept that to herself.

"Do you want me to call your mom?" she asked. "You can cancel."

"No. No. I want to do it. Anyway, it can be like ironic or whatever. Plus it's silly to turn down the paycheck when I get it. Which I will. I might swing Sam Pleasant too."

"I'll be there to hold your veil," Amanda said.

"You still going to your friend's little wedding this weekend?" Dru asked as they joined the line of cars waiting to take Cahuenga back over the hill. Amanda fixed a little smile on her face and nodded.

"My flight leaves at one." Which was sort of the truth. She was driving out to Charming at one the following afternoon. Another bit of information Dru didn't need to know. She was under the impression that Amanda was going to the wedding of one of her college roommates in San Francisco. If she knew she was going to Helene's wedding she would lose her mind. Or worse, demand to come along. Amanda prayed Sam Pleasant wasn't going to be there.

"Well, have fun. You still have to show up first thing Monday morning. Don't get too sauced. I can't imagine what you're like hungover. Though I know they'll be no evidence of it. You're like the only person I've ever met who refuses to be photographed. You're such a freak."

"You know I don't drink and when you're sober there's no need for pictures. I'll have the memories to forever live in my mind. Clear and untainted by the stain of tequila shots. I'll be fresh and at your beck and call, like always."

"Don't act like you don't love it. You were nothing before me," Dru said before she laughed. Amanda knew she was only half joking. Amanda just smiled and forced her eyes back on the endless line of traffic in front of them.

"You're going to run lines with me tonight?" Dru asked a few minutes later as they finally passed the Hollywood Bowl.

"Of course. I wouldn't miss it."

Amanda thought she heard Dru mutter a quiet thank-you, but she couldn't be sure.

* * *

It was after nine when Amanda returned to her little studio bungalow. After she'd convinced Dru to eat some dinner, they ran lines for the Spright project, then Dru asked her to stay a little longer while she reorganized her shoes. Amanda didn't mind.

Okay, to be honest, she did. It had been a long week and she still needed to pack for her weekend away, and she was hoping to get home so she could make a quick phone call to her parents before they went to bed. But Dru didn't want her to leave. It happened every time her mother ditched her for long periods of time. This week, she was hanging out with some housewives at a former soap star's mansion. With Dru filming the show and Amanda there to keep her company, Kaidence didn't see a need to check in in-person. Dru didn't like to be alone. Amanda understood, but she didn't pay her enough for that kind of overtime.

She opened the front door to her place and turned on the lights. Just as she set down her things, she heard her phone chime. It was a text from her mom.

Night night, my hardworking girl.
We love you!

Amanda sighed and pushed down the sudden feelings of loneliness brewing inside of her. Her parents had all the faith in her when they loaded up their cars and helped her move out west. She knew things wouldn't be easy. She knew she would have to put in her time, pay her dues, but she never thought this was where her journey would bring her. She thought about the screenplays gathering dust in Final Draft files on her personal laptop.

Looking at her phone, she considered calling her mom back, since she was still awake. She decided against it though. She didn't need to cry and if she talked to her mom, just the sound of her voice would have her bursting into tears. There were kind people in LA but no one like her parents, and sometimes she needed to pretend there wasn't a different, far away place where she felt truly at home and truly loved. Less alone. If she let the homesickness settle in, the regret and self-doubt would immediately follow. She settled on a text.

> Good night, Mom!
> I'll call you tomorrow.
> Hug Dad for me.

A moment later she received a text from her dad.

> I feel the love.

She took her time getting ready for bed. Something she didn't understand was nagging at her as she washed her face and brushed her teeth. Something beyond the loneliness. When she climbed under the covers and tried to get back to her *Sailor Moon* rewatch, she couldn't focus, even though she knew the dubbed dialogue by heart. Grabbing her phone off her charger, she flopped onto her back and found herself pulling up Sam's *GQ* interview.

She knew better. No good would come from even thinking about him any further, but the idea of Dru trying to get with him made her stomach hurt. It didn't matter if Sam took her up on her offer. For the first time ever she and Dru wanted the same thing. Something about that was so wrong.

She skimmed the article, trying not to look at the devastatingly beautiful picture of him walking a black horse down a trail as she looked for the declaration of his single status.

> *Pleasant is so gracious, letting me visit him on his family's ranch. I understand the honor that has been bestowed upon me when his rather particular horse, Majesty, accepts a carrot from my open palm, but I know I would be making a terrible mistake if I don't ask the twenty-eight-year-old what he's looking for in a partner and if there's a current partner helping to make those wishes come true.*
>
> *"I gotta say I'm pretty private about that stuff. About many aspects of my personal life, but I know how this goes. I know how people like to guess, and guessing never works out for anyone."*
>
> *At this point Sam smiles and gives Majesty a loving pat, and I know my husband would understand if I asked for a divorce on the spot.*
>
> *"I am single at the moment. I got out of a relationship right before I booked this project and decided to focus on work for a while." And as for the future? "I want what my grandparents had, what my parents have. I was lucky to be raised by people who love each other very much. I was lucky to be raised in a very loving home. I want to keep that going. Not that I'm looking now." He laughs again and I find my finger hovering over my husband's number. "But one day I will be looking for someone who wants to fill a home with laughter and sick dance moves."*

The article went on to talk about Sam's older brother trying to out–Milly Rock him and the sight of his then eighty-two-year-old grandmother, two-time Oscar winner Leona Lovell, demonstrating her version of the Harlem Shake. The real one, not that weird viral video thing. The words started to run together and Amanda found herself going back and looking at the photos. When the sound of his laugh echoing in her ear brought everything back to the surface, she knew she had to make a decision.

She loved Helene dearly, and cherished their friendship, but maybe after the wedding she should pull back from trying to engage with her so much socially. They were in two different worlds, not that Amanda thought Helene's A-list status made her unworthy of Helene's friendship, but things had run smoothly between them when their friendship involved Amanda slipping over to Helene's house for a quiet night in with her girlfriends. Oscar night had been the first time she'd really stepped out with Helene and now there was her wedding, which Amanda knew would be something close to magical. But it wasn't Amanda's reality. Not to mention, Dru would absolutely freak out or try to take advantage if she found out Helene even knew Amanda's name.

And Amanda knew if she kept playing with the type of carefree fire that had landed her in Sam's hotel room, she would find herself worse than alone. She'd find herself with a broken heart.

Chapter 4

Sam left the barn and made his way back to the lodge. He thought a long morning ride with Majesty would lift whatever dark cloud that was messing with his mood, but it didn't work. He'd finished up all his post-Oscar interviews, had a few meetings, then pretty much fled back to his family's ranch to get some much-needed rest. He was happy to be back home with his brothers, his soon-to-be sister-in-law, and his cousins, not to mention his horse. After a good forty-eight hours of rest and his grandmother's amazing cooking, he still felt off.

He walked through the grounds, trying to appreciate the perfect February weather. The sun was shining in a cloudless sky, but there was just enough of a breeze coming off the mountains to keep things comfortable. Preparations for Helene's wedding had begun months ago, but now the staff was buzzing around getting everything ready for the weekend's festivities, starting with tonight's rehearsal dinner and square dance. Sam had about three hours to fix his face and his mood so he could be a good friend and host when Helene and Ignacio's other friends and family arrived.

He came up to the lodge and made his way around

back, and toward the stairs that led up to Zach and Jesse's office. He stepped back just as the door swung open and Zach stepped out.

"Oh, hey. You heading up?"

"Yeah. Can I borrow your truck? I need to head back to the house and change."

"Yeah, sure." Zach pulled his keys to his pickup out of his pocket and handed them over.

"Thanks," Sam said. For some reason he sounded like one of their dogs had just died. He really needed to snap out of it.

"Man, you alright? Walk with me," Zach said as he headed toward his new white pickup. "I won't say you've been moping, but you should see your face right now."

Sam turned the keys over in his hands, then looked up at his older brother. Nothing bothered Zach. As long as the ranch was up and running and his fiancée Evie was happy, the man didn't have a bad day. He also didn't have Sam's artistic spirit. He knew he could talk to his brother, but he wasn't sure he would understand.

"Honestly, I don't know."

"What's going on? Talk to me."

"I don't know! That's the problem. I made the movie. I won the award. John has a ton of scripts for me to look at, directors want to talk to me. Majesty is in great health."

"Hey, we always look after her when you're gone. Evie takes her out every day she's here."

That was enough to make Sam smile. Evie hated his horse and Majesty hated most humans, but somehow they'd come to an understanding. If only the happiness and well-being of his beloved horse was enough. "You know I appreciate that. Evie's a real one."

"She is, but you? Sounds like you're just overwhelmed."

"Maybe that's it. I don't know why I'm complaining."

"'Cause you're human. You set a goal and you reached it. You also have the rest of your life ahead of you. Ask Miss Leona. You think winning an Oscar instantly solved her problems? Shit, she had to help raise the three of us. We turned her gray under those custom wigs."

Sam laughed for real this time. "True."

"Listen, you got some time off. Hang around here as long as you like. I know Jesse loves having you around."

"I don't know about that."

The whole family was spread out over three fairly large houses on their own private cul-de-sac. He had an apartment in LA, and now that Evie's restaurant was up and running in New York, he was welcome to crash in the family town house in Harlem, but Pleasant Lane was always home. That was until Zach kicked him out of their house and made him crash with Jesse. He loved Evie, but since the minute they'd gotten engaged and convinced their grandma it was okay for them to be living in sin, Sam had been playing musical houses around the cul de sac, switching between his brothers' and grandmother's homes. His cousins Lilah and Corie were already living in Miss Leona's. He could sleep over there, but his grandmother had enough to deal with. He'd suck it up and stay with Jesse. Didn't mean he had to like it.

"What happened?" Zach laughed.

"I got a forty-minute lecture about condiment placement last night. I accidentally moved the steak sauce onto the wrong shelf."

"You can come stay at my place until Sunday night, but Evie's back Monday morning."

"No, it's fine."

"I was gonna say you could help Jesse with his dating

profiles. Might help take your mind off things, but maybe not."

"Wait, back it up. What dating profile?"

"Evie convinced him to try out a few dating apps."

"There are, like, seven eligible women in this town. Why doesn't he just go down to Claim Jumpers if he's looking for local love?"

Zach shrugged. "She signed him up for one of those weird ones that matches moderately wealthy people."

"Uh, I'm definitely going to talk to him about that. Speaking of dating, Walls said some shit about how I've been sulking since Natalie and I broke up. You think I've been sulking?"

Zach stepped back and looked Sam over for a second.

"I wouldn't say sulking—"

"Wow. Really?"

"Listen, you two broke up and you only brought it up to me once in any official capacity, but there was a mood shift. I just thought you were stressed out about the movie. That script was heavy."

"Yeah. I guess I did too."

"But now?"

Sam almost told his brother about Cha-Cha. Days later and she was still hovering in the back of his mind. He thought about asking Helene if she knew anything about her, since they'd been together at the party, but it was her wedding week. Plus, he didn't want to let it slip that he and Cha-Cha had slept together and Sam hadn't even managed to catch her name.

"Nothing. It's nothing. I just—Walls was giving me shit about ignoring all the women who've flooded my DMs this week. After the win."

"You really taking relationship advice from Walls?"

Zach's eyebrow went up under his tan Stetson. "I know that's your homie, but it's Walls. That's like going to Corie for a soft shoulder to cry on." Their play cousin/Miss Leona's assistant was a few degrees below cold-blooded.

"I just want a girl to love me for me," he said dramatically.

Zach let out a hearty laugh. "You're a Pleasant. That was never going to happen."

"Oh? So what about Evie?"

"Do you see this face, man?"

Sam rolled his eyes.

"Ninety percent of what we got going on is because of this pretty-ass face."

"Yeah, okay."

"Nah, I'm playin', but Evie can't stand my ass and everyone knows it. If she didn't love the real me, there's no way she would have agreed to marry me. So yeah, you're onto something. But I don't know how to help you or Jesse."

"Is there any helping Jesse? Really? He needs a combination of Mom and Corie with the patience of a saint. I'm not sure a woman like that exists."

"Well, what are you looking for?"

"I'm not sure," Sam lied 'cause at the moment he knew exactly what he was looking for. He just had to figure out her name. He just knew what it would sound like if he said it out loud.

"Well, if you're feeling lonely, man, it might not be a bad idea to get back out there. If it's something else, there's no bad time to talk to a therapist. Evie and I have started going together. It's tough, but . . ." His brother shrugged.

They'd had a therapist on set when they were filming

Sky. Sam had met with Dr. Gilliam throughout production and three more times after they'd wrapped. She'd been happy with the way he was processing the dark source material they were working with and kindly reminded him her door would be open if he wanted to speak with her again or if he just wanted a referral. He felt comfortable reaching out to her, but he had a feeling this particular thing wasn't something he needed to see someone about.

"Maybe I should get back out there. It has been a while."

"Get back out. Just do us all a favor."

"What?"

"Do not tell Mom."

Sam laughed as he leaned back against the truck. "You know I'm not stupid."

"She will fly back here. She will have every eligible maiden from here to San Francisco lined up at those Big Rock gates. She will call up every soror with an unwed daughter—"

"I know, I know."

"She'll hit the pageant circuit, man. You're not Jesse. She'll have no problem selling any parents on you. Plus, you're her baby."

Sam rolled his eyes even though he knew it was true. Parents weren't supposed to play favorites, but Zach was their dad's favorite and he was their mom's. She'd never done a damn thing to hide it. There was no reason to feel bad for Jesse. He was their grandmother's favorite and that took the cake. Either way, Sam knew both his parents were still waiting to see all of their sons married off in their weird old-school way. And he knew his mom was beyond impatient for a grandchild. Zach and Evie were on their way there, but if she could double her odds, she wouldn't hesitate to start playing matchmaker.

Sam had a much better, simpler plan. He'd do his best to track down Cha-Cha on his own, just to talk. Just to see if that spark he felt was real, and if that didn't work, he'd wait until Helene got back from her honeymoon and casually ask how her friend from the after-party was doing.

The look on Helene's face when she climbed out of her car changed Sam's whole mood. Yeah, he was still a little out of it and he had mentally committed to finding a woman who might want nothing to do with him, but at least this week he could focus on his friends and their union.

He'd showered and changed, then met up with Jesse, Zach, and Delfi, their family friend who was also the ranch's recently promoted general manager. Zach had since stepped back from his more hands-on approach to greeting important guests, but since Helene was an A-list priority and a friend of Sam's, Zach wanted all hands on deck to assure her and her family that the boatload of money they'd shelled out to clear the ranch for three days would be well worth it. Jesse never greeted guests, only business associates and important vendors, so Sam figured he was taking this opportunity to quietly fawn over Helene in person. Helene had that effect on people.

She and her sister, Robyn, arrived ahead of the rest of the wedding party so they could have a quick chat with the wedding planner, Joan, then catch their breath before the festivities kicked off.

"So we'll have one of our valets, Will, bring your things over to the Bluebird cabins and then we're all set for the rehearsal at four. If you need absolutely anything you let us know," Delfi said.

"Thank you again, you guys. I'm excited to be here. I'm

so excited to be getting married here. I'm just excited," Helene laughed.

"We're excited for you," Sam replied.

"Ignacio and his family should be here in about an hour and so will my parents. We're gonna head to our room and then I'll probably mosey back over and meet them."

"Great," Delfi said.

Just then the double doors to the lodge opened and Will ushered another guest inside. The whole group turned to see who was joining them.

"You're here!" Helene squealed. She rushed across the lobby and pulled the slightly shorter, but much fuller woman into her arms.

Sam looked around Joan's shoulder and had to squint to make sure he wasn't seeing things. When Helene stepped back, gently taking the woman by the shoulders, he knew for sure he wasn't crazy.

Cha-Cha was on the scene. She looked different from the night they'd met. No shiny sequin jumpsuit and rocking about 75 percent less makeup. She was wearing jeans, a T-shirt with some *Sailor Moon* fan art on it under a hooded cardigan, and a pair of ice-blue Chucks. Her long triangle-part box braids were pulled back in a ponytail, but she still looked as beautiful as Sam remembered, her full lips and her high cheekbones practically glowing. Sam was glad to have confirmation that he hadn't been a fool trying to get with her. She was a ten.

"I'm so early," she groaned, apologetically. "I thought there was going to be a lot of traffic and I didn't want to be late."

"Are you kidding? Never in the history of weddings will anyone complain about people showing up on time. This is cosmic balance for the fact that my cousins will definitely be late." Helene looped her arm through Cha-Cha's and brought her back over to the group. Sam didn't miss the way her eyes flashed wide when she saw him. A second later though, the shock or maybe the horror that had registered at seeing him vanished. She fixed her face with a sweet, friendly smile and seemed to focus her attention on Zach.

"Everyone, this is my friend Amanda." Helene went around and reintroduced everyone.

"Thank you so much for having us. You have such a beautiful place here," Amanda said.

Zach replied, giving Amanda his usual brief rundown of the ranch, but Sam wasn't listening. He was too busy focusing on how hard Amanda was trying *not* to focus on him. She looked over at Helene and then Delfi.

"I can just hang around here for a bit. I think I might be too early for my check-in," she said, like she was terrified to impose or break the rules. This Amanda was different from the Cha-Cha he'd been with at the start of the week. The woman he'd met on the dance floor had been brash and assertive. Amanda seemed almost shy and reserved. Or maybe she was just going out of her way to be polite. Either way, Sam was even more intrigued and pleasantly surprised. He'd made up his mind to track her down. He never thought the universe would drop her right into his lap.

"Nonsense. We can get you set up right now," Sam heard himself say. He knew Delfi was silently punching him in her mind, but she was on the clock. She'd give him an earful about how he might be a Pleasant, but he didn't work at the ranch and he didn't run shit around these parts. She'd also probably try to get him in a headlock and threaten to tell Miss Leona if he overstepped again. All in good fun, of course. But for now, she smiled wider and did her best to set Amanda's worries to the side.

"Absolutely. Amanda McQueen?" Of course Delfi had the whole guest list memorized; most of the staff would. It was just how they did things at Big Rock Ranch.

"That's me."

"Wonderful. You'll be staying right here in the lodge. Come with me. We'll have Laura here get you your key." Delfi gently touched Amanda's shoulder and guided her back to the desk where one of the newer guest clerks Sam didn't know very well was waiting.

"Your friends are rolling in so I'm heading back to work, but it was great to meet you," Jesse said to Helene.

"It was lovely to meet you finally." He gave her his signature stoic nod before he peeled away and headed back to his office.

"I'm going to do the same. We'll see you ladies in a little bit." Zach said his goodbyes and then followed after their older brother. There was no reason for Sam to hang around, but he couldn't get the message that it was time to go down to his feet. He watched Amanda as she smiled at Delfi and Laura behind the desk. He had to get her alone so they could talk.

"Everything okay?" Robyn asked. Sam snapped out of his trance. He'd definitely been staring.

"Um, yeah, all good. Helene, I'm gonna head back to the house, let you ladies do your girly things," he teased. "But I'll be there for the rehearsal."

"Great. Thank you again. Your whole family—just, thank you."

"Of course." He shot her a wink and headed for the door. He couldn't stop himself from tapping Amanda's shoulder. She looked back at him, her throat working as she swallowed. "It was nice to meet you," Sam said.

"Likewise," she replied before she took the keycard Laura handed her. Sam could see the pleading in her eyes. She was just as surprised as he was and what's more, Sam was pretty sure he wasn't the only one who'd kept pretty quiet about their rendezvous. So Helene didn't know. Maybe Amanda didn't want her to know. It was silly for Sam to speculate. Later, when things quieted down or ramped up and there was so much going on no one would notice if he and one of the wedding guests slipped away, he'd pull Amanda aside and see where her head was at. And if she wasn't interested in getting to know him any further he could at least give her a hard time for stealing his Oscar.

Chapter 5

Amanda was proud she'd managed to wait until she'd gotten to her room to have a mini freak-out. The chances of running into Sam on the Pleasant family ranch were pretty high. She'd known she'd be risking another encounter by showing up on his turf. And she'd prepared for that, spent half of the two-hour drive rehearsing exactly what she would say, what excuses she would use to avoid him if he wanted to revisit what had happened between them that Sunday night.

She just hadn't thought he'd be standing in the lobby right when she walked through the doors. And she definitely hadn't expected him to have gone full cowboy boy with his thigh-hugging jeans and cowboy boots. His white cowboy hat had been in his hand, because of course he'd be raised not to wear it indoors. She'd ignored the way the orange-and-green-plaid shirt he had on did nothing to hide his cut biceps or his sculpted chest.

All of that had been too much to take in. The fact that he'd been with Helene and her whole behind-the-scenes wedding-day crew that included his ridiculously handsome brothers really tested the limits of her reflexes. She'd had to stop herself from gasping and running back toward the exit. Or drooling. Seriously, a family should be limited to one smoking-hot son. Three is just unfair.

She'd found the rest of her brain cells when Sam had left the lobby after lightly touching her arm. Still the panic had already set in and now she worried it wouldn't dissipate until she was safely back in LA.

Amanda let out a deep breath and sank down on the love seat in her adorably faux-rustic suite. She'd only seen a fraction of the property, but it wouldn't be a stretch to say that Big Rock Ranch was a beautiful ranch. Just pulling up to the main lodge with the picturesque mountains rising high in the distance made Amanda feel so grateful for the invitation. And the time off. Dru had texted five times on the drive over. Nothing important, just backhanded and covert requests for reassurance before she went into her audition. She clearly wanted the part even if she'd pooh-poohed it the day before.

An odd tightness flared in Amanda's chest just thinking about returning to work on Monday. She didn't belong at this wedding. The only reason she wasn't booking it back to the freeway was her love for Helene. She couldn't bail on a friend, not on her wedding day.

That didn't stop the feeling of dread that was looming over her. She allowed herself one night here and there to step outside of Dru's cycle of misery, but a long weekend in this magical place with its five-star accommodations would be just enough to recharge her for another few months. She had to be careful though that she didn't relax too much and be forced to beg for work at the ranch. That just wouldn't do.

Amanda sighed and shook her head, smiling to herself a bit, then went to grab her dress for the rehearsal dinner.

While she wasn't in the wedding party, Helene had still invited her to come and hang out. Hopefully, Sam had just popped by the front desk to say hello and she wouldn't see him again for the rest of the weekend. Amanda knew it was a long shot, but if anything she was optimistic. She laid out her dress, and just as she was considering the travel steamer her phone chimed with a text. For once, it wasn't Dru. Amanda's mood immediately shifted as she read Helene's text.

> Come get ready with me in our cabin!
> We're over in Bluebird.

> Okay! I'm on my way.

> I want to discuss how hot the
> Pleasant brothers are before
> I become a married woman.

> Definitely on my way. LOL

Amanda responded, even though she was far from LOLing.

She gathered her things and headed to the lobby. Back at the front dcsk, Laura handed Amanda a beautifully illustrated map of the property, then offered to have a nice young man named Will give her a lift over to the cabin where Helene was staying. Amanda almost turned the offer for a ride down. She could take a nice long walk around the property and scope things out for her herself, but when she took a closer look at the map she didn't think lugging her things what appeared to be a smooth half mile to the private cabins was the best idea. She happily hopped into one of the ranch golf carts and let Will zip her across the property. She tipped him with the cash brought expressly for that purpose, then hurried up the three short steps of Bluebird cabin. Helene opened the door before Amanda could knock.

"Hey! Come in."

Amanda stepped inside and embraced her friend and then her friend's sister, Robyn.

"You're sure it's okay I came by? I don't want to get in the way of your bridely activities," Amanda said as she set down her stuff on the arm of the sectional near the front door.

"It's more than okay. I barely got to talk to you on Sunday and I'll barely get to talk to you this weekend. Let's squeeze in some QT while we can. Besides, I got this huge place just for me and Robbie. Plenty of room for us to spread out."

"No kidding." She glanced around realizing Bluebird was more of a three-bedroom house than a cabin. "Um, speaking of Sunday night, there's something I think I should let you in on. But I need an extreme vow of silence."

"Of course," Helene said gravely. Robyn nodded in kind.

"I'm a steel trap," she said.

"She really is. What's going on?" Helene asked.

"First, let me say thank you so much for inviting me out. I know I bail a lot because of my schedule, but it means a lot to me that you still try to include me in your life. Especially moments like this. You are a great friend."

"Damn, girl. Stop! I need to save my tears for my vows," Helene said, lightly swatting at her arm.

"Okay, okay. So I wasn't going to tell you this because you know me. I don't like my business all out there."

"Ignacio had to stop me from forcing guests to sign an NDA."

"She's not joking," Robyn said.

"This is why we're friends," Amanda laughed before she cleared her throat. The truth she was about to share sent a sobering chill over her skin. "Also it's your weekend and I didn't think it was a good time to bring up my own petty drama, but recent developments have forced my hand."

"Okay, now you really have to tell me."

"Sunday night when I left Kata and Rina's party?"

"Yeah?"

"I didn't go home. I went to Sam Pleasant's hotel room and we had adult relations. Like all night long."

"Amanda!" Helene gasped, enunciating every syllable. "I am shocked."

"I'm impressed. Never thought he'd be into thick girls," Robyn shrugged. She and Amanda were around the same size. Big girls had been pulling fine men since the dawn of time, but everyone knew how Hollywood social culture worked.

"Same, but that's not the issue," Amanda went on. "I—um, I never told him my name."

Another gasp from Helene.

"And I kinda bolted the next morning before he woke up. And I also kinda stole his Oscar statue. By accident! I returned it. He got the rest of my emergency condoms and some Fenty lip gloss I now need to replace."

"Okay, I need to sit down." Amanda and Robyn followed Helene over to the sectional in front of a massive fireplace.

"So you had a for-real covert fling with Sam Pleasant. When I say I'm proud . . ."

"Stop," Amanda laughed.

"No, seriously. You were so stressed about coming along in the first place, but, honey. Talk about living it up. Mama is so proud."

"Yeah, okay. It was actually one of my finer moments. However, I didn't realize this was his family's ranch until yesterday."

"Oh, so you tried to hit and quit and then you just ran into him in the lobby."

"Yup."

"Okay, so what's the play here?" Helene said, clasping her hand under her chin.

"What do you mean what's the play? There's no play. I just didn't want you to wonder why I was hiding behind an ice sculpture all weekend."

"Oh God. I didn't even ask. Was it bad?"

Amanda sighed. "No, it was amazing, BUT! That doesn't mean there's a play. It happened. It's over."

"Do you want it to be over? I mean Sam is pretty private too, but I think he and I are close enough for me to give him a little wink wink nudge nudge in your direction."

"And then what?"

"What do you mean?"

"I've used up all my goodwill and PTO with Dru this fiscal quarter."

"I'm not going to say it, but you know what I want to say."

"I know."

She loved Helene, but Helene really didn't understand Amanda's life. Helene understood how hard of a town Hollywood could be, being a young dark-skinned Black woman herself, but Helene came from money and that money had subsidized her lifestyle until her acting career took off. Amanda's parents were amazing, but they weren't "pay her grown-ass bills" rich. She had some savings, but living in Los Angeles wasn't cheap and she couldn't afford to be unemployed. She didn't want to delve into the complex feelings that came with leaving Dru alone to deal with her mother, while also worrying if Dru would sabotage her job prospects if and when she announced she was moving on. She knew it wasn't healthy or good, their bizarre codependency, but right now wasn't the time to quit. However, that wasn't the issue at the moment.

"Dating just isn't on the schedule right now. Hell, flirting isn't. We had a nice time. Let's just leave it at that. I don't want you spending your wedding trying to play matchmaker for someone else. Okay?"

Helene's bottom lip jutted out just a bit. "Fine."

"I'm so annoyed he knows my name," Amanda said through a playful scowl.

"What kind of anonymous kinky shit were you two up to?" Robyn asked.

"Yeah, I know you said leave it, but I want details," Helene added.

Amanda felt her cheeks heat. "Nothing. I just—I didn't think he was serious when he started chatting me up and when he made it clear he was, I wanted him to work for it. Also I wasn't out looking to smush. I just wanted a night off."

"Okay, so he didn't even know your name until an hour ago," Helene said. Amanda could practically see the gears in her head turning. She should have kept her mouth shut. "But you don't want to make anything of it."

"No. I just want to see my beautiful friend wed to her true love."

"Fine." Helene stood and made a show of smoothing the seat of her maxi dress. "I'll focus on my stupid wedding. But when I get back from my honeymoon I'm getting all up in your business."

"Why?" Amanda laughed.

"'Cause the whole time I've known you I've been careful not to bug you about your love life. I wanted to respect it, but now—"

"Now she knows there's a freak in you," Robyn went on, rolling her eyes.

"If there's anything I love more than my man and my art it's inserting myself into people's love lives. I'm gonna try to get the Big Pleasant's phone number for my baby sister before the weekend is out."

"Oh, hell no," Robyn said, her eyes wide with sudden horror.

"Why not?" Helene replied. "He's fine as hell. All three of them are."

"Yeah, but he's so big and he doesn't smile. I'm down for a challenge, but I don't want to crack that giant grumpy egg."

"They're like the Three Bears. One big, one medium, one mediumer. All pretty hot," Helene said. She wasn't wrong. While Sam was the shortest of his brothers, he was far from little. And unlike Baby Bear, everything about him was just right, Amanda thought before she immediately made herself swear she would never utter those words out loud to anyone.

"We can all agree that Sam and his brothers are very

attractive," Amanda said. "Now let us never speak of them again."

"Fine," Helene laughed. "Let's talk about me instead!"

"Let's!" Amanda agreed. "I don't have anything to toast with at the moment, but here's to you, our darling Helene. I am so happy to celebrate your happily ever after."

"Amen!" Robyn said, her palms turned upward.

Helene smiled even wider, tears glinting in her eyes. "To me and my man."

True, Amanda didn't have time for anything other than keeping up with Dru, but in her heart, deep down, she hoped that one day she would find something close to what Helene and Ignacio had found together. Love, respect, and friendship.

Her phone buzzed with another text from Dru. She sighed.

One day, maybe. But clearly not now. And not with Sam Pleasant.

As soon as more of the wedding party and members of Helene's family started to arrive, Amanda did what she did best: She faded into the background. Normally she'd volunteer her services as a friend of the bride, but she understood how these things worked, the hierarchy at play when it came to bridesmaids and friendships. Plus the planner and her assistants were also at the ready. Amanda would step up if needed but for now, it was time for family and close friends to bond with the bride and groom.

She followed the wedding party over to where the ceremony was being held. Rows and rows of chairs were lined up in what seemed to be an open field. Close by was a barn and there were a few horses grazing in a pasture. The whole setup was downright cinematic. Amanda had set her phone to vibrate—in case Dru had an emergency—and gave herself permission to just take it all in.

She grabbed a seat in the last row and watched as the minister and the wedding planner herded everyone into their proper place. Something brushing her leg caught her attention. She looked over as this large black Lab had made its way over to her.

"Well hello," she cooed, scratching the dog's chin. It sat obediently, like it was waiting for her to give it some instructions. "I don't have any treats for you. I'm sorry."

"She doesn't need any treats."

Amanda looked up just as Sam Pleasant eased himself into the row. He'd changed into a navy blue suit, but he was still wearing that damn white cowboy hat. Amanda did her best not to swallow her tongue. Somehow she managed to playfully roll her eyes instead.

"Is this seat taken?" he whispered as he sat down beside her just as the first of the ushers practiced walking the mothers of the bride and groom to their seats.

"Yes, it is, as a matter of fact. I'm having a very important and private conversation with—"

"Clementine. Her name's Clementine." He flashed a smile that could light up the night sky. What was she thinking hopping into bed with someone that good looking!

"Yes. My good friend Clementine and I have some very important issues to discuss."

"Like how you like to use men and leave them cold and alone."

"I like to think I left you in a big comfortable bed feeling more sexually satisfied than you've ever been in your whole life."

"Well then, you should definitely tell her that you're somewhat of a thief."

"Excuse me. That was a mistake and I returned it immediately. I assume your management team gave it back to you?"

"They did, but that's not what I meant."

Amanda looked over into his deep brown eyes as he paused for dramatic effect. In the back of her mind she wondered how many women had fallen for this routine. The eyes, the smirk, his whole face, really. The polished cowboy act. And now an Oscar winner. He had to have women chasing him noon and night. She knew one had already proudly slid into his DMs. The thought of Dru taking her crack at him sobered her right up. She cleared her throat and focused back on the dog.

"What did you mean?" she asked.

"You stole my heart."

"Oh. Okay." Amanda chuckled quietly, then leaned forward and cupped Clementine's sweet face. She'd never seen such a shiny coat on a dog, but she didn't want to tell Sam. She had a feeling it might go to his head. She settled on something he could take credit for. "Your dog daddy is full of crap, did you know that?"

"She's not mine. Clem belongs to my brother Jesse. That pretty girl over there is mine." Amanda looked on the other side of the pasture and saw some mixture of cattle dog and mini horse basking in the sun. She watched Sam as he leaned over and snapped his fingers twice. The dog's head perked up and as soon as she saw Sam she came trotting over. She stopped at Amanda's side and nudged Clementine out of the way. Amanda smiled to herself and did her best not to cry tears of joy. This was her happy place. Wide-open spaces and surrounded by adorable dogs.

"Oh, it's your turn for pets, is it. Hello, beautiful," she cooed softly. "Yeah, that's right. Ignore your dog dad. You'll get the loving you need right here. What's her name?"

"Euca. She lives here full-time with my grandmother, but she's still my sweet baby girl." He reached over and scratched Euca behind the ear. Amanda ignored the way his fingers brushed hers in the process. She turned and looked back toward the mountains again. "This whole place is beautiful. The views, the cabins, the dogs. You grew up here?"

"I did, but I can't take credit for the beauty of it. My grandfather really turned this place into what it is, and my brothers have spent the last seven years putting their own shine on it. We're just borrowing the land the Earth has provided and the splendor all around you, you can give that up to God."

"Do you always lay it on this thick? You're not making me regret my decision to ditch your ass right now."

"I'm just messing with you. I'm surprised to see you here actually."

"Likewise."

"Are you having any regrets, Cha-Cha?"

"Cha-Cha?"

"That's what I've been calling you, in my mind."

Amanda wouldn't have been surprised if her body picked that exact moment to start ovulating. She swallowed, then schooled her features though and focused on the easy task of petting two dogs at once. "You've been thinking about me, have you?"

"I have."

Amanda froze as Sam tipped up the brim of his hat, then leaned over. His breath lightly brushed the shell of her ear as he spoke. "But next time we're together, I'd like to call you by your real name. Amanda, is it?"

Right at that moment, Amanda knew she should have ended this conversation before it began. Politely excused herself from Sam and his adorable dogs and walked the grounds or hidden under her bed back in the lodge until it was time for dinner. Anything to avoid him because even though everything out of his mouth was corny and over the top, it worked for her. Every second she spent at Big Rock Ranch, she knew she was in big trouble.

Chapter 6

To buy some time, Amanda deliberately turned to watch Helene as she made her way down the aisle on her father's arm. She was wearing a light cardigan over the flowing cream maxi dress she'd changed into. She wanted to make sure she chose her words carefully, and she wasn't sure she could do that if she was looking into those brown eyes shaded by the brim of that white hat.

"First of all, young man. Have you ever considered I wanted that one-time thing to be just a onetime thing."

"I was hoping you wouldn't say that."

"Well, lucky for you it's not true." Amanda refused to look at him, but she didn't miss the quiet chuckle he let out. "But there are a few things you need to know about me."

"Fill me in, girl."

"For one. I am a very private person and while no one is paying attention to us now, maybe don't broadcast what might be happening over here by practically licking my neck while you're talking to me."

"Excuse me." Sam groaned as he sat up a bit and moved so there was now an empty seat between them. Euca and Clementine shimmied by and wasted no time filling the space. Amanda still refused to look at Sam's face, but she didn't miss the way his strong, but manicured fingers slid over Clementine's fur. She hadn't forgotten the way they felt on her skin, how they felt between her legs. "Please. Go on."

"There's one night, but if we're moving to the massive commitment of a two-night stand, I feel like you should get to know me just a little bit."

"Okay, so let me get to know you then. What you do? Where you from? What your mom and dem like?"

Amanda smiled despite herself. "I'm from Rhode Island. My mom is a nurse at the health center at the U Providence campus. I'm an only child."

"And what do you do?"

"Um—I'm a writer." Which she was, when she had the time. Which she hadn't lately. And maybe she didn't get paid for it either. But she did write, and if she was honest with herself, she was pretty damn good at it.

"Oh. Alright. What are you working on now?"

"I have a few top-secret things in development."

"I understand, no need to give me details. Give me a hint though. Sci-fi? Horror? Comedy? A sweeping romantic saga? Please tell me you're bringing back full-length feature porno."

"I don't know where you've been. The full-length feature porno is alive and well. Um, it's a cross between *Lost in Space* and *Pirates of the Caribbean* with four hundred percent more Black people and a love story that isn't cursed. But there is magic." That was the elevator pitch for the script she'd been sitting on. A script that would never get made.

"Damn, that sounds amazing. Little sci-fi, fantasy action. I like it."

Amanda suddenly didn't feel comfortable talking about herself anymore. "How long have you known Helene? Did you two meet at Juilliard?"

"Actually, I didn't go to acting school. I didn't go to college."

"Really? Not that you needed to go to college. I just—"

"I was performing on the rodeo circuit with my brother, and he and I got a chance to do stunts for that movie *Rodeo Kid*. Did you ever see that?"

Amanda covered her burst of laughter. "Oh my God. I ran that movie into the ground. I used to have such a huge crush on Bryan Michael Weston."

"Okay, so I did all of Pudge's stunts. Helene's dad produced that and I met her on set one day. We reconnected on *Inferno*. I was working steady through my teens and then got called in to actually speak on camera during *Patriot's Promise*."

"Now that movie was terrible. I'm sorry," Amanda blurted out, but Sam seemed pleasantly surprised by her honesty.

"Thank you. It was complete garbage, but they cast me right as I finished up my GED. Came to a deal with my parents that I would go back to school as soon as the work dried up and I'm very fortunate it hasn't yet."

"And now you're officially Hollywood royalty. Wielder of the golden knight."

"You know, some sex-crazed woman tried to steal my statue from me? Can you believe it?"

"Anyway."

A strange look came over Sam's face as he continued to run his fingers over Clementine's shiny coat. Amanda realized she'd stopped lavishing Euca with the proper attention, but she didn't seem to mind. The dog let out a sigh and made herself comfortable, resting her head on Amanda's feet.

"Can I be real with you for a second?" Sam said.

"Yes, of course."

"Whatever I'm feeling? Right now? It's a combination of surreal and anticlimactic."

Amanda was not expecting him to say that. She glanced up as the minister had them reset for another run-through, before giving her full attention back to Sam. This ceremony was rather involved. "What do you mean?"

"I feel this sort of . . . drop, like I expected something else to happen, something bigger."

"You wanted our Lord in heaven, our savior Jesus Christ himself to descend from the heavens and present you with the award himself?"

"Okay. Okay, I know I sound a little poor little rich boy right now."

Amanda winced, but nodded all the same. "You kinda do, yeah."

"I can't explain it."

"Well, if you're struggling with some sort of letdown, look at it this way, you accomplished something so many people dream of and you did it with a part you should be proud of. Did the movie get a little white saviory? Yes."

"Damn. Tell me how you really feel."

"I mean, you didn't notice that when you read the script?"

"Amanda, listen, I'm a super-famous, very important actor. I'm not accustomed to people speaking to me in this manner."

"Sorry, Your Highness, but I don't know or like you enough to protect your feelings."

Sam let out another deep laugh that made her thighs

melt. She should really get up and take a lap, just to cool off, but she stayed right where she was.

"All I'm saying is, even though the movie wasn't exactly what I would have wanted, you were amazing in it. You gave one of our ancestors a voice and the Academy actually acknowledged that. People know Josiah Williams now in a way they didn't before thanks to you. Be proud of that. Also you and your grandmother are both Oscar winners. Your whole family should be over the moon."

"They are. They are. And you're right. Thank you for that blunt, but much appreciated perspective."

"You're welcome. Now for your next project can you please do something that requires more male nudity?"

"Listen. If you have the porn script ready just say so."

Amanda looked over at him again and that blinding smile let her know she was in deep, deep trouble.

She was gonna have to sleep with him again. She'd be a fool not to.

Sam was still a bit in shock. He'd been thinking about two things all week: his career and finding Cha-Cha again. He'd never thought he'd find himself sitting with her during the opening ceremony of Helene and Ignacio's wedding Olympics. And he didn't expect his attraction to her to grow exponentially during one conversation. He prided himself in having a team, hell, a family that kept it real with him. But beyond the many opinions the Internet had to offer, his cousin Corie was the only one to question the themes in the film. He loved Corie, but she dragged everyone and everything, so Sam spent most of his time taking her opinions with a grain of salt.

Sam understood. They all wanted to encourage him in

his craft, still no one had given their complex perspective as succinctly as Amanda McQueen. He was gonna call her Cha-Cha though until she said otherwise.

"So you're here for all the wedding party things but you're not in the wedding party. How did that work out? How did you and Helene meet?" Sam asked.

"Ugh, our meet cute was actually kind of a bummer."

"What happened?"

"It was in a Starbucks out in Malibu. I walked in as another customer said some pretty racist things to Helene and she was just in shock. She didn't respond. I told the lady off and then sat outside with Helene until she felt okay to drive home. You know, sometimes your adrenaline's so high you almost feel dizzy?"

"Oh yeah. I've been there. Rodeo circuit was full of good ole boys who wanted my dad and my brother gone. You get your racist studio exec here and there, but I heard the worst of it standing right by the chutes."

"I don't know what a chute is, but yeah, you get it. She asked for my number so she could thank me properly when she was more clearheaded and we've been friends ever since. She invites me to things all the time, but my schedule is weird and I don't always get to make it out. This whole seeing-each-other-twice-within-seven-days thing is an anomaly."

"Ah, okay."

"I'm here a day early because again Helene is amazing and just wanted to give me a little time away from Los Angeles. I appreciate the break."

"Oh, well, if it's a little R and R you need, you've come to the right place, little lady. I do have the hookup around these parts and could get you access to all the ranch's fine amenities."

"Okay, slow down there, Tex. I'm just here to chill."

"Nah, you didn't come all the way out here just to chill. I'm serious. Perks of knowing a Pleasant. In the biblical sense." Sam waggled his eyebrows and was rewarded with another of one of Cha-Cha's sexy smiles. "For real. You're not in the wedding. I'm not in the wedding. They will not notice if we disappear for a while."

Her smile dropped and she looked over at him like he had lost his damn mind. "Are you kidding?"

"What? Helene has seven hundred people in this wedding and the staff of the whole ranch is at their service. You won't be missed."

She sucked her teeth. "No, I mean we're in the middle of an open field, so unless you want to army crawl to that barn way over there using the dogs as cover—"

Sam laughed quietly at that particular visual.

"I'm not just walking off with you during this rehearsal."

Sam knew his reasons for being so private. Celebrity came with a cost. He did what he had to in order to keep his business under wraps, but it seemed a little strange that Cha-Cha was suddenly throwing down her own verbal NDA. They weren't walking down Melrose. They were on private property for an event where photos were expressly limited to the wedding photographer.

"Listen, if you don't want to be seen with me, I get it," he said, only sort of joking. The sudden softening of her expression made him wish he could take it back. "Hey, I was just playing. I didn't mean—"

"Listen, I know you're just a regular guy who looks

ridiculously fine in a cowboy hat, but you're also Sam
Pleasant. The other night still doesn't feel real. I just need
a minute to adjust."

"Yeah, we can do that."

Sam sat back and focused his full attention on the spectacle being choreographed in front of them. There had been
hundreds of weddings at the ranch, but this might be the
one to top them all. The silence between him and Cha-
Cha stretched out and all Sam could do was start cata-
loging all the other questions he had for her, when he was
done making her feel completely awkward.

"I really want to pet a horse," she whispered suddenly.

"Say again?"

"A horse. I love horses, but it's been years since I've
seen one in person."

"Sometime this weekend when no one is looking, I will
introduce you to a very special horse. My girl Majesty."
Sam reached into his pocket and pulled out his phone.
Of course a picture of Majesty graced his cell's lock
screen. And his home screen. And the wallpaper on his
laptop and his tablet.

"Oh, I know this horse. From the *GQ* spread."

"You read my *GQ* article?"

"By accident. I was flipping through looking for some
cologne ads."

"Hmmm. I'll also introduce you to my brother's horses,
Steve and Bam Bam."

"I know nothing about Bam Bam and I already love
him."

"I'm sure he'll love you," Sam said. Then he went ahead
and took a risk. "I know I just met you and this might
sound crazy, but could I get your number?"

"No," she replied with crisp ease. Sam had forgotten

the acute sting of rejection, but it took hold right in the center of his chest, burning as it spread.

"I'm staying in room twelve though. If you can be cool, maybe stop by after tonight's festivities. Or tomorrow night."

And he's back in the game!

"I can do that."

"I look forward to it. Now tell me more about Bam Bam, my new favorite horse in the world."

For such a festive evening, a dark cloud had somehow settled over Amanda's mood. Was this what it felt like to have the most basic of crushes on someone? She hadn't looked at a guy romantically—or sexually—since she'd started working for Dru. She couldn't stress enough how her night with Sam had been a colossal fluke, but there she was trying her hardest just to enjoy the lovely bonfire the ranch staff had planned for Helene and Ignacio's guests.

She couldn't though. Her stomach wouldn't stop fluttering every time Sam caught her eye. This insistent heat that had crept up her neck when he'd whispered in her ear all those hours ago had spread, bringing a tingle with it. Over her cheeks, the crown of her head, and down between her legs. Amanda couldn't stand it.

She'd gotten a few moments with the bride and groom after dinner and before they headed over to the dance hall for a little square dancing. She spent the rest of the evening keeping mostly to herself or making quick but polite small talk with their friends and family. She'd gotten trapped momentarily by an uncle, the key demo typically attracted to her full curves, but she was able to spin away as soon as she saw Helene's sister heading toward the restrooms.

Sam had been there the whole time, keeping a careful distance, but she watched him work the room, charming everyone in sight, stepping off to the side to check in and share a quick laugh with the ranch employees.

She wondered what it was like to be so out there all the time. She was an absolute pro at making herself invisible. Since she'd arrived that afternoon, she'd successfully avoided no fewer than five professional photo opportunities. Sam wasn't the guest of honor, but there was no way Amanda could miss the way everyone in the room gravitated toward him. Adoring gazes followed him everywhere he went. It wasn't shocking. He was so damn fine and he looked poured into the suit he was wearing, and somehow the wool-lined jacket he popped up in during the bonfire made him look even sexier. It was a lot to take in, and as the night went on Amanda came to a decision.

After she banged Sam one more time, she had to move on. He wasn't for her, even in a casual sense. She could see herself in another life waking up early in the morning and stepping out onto the porch of one of these high-end cabins. Looking out over their children as Sam rode his black stallion across the range. But life wasn't one of her fantasies. In thirty-six short hours she'd be in traffic on her way back to LA. Back to life as an assistant. She was still proud of her work, even if she'd fibbed about it a little, but D-LIST ASSISTANT STRIKES UP FLIRTY FLING WITH A-LIST RISING STAR was not a gossip headline she wanted to see.

She wasn't going to give Sam her phone number. He'd text or call and she'd respond, she'd answer and she knew that would only lead to disaster. Whatever was going on between them would stay right here on Big Rock Ranch.

Around ten while a friend of Ignacio's was entertaining everyone with a rousing rendition of "Back That Azz Up" on acoustic guitar, Sam's brother Zach popped up. Amanda watched from across the fire as he checked in with Helene and Ignacio. A few minutes later Sam and Zach disappeared into the night.

"Having fun?" Robyn asked.

"I am. I think I'm going to turn in though. I keep toddler hours. I'm up way past my bedtime."

Robyn smiled, then pulled her in for a light hug. They both made their way to the other side of the log sitting circle. Helene saw them coming and stood just as they reached her. "Join us for breakfast tomorrow, yeah?"

"Wouldn't miss it."

"Great. Let me get one of the boys to walk you back," Helene said.

"Oh no. I'm fine." It was dark, but there was a clear lantern-lit path all the way back to the lodge. Besides, she was ready to be alone. It had been a long day.

"Nonsense. Tom?!" Amanda looked over at one of the groomsmen who was a few feet away, texting like mad on his phone.

"Yeah," he said without looking up.

"Walk my lovely friend back to the lodge."

"Yeah sure."

"He's a real gentleman. Promise," Ignacio said with his broad smile. They said their goodnights and Amanda started back for the lodge. Tom fell into step beside her, thumbs still moving over his screen.

"Sorry," he mumbled as they walked. "Work thing."

"Completely understand." And she did. Dru had texted her three times about a pair of boots she wanted to buy but couldn't decide on.

When they reached the lodge, Amanda thanked Tom for

the escort. He turned and headed back toward the party with a goodnight that was more of a grunt.

Exhaustion flooded over her as she made her way through the lobby and back to her room. She was shocked and a little worried to find a note tacked to the door under the iron-crafted number twelve. A smile hit her lips when she read the words on the piece of ranch stationery.

Miss McQueen, Please call the front desk when you return to your room.
                                          —a friend of Bam Bam's

She used her keycard to let herself into the room and went right for the phone beside the massive wooden bed. She dialed zero and the phone started ringing.

"It's a beautiful night at Big Rock Ranch. This is Naomi."

"Hi, this is Amanda McQueen in room twelve. There was a note here for me to give you guys a call."

"Hello, Miss McQueen. We hope you enjoyed your evening."

"I did, thank you."

"Mr. Pleasant had to return home, but he had us prepare some dessert for you. A late-night snack, if you will. Could we interest you in a s'mores pie with our house-made vanilla bean and almond ice cream? It's one of my personal favorites."

Climbing into her pajamas and eating feelings sounded like a great idea.

"I'd love to try the s'mores pie. Thank you."

"We'll get that over to you."

Amanda thanked Naomi one more time, then hung up the phone. She changed into her super-sexy sweats and a tank top featuring her favorite *Adventure Time* fan art. After she washed her face and pineappled her braids on top of her head, there was a knock on her door.

"Your s'mores pie for you, Miss McQueen," she heard a young woman's voice call out in a stage whisper. Amanda rushed across the room and opened the door. There was a girl close to her age wearing the signature white, green, and blue plaid shirt and carrying one of those warm skillet plates piled high with gooey goodness.

Behind her was Sam, with two flutes and a bottle of champagne.

Chapter 7

"Good evening, Miss McQueen. We have your super-delicious s'mores pie. Where would you like it?" The girl's name tag said TAWNY.

Amanda glanced around and looked at the small coffee table between the love seat and the fireplace. "Um, right there is perfect. Thank you." After she set the dessert skillet down on top of a small protective mat, she produced some spoons seemingly out of thin air.

"There you are. Enjoy," Tawny said, her voice sweet and bright. Amanda slid her the bit of cash she had waiting in her palm and then stood by as Tawny left the room. Sam was still standing in the hallway.

"I thought you'd called it a night," Amanda said, fighting a smile and failing miserably.

"Ah, no. My brother was heading back and I figured I'd go with him. Didn't want to make it obvious that I was waiting for you."

"Oh. Would you like to come in?"

"I would love to." He stepped inside and closed the door behind him. Closed her inside with him. Inside another hotel room with Sam Pleasant. How did this keep happening?

He carefully set down the champagne bottle and glasses, then removed his hat. He nodded toward a set of oddly shaped hooks by the door.

"Do you mind?"

"If I say I don't, that doesn't mean we're betrothed or anything, does it?"

"No, it just means I'm asking before I hang my hat any old place. Just trying to respect your space is all. Ma'am." Amanda rolled her eyes at the entirely unnecessary twang he added at the end.

"Knock yourself out, Tex."

Sam threw her a devastating wink and settled his white hat safely on the hook. He turned then and took her hand and led her over to the couch. They sat together, just enough space between them for Amanda to pull her knee up to the cushion. The huge scoops of ice cream were melting atop the warm pie, but Amanda couldn't bring herself to care at the moment. Sam draped his arm over the back of the couch and lightly brushed her shoulder.

"Did you enjoy the rest of your night?" he asked. For some reason she didn't expect such a simple but sincere question. She expected more lines. More come-ons, more jokes. Instead she got that soft look in his eye. The same one she'd caught a glimpse of before they'd tumbled into his bed at the W.

"I tried."

"That bad, huh?"

"No. I had a great time. The square dance was amazing. I haven't been to one since Girl Scouts."

"Oh, I bet you were the cookie champ."

"No. One year I pooled all my resources to help this other girl win 'cause her parents were getting divorced? That made me feel like a winner."

"I would say so," Sam said, chuckling a bit.

"I just wish I'd had a proper pair of cowboy boots so I could have really gotten into the spirit. My wedges got the job done, but I would've really liked to have committed to the whole ranch aesthetic if I'd known it would be so involved."

"Oh, you need some proper boots. Your feet haven't truly lived without them," he said gravely. She had a feeling he was right.

"I'll add them to my footwear bucket list. So what's next for you?" Amanda nudged his knee, then realized it was time to stop neglecting their dessert. She grabbed a spoon and dug in as Sam replied.

"I'm taking a little time off. I've been filming and traveling for the better part of two years. I'm exhausted. I missed my family too."

"Must be nice to be home," she said before she took another bite.

"It is."

Just then Amanda heard her phone vibrate once on the bed.

"I missed seeing my brothers and my grandma."

"I'm sure they are glad to have you back. Are you gonna get in on this? 'Cause I will eat the whole thing," she said, going in for another spoonful. "This ice cream has angel tears in it or something."

"Yeah, I'm gonna have some, but first, a toast."

"Oh, to what!"

"Hold on." Sam grabbed the bottle of champagne and made quick work of the foil and the wire before he twisted the cork off into his palm with a light pop. "There's no reason to send a cork flying."

"I agree with you."

Amanda watched his confident hands as he filled her glass and handed it to her.

"Here's to us," he said.

Amanda felt her eyebrow jump up. "To us?"

"To us. And the do-over story we have to tell our grandchildren."

Laughter sputtered out of Amanda. "What?!"

"What? You want to tell them how you seduced and then robbed me on Oscar night?"

"I mean, yeah. It's a better story than telling we met at a wedding. Sometimes you need to know that your grandma liked to steal."

"Like I said, to us."

Amanda rolled her eyes as she gently clinked her glass to his. She fought the urge to toss back the champagne and took a small sip. "You know, you're going to feel real silly when you wake up Monday morning and realize I was just a figment of your imagination."

"Oh really!"

"You know all this is too good to be true," Amanda said, and she flipped an imaginary hunk of hair off her shoulder. Sam laughed in response, but his deep chuckle died on his lips as Amanda slid her fingers over his thigh. She savored how nice his muscles felt under the perfectly tailored dress pants.

"Be careful now," he said quietly.

"Or what?"

"I'm gonna sex you into a coma and make off with your horse."

"No, please. Not my horse," Amanda begged.

"You know what they say when you take something with you?"

"What's that?"

"That you didn't want to go," Sam said.

"No, no. That's if you leave something behind. It means you wished you could stay and you're looking for a reason to come back. If you take something that just means that. You like. To steal."

Sam shook his head, another smile spread over his face. "Imma kiss you now, Cha-Cha."

Amanda leaned forward, making it clear that was exactly what she wanted. Her eyes slid closed just as their lips met. Before, there was kissing, but it was that sort of anonymous stranger kissing. Good, fun, but almost as a formality. This kiss felt different, more intense. The payoff for a day of discreet flirting when she wished she could do so much more. She knew she couldn't keep Sam, but she gave herself permission to enjoy this kiss.

She took all the moments she needed to savor the soft, perfect fullness of his lips. She didn't shy away from the way his tongue slid into her mouth and brushed against hers. She only stopped his hand from moving farther up her thigh when her phone started buzzing incessantly on the bed.

Amanda pulled back, breaking the warm connection between them.

"I should grab that. It could be my mom. One second."

"Yeah," Sam said as he let out a deep breath. The way he scrubbed his hand over his face as she walked over to the bed sent a little tingle over Amanda's chest. She was glad she wasn't the only one affected by the kiss. Amanda reached for her phone, dread draining the joy from her body as Dru's name scrolled across the screen. She silenced the ringer, then turned back to Sam. There was no way she was answering with him still in the room.

"I hate to do this, but I have to take this. My friend is—"

"No. Absolutely." Sam cleared his throat, then stood carefully. He failed to hide the erection pressing against the seams of his pants. Later, when she wasn't dreading a conversation with Dru in front of him, she'd be flattered by the presence of it. She watched him as he came around the back of the couch and kissed her on the cheek. When he pulled back, there was an intensity to his eyes, something she wanted focused on her the next time she found herself under him. And there would be a next time. One last time before she had to turn back to her real life.

"Tomorrow?"

"Tomorrow."

He leaned closer again and kissed her one more time on the lips. "Get some sleep. 'Cause tomorrow, we're going to wear this bed out."

A burst of laughter came from Amanda's mouth as he backed toward the door. "Okay. Then. I'll make sure I stretch too."

"Night."

"Good night, Sam." He grabbed his hat off the hook with a wink, then slipped out the door.

The air rushed out of Amanda's lungs as soon as she heard the door click shut behind him. Sam Pleasant was dangerous. Lucky for her she didn't have the time or live in the alternate reality where pursuing him made a lick of sense. No, all she wanted was tomorrow and she was giving herself tomorrow, dammit, even if it meant blocking Dru's calls.

Her phone vibrated in her hand again several times as Dru fired off a series of texts.

Call me back you fucking hag.
I didn't get the part.
They already gave it to Lacy.

"Oh God," Amanda groaned out loud. Lacy. Frenemy Number One. The two had known each other since they were kids, and if there was anything they both loved more than the attention that came from acting it was getting under each other's skin.

Amanda hit the phone icon next to Dru's name and braced herself for one hell of an outburst. Dru answered, screaming. Some of it was unintelligible, but Amanda managed to get the central themes of her rant. She waited patiently until Dru was out of steam.

"Did either of you know the other was up for the part?" she finally asked. Lacy was white, blonde, tall, and slim— she and Dru would normally not be up for the same parts by Hollywood standards.

"I mean, I told her I was going in for it, and she told her agent she wanted to read for it."

Amanda closed her eyes and managed not to sigh. Of course she did. Lacy was still upset that Dru had booked *Andromeda* over her.

"I'm very sorry she did that to you. What can I do?"

"Not a damn thing, but maybe next time do your home-work. You know I don't like going up against her for parts. I usually get them and then when she does, she's extra petty about it. It's not good for our friendship."

"Hmm, you're right. I'll pay closer attention next time," Amanda said, like she actually had access to Lacy like that. Her mother, Justine, was her manager and her PA. She did everything for her daughter. She would never tip Amanda off to her comings and goings. Dru knew that, but the truth wasn't relevant to this conversation.

"When are you coming back?" Dru huffed.

"Like I said, Sunday night. Why aren't you out tonight?"

"I am. I'm in a car."

"Oh."

"I was out with Lacy. I just left her ass at Cargo."

"Oh okay. Well, go home and get some rest."

"No, fuck that. I'm going to meet Kellie at Lux."

"Or go meet Kellie at Lux." Kellie was another fair-weather friend, but as a top-tier social media influencer they at least didn't find themselves competing for work. Guys, on the other hand, were another issue. Hopefully, there were enough men at Lux to keep them both distracted.

"Be safe," Amanda said.

"Yeah, whatever." Dru ended that call.

Amanda chewed the inside of her lip and sighed as she looked at the dark screen. She looked across the room and caught sight of the top of the champagne bottle peeking over the back of the couch. She tossed her phone on the bed and went straight for the bottle. After a deep swig, she considered the remains of the dessert. The ice cream was completely melted, but the sweet smell still lingered in the air. She reached for the spoon and took another bite, then washed that down with another sip of the champagne.

At least her night had gone according to her original plan. Alone with ice cream and pie in her pajamas.

Sam sat behind the wheel of Zach's truck, pushing back on his rising disappointment as he waited for the gates to Pleasant Lane to open. The slow parting of the heavy wood and steel was usually a comfort to him. After a long drive from Los Angeles or fresh off a flight to Ontario Airport, through the town he never really felt good calling home, arriving at this family cul-de-sac hit a reset button for him. He knew what waited on the other side. He knew he'd have the space and the freedom to refill his well before he went back out to deal with the BS parts of his chosen path.

But he'd had no plans to pull back through those gates tonight. He should have been back at the ranch, slowly, sweetly putting in his best work between a certain pair of luscious thighs. He should have fallen asleep with a certain Cha-Cha in his arms. He could have easily seen himself waking her for an early morning kiss so he could sneak out before the other guests started milling around. He should *not* be alone in Zach's truck waiting for his cock to deflate, thinking about who he was going to risk waking up, his brothers or his grandmother.

He didn't think Amanda *owed* him a thing. The complete opposite. But man, did he wish the night had gone differently. He didn't know what was wrong with him. His attention had never been snatched up by a woman so quickly. So easily. He wasn't sprung, exactly, but damn, was he interested. He wanted more time with Amanda. He wanted to get to know her. He was relieved that his desire to see her again wasn't completely unfounded. She'd been shocked to see him, but there was no mistaking the heat between then, or the bold-ass way she knew how to flirt.

The gate stopped at its fully opened position and Sam drove through, down the dark lane lit every twenty-five yards by iron lampposts. He drove past Jesse's house and his grandmother's home at the center of it all and pulled the truck to a stop in Zach's driveway. He cut the engine, then hopped out, locking it before he dropped the keys in the terra-cotta pot on his porch. He took his time walking back toward his grandmother's house. He heard a few high-pitched barks as soon as he stepped on the porch, but Poppy quieted down as soon as he put his key in the door.

"Hey, girl," he whispered to the terrier mix as he scooped her up from the floor. "You up all alone?"

"Is that my baby baby?" he heard his grandmother Miss Leona say from down the hall. He walked into the kitchen and found her standing at the kitchen counter in her billowy pajamas, with a hot cup of something in her hands. He crossed the title floor and kissed her on her cheek, catching a whiff of the hot and very spiked cider in her mug.

"It's late, young lady. What are you doing up?" he asked.

"Oh, the girls are still out. I can't sleep until I know all of my babies are settled back in the barn."

"Lilah and Corie are grown, Grandma. They could be out all night. No need to wait up for them," Sam said, knowing she wasn't going to listen to him, no matter what he said. Her grandma mode was strong, and Lilah was the baby of the whole Pleasant bunch. Ever since she took off running from the bunk-ass arranged marriage his uncle had tried to stick her in, she'd been living with their grandmother. Lilah was smart as hell and savvy to boot, but she was soft-spoken and kind of shy. When she went out with Corie, who was always looking for trouble, even he raised an eyebrow at the quality of their evening plans. Miss Leona felt responsible for her while she was figuring out what she wanted from her life without her father interfering.

"You know damn good and well I'm not worried about Corie," his grandmother said. "I'm just up in case Lilah needs me to bail Corie out of jail."

"Makes sense. You want me to wait up for them?"

"Oh no. They should be back soon. They just went to

Claim Jumpers." The cowboy dive bar on the other side of town was where all the locals went to kick back.

"Gotcha." Sam set the dog down and took a seat at the kitchen island. He took his hat off and set it on his knee, then scrubbed his hands over his face.

"Everything going okay with Helene's wedding?"

"Yes, ma'am. Happy bride. Happy guests. I think tomorrow will be real special for them."

"Well, I'll be there for the ceremony."

"Not staying for the reception? Don't you want to catch the bouquet?" Sam teased. His grandmother hadn't so much as looked at another man since his grandfather had passed away nearly twenty-five years ago. Sam only had a handful of memories of Grandpa Pleasant, but he did remember how happy his grandmother had been in his company, how they behaved like teenagers until the very end.

"I can't. I've made other plans. I have a date."

Sam pressed his hand to his chest and leaned all the way back. "Ah. Excuse me?"

"I have a date."

"Well, go on, girl. Tell me about him."

"I will not. And you will not tell your brothers, especially Jesse. He's already all up in my business, getting in the way. You know nice Mr. Chester?"

"The organ guy." He played the organ at Miss Leona's church.

"Yes, honey. The organ *guy*. He asked me out to a nice lunch. Jesse got puffed up. You know how he does—"

"I do." His brother didn't have a temper, exactly, but he had a temper. It didn't help that he was six-foot-seven and built like warehouse, forget a barn. He kept his temper in check most of the time, but while Zach, Lilah and Corie took care of Miss Leona's day to day needs, Jesse had knighted himself his grandmother's protector. Trying to save her from any and all elderly would-be grifters looking to swindle her out of her money and her heart. But Mr. Chester was far from the type. He was a sweet old man who had always been kind to their family. Too bad Jesse had ruined his chances.

"Okay, so this new guy slid in while Jesse was swimming laps or something."

"Why do you have to make me sound all common? Slid in. Please."

"Well, you won't give me details and you're being all covert. I have to assume he's being covert too."

"No one is sliding in anything. I'm just trying to keep most of my grandchildren out of my business. But if you must know, he's a widower. He's a nice man. He still works. He has one grown daughter who is doing very well for herself."

Sam was pretty out of the loop when it came to the happenings of the over-eighty set. She could have been talking about anyone. "Well, you let me know if it starts getting serious. I want to talk to the young chap."

"Mhmm. I take it you're sleeping over here tonight."

"I didn't want to wake Jesse up and the rest of the dogs. Do you want me to wait up for Lilah and Corie?"

"No, baby. You go on to bed. You can stay in the Sunshine room. It's all made up for Evie, but I'm gonna stick to my word and let her sleep over there when she gets here tomorrow."

"How kind of you," Sam laughed as he came back around the island. "Don't worry, they'll be married soon enough. Good night, Grandma."

She sucked her teeth. "Miss Leona." It was what everyone called her, all three of her sons and all of their children.

Except Sam. Lilah may have been the baby, but Sam got away with more.

"You know I can't call you that. It's so impersonal. So cold," he teased. His grandma rolled her eyes and tapped her fingers against her cheek. He gave her a light kiss and a hug, then headed down the hall toward the guest rooms.

Talking to his grandmother put a smile back on his face. It also made him look forward to seeing Amanda again. They couldn't spend the night together, but it would be nice to text her before he knocked out. Say goodnight, tell her how much he enjoyed being with her for the short time they had. Maybe tomorrow, he'd remember to get her number.

Chapter 8

Amanda felt strange. It was the only way to describe the uneasy feeling that had been following her all day. She'd tried to get some good, restful sleep. It was the most responsible thing to do in a nice hotel room, and the bed in room twelve was freaking divine. Perfect mattress, warm blankets and feather pillows to die for. She could've taken a two-week vacation on the bed in room twelve. Too bad Dru had been blowing up her phone on and off until two a.m. Amanda should have expected it. Yes, she had her weekends off, but Dru had geographical anxiety when it came to Amanda, especially when Kaidence was busy. It hadn't helped that Dru had been drinking. Still, Amanda had answered her calls and replied to her texts until it was clear Dru had fallen asleep. She'd passed out herself and woken up to the ascending twinkling of her alarm. She'd slept soundly, but she'd needed at least four more hours.

She'd pulled herself together and made her way over to the Copper Canteen for the ladies' breakfast with the bridal party. That's when things had started going downhill. Helene's cousin Oni had to go and bring up Sam. Helene and Robyn kept their word and their mouths shut about what they knew about Amanda and her unique situation with a certain actor. They didn't stay on him too long as a topic of conversation, but for seven or so minutes nearly every woman in attendance, including Helene's mother, presented their opinions on Sam's devastatingly good looks, his Oscar win, and his single status, testing all of Amanda's limits.

More than one member of the bridal party had made it clear Sam could get it before they'd moved on to the all-important topic of who had done bridesmaid number two's eyebrows. Before the weekend was out, one of these single ladies was going to take a crack at Sam Pleasant. Amanda just smiled and laughed along with the conversation, ignoring the glance Helene passed her way. She understood. Sam was gorgeous. He was famous. He was available. Who wouldn't want to get with him?

Of course, Amanda hadn't breathed a word about the night they'd spent together or their abbreviated dessert break, but it had been a special kind of awful listening to them talk about a person she had to admit she had some pretty confusing feelings for. And she definitely wasn't jealous. It wouldn't make sense for her to be jealous. She and Sam weren't a thing, and whatever had happened between them was, by definition, a secret. But still, an odd pang pinched at her neck every time another woman mentioned his name.

And that seemed to be the theme for the day: glee for the happy couple and their beautiful union, and absolute shock and excitement over the fact that Sam Pleasant's fine ass was in attendance. By the time they'd gotten to the reception Amanda felt even more confident in her decision to completely disappear from Sam's life when the wedding came to an end. For one brief moment she'd thought about what it must be like to actually date someone like Sam, the constant comments, the constant competition. She didn't want it. It didn't matter how badly she wanted to see him wearing nothing but that cowboy hat.

They'd spoken to each other twice throughout the day, but only in passing. He'd offered her a polite hello that was devoid of sexual innuendo before the ceremony. And he'd checked on her again, simply asking if she was enjoying herself during the cocktail hour while the mariachi band Helene's father had requested was entertaining the mingling guests. He'd sat with his grandmother, thee Leona Lovell, during the ceremony and they were placed at different tables during the reception.

It would have been interesting to spend the event on his arm, even though she had to check herself hard and fast for even considering it, but as the night went on and dinner turned to dancing, the invisible wall between them proved to be a blessing. It forced Amanda to really examine the impact her attraction to Sam had on her overall horniness. And that's all it was, purely sexual. Beyond that there were no real feelings.

He was funny and charming, and on the surface, thoughtful and considerate. Amanda couldn't ignore the way he doted on his grandmother until she was ready to call it a night. Sam Pleasant was a great guy, but what did that mean to her? Nothing. Definitely not enough to throw her hat in the ring with his hundreds if not thousands of lady admirers. Even if only a dozen or so had a real chance. On paper there was a lot to like about Sam Pleasant and she was sure, beyond what she'd already witnessed, he had even more to offer a lucky girl. Still she knew that none of it was for her.

It was so clear, Amanda should have felt good about the bullet she was going to dodge. The one where he realized she wasn't actually his type. Or when she remembered that she would probably die alone, adjusting Dru's IV in whatever assisted-living facility they'd both been stuck in by the kids Dru would eventually have with a pro-basketball player who refused to marry her. A calm, pleasant feeling should have washed over her. She should have felt light and carefree, able to enjoy the rest of the evening and the DJ's impressive selections as she cut up her own corner of the dance floor.

Instead she found herself off to the side, nursing a glass of champagne as she swayed to the beat. Her smile refused to leave her face as she watched Helene, arms draped over her new husband's shoulders. She was happy for them, and really the whole day, the whole weekend so far had been so much fun. She just wished she didn't feel so lonely.

She swallowed the lump in her throat and chased it with a sip of bubbly alcohol. She caught sight of Sam on the other side of the dance floor. He was talking to some other ridiculously hot guys. Amanda knew men like that flocked together. It only made logical sense. But it didn't matter, she reminded herself. Men like that were not for her. She didn't mean that in a low self-esteem-y way. She was a catch, dammit. But the world of A-list celebrities was silly and over the top, and sometimes it hurt to look at it. She could be a friend on the periphery, she could watch from the sidelines, but she couldn't participate. Not in any real way. Amanda glanced down at the now-empty glass in her hand.

She needed to stop drinking.

When she looked up again, at first she'd lost sight of Sam. Not that she was looking for him. A mixed bag of emotions rushed through her when she saw him making his way from the DJ's table to her general direction. She figured there was some other famous or photo-ready person somewhere between them, and there was. She spotted at least four, but that didn't stop him. He was coming right for her. Amanda's palms were suddenly warm, her fingers unsure. She set down the glass on the dessert table behind her, then straightened her shoulders as she slowly released a deep breath.

Just as Sam reached her the opening notes of "I Only Have Eyes for You" came through the speakers. The DJ took to the mic. "Just want to slow it down again, just one more time. This one is for all the lovers out there, young and old. And the bride and groom."

The sentiment echoed around the room as Sam reached for her hand. "Care to join me on the dance floor?"

She fixed him with a stern glare and whispered, "Keep clean and above the belt."

"Ma'am. I'm a gentleman. Everything about me is nice and clean."

"Uh-huh." Amanda rolled her eyes, but that didn't stop her from following him out to the dance floor. Also didn't stop her from hearing some comments from the peanut gallery.

"Oh, that's so nice," one of Ignacio's guests said in what would never have been mistaken for a whisper. "She's been alone all night."

"Who is she?" her companion said. Seriously, had no one ever learned to whisper? Sam had heard them too.

"I think it's one of Helene's cousins."

Amanda bit her lips and forced herself not to laugh. Of course Sam's attention was all about pity when it came to her.

"How come when you show up to these things without a date it's seen as sexy, but when I do it, it's pathetic?" she asked as his hand slid around her waist. She forced her body not to respond. She managed to keep herself from pressing closer and soaking in his warmth, inch by inch. Instead, she draped her arms loosely over his shoulders, leaving plenty of room for the Lord. He seemed to catch her drift, but that didn't stop a devilish grin from touching his lips.

"Nah, nah, I didn't come here without a date. I came here with my grandmother. I'm sure that sent my stock through the roof."

"That's sick," Amanda teased. "Using thee Leona Lovell like that. She's royalty. Show her some respect."

Sam let out a low chuckle as his tongue swept out and wet his lower lip. "Do you want me to prove a point?"

Amanda's eye sprang wide with shock. She glanced around and caught the handful of people still watching them, including Loud Mouth and her friend. "Absolutely not. No."

"You mean you don't want me to pull you close and kiss the hell out of you in front of all of these people? Let them know if I had the choice I would have spent the whole day by your side?"

"What about your grandmother?"

"I have two brothers and two cousins who would have been happy to escort her."

Amanda fought the urge to rest her head on his shoulder and finally said the thing she had a feeling she'd regret one day. "I don't think you should come to my room tonight."

"Oh yeah?"

"Yeah. I—uh, I don't think this is a good idea."

"Was it something I said?" he teased even though a sad smile crept across his face.

"No. This is a textbook 'it's me, not you' situation. You're—well, so far so good."

"What does that mean?" Sam laughed.

"I'm trying not to gush over you. We're not there yet."

"And we won't get there, is what you're saying."

"I keep running into you by accident and I know you're not trying to boo me up or anything, but if you come to my room tonight? I just know me. I'll want to run into you again on purpose and I just can't."

"I see."

"My life's kinda full right now and not in a fun way. When I do start running into someone on purpose, I don't want my life to get in the way."

"So we part as friends," Sam replied. "Friends who desperately wished they had slept together at least a dozen more times."

Amanda let out a hideous snort. "You have a lot of friends like that?"

"Nah, Cha-Cha. Just the one."

"Mr. Pleasant. I've had a wonderful time."

"If you change your mind—"

"I'll book a room with Naomi." Amanda watched Sam's face closely, noting the hurt he was trying to hide. Finally he gave her a little nod, letting her know he understood, that he wouldn't push her any further. She dropped her gaze to the knot of his tie, and they spent the rest of the song swaying together in their own corner of the dance floor. When the song ended she wanted to leave him with a final bit of advice, maybe hint at the idea that he should ignore any DMs he received from Dru, but she decided to stay out of it. If he took her up on her offer, it would just serve as further proof that Amanda had no business messing with Sam. She stepped back, taking his hand as it slipped from her waist.

She reached up and slowly, but playfully drew the backs of her fingers down his cheeks.

"You'll find another girl like me, Tex. I promise," she said in a deep Southern drawl.

"Don't make this worse than it already is. You best go, missy. Leave a cowboy to his broken heart," he responded in kind. Amanda chuckled a bit as she gave his fingers a light squeeze, then walked away. This was how they needed to leave it, with laughs and no hard feelings. Nothing had really happened between them anyway, just some pelvis-quaking sex and part of a really decadent dessert. Speaking of which . . .

Amanda grabbed a piece of cake and headed back to her table, where Helene's actual cousin was sitting, rocking her sleeping toddler. She could still see Sam on the other side of the room. The smile had returned to his face as Loud Mouth stepped up and started to dance with him.

"Oh, I haven't had any cake yet," Helene's cousin said as Amanda made herself comfortable.

"You want me to grab you a slice? Your hands are full with the baby," Amanda replied.

"No. I'll get one before we head back to our room. Are you having fun?"

"I am," Amanda said, even if it wasn't the whole truth. For once, she couldn't wait to get back to LA, where her regular life was underwhelming and exceedingly less complicated.

* * *

Around midnight when the after-party started to dwindle, Sam decided to call it a night. Overall the wedding had been a complete success. For one, an actual wedding where both the bride and groom had shown up on time and enthusiastically said I do had taken place. And as the afternoon had rolled into night, a lot of the guests had gone out of their way to tell Sam how much they were enjoying their time at Big Rock Ranch. Sam couldn't have been happier for his friends, so he'd felt like a total ass sporting a fake smile for the rest of the reception. He'd danced and mingled, declined more than one indecent proposal, but overall he'd had a pretty good time himself, until Amanda had let him know that whatever he'd seen happening between them that night and beyond was no longer in the cards.

Amanda had split an hour before, not that he'd been paying attention. He'd caught sight of her a few more times as the night had gone on. As she'd enjoyed her slice of cake, when Ignacio's brother had pulled her back out on the floor to dance to some Latin remix of the new Normani track. When she'd hugged Helene and Ignacio good night. She'd headed back toward the lodge with another female guest by her side. Sam knew no one had caught on to the way the heat between them had thawed. Still he didn't think it would be a good idea to take off right after she'd left. He'd waited until the mood of champagne and wedding hookups amongst the stranglers became too much to handle, then headed back to the barn, where he'd parked Zach's truck.

The place was quiet when he got back to Pleasant Lane. He let himself into Miss Leona's house, then made his way down to the guest room. He should have passed right out. It had been a long few days, and he still hadn't recovered from the adrenaline rush from being under the spotlights on that Oscar stage. He was exhausted, but he lay awake in bed, just staring at the ceiling, wondering what the fuck was wrong with him.

Sam didn't know what he expected. Actually, that was a full-blown lie. He'd expected he'd enjoy Helene and Ignacio's wedding. He'd expected to enjoy a few laughs with his grandmother, and when she'd had enough he knew Jesse would come pick her up and take her home, leaving Sam to openly ogle Amanda late into the night until she gave him the signal that she was ready for the two of them to head back to her room together. He had condoms at the ready. He had more champagne chilling, a short menu of late-night snacks on deck just in case they needed to refuel between what he'd hoped would be round three and four. He'd expected to wake up early tomorrow morning and kiss Amanda, finally get her phone number, and sometime next week, he'd expected he was going to call her up and ask her out on a proper date so they could really get to know each other.

He wasn't sure what exactly had gone wrong. Not that it mattered. Amanda had told him where she stood and all he could do, what he planned to do, was respect that. She just wasn't into him.

Sam had to face it. He was an optimist and a hopeless romantic, and both of those things sometimes got in the way of reality. Amanda had made it clear the first time she'd skipped out of his hotel room that she wanted nothing to do with him beyond their one-night stand. Running into each other again had been pure coincidence. He'd been so amped to see her again some of the sparkly dust that clouded his brain from time to time had him mistaking that coincidence for destiny.

On planet Earth, however, that wasn't the case. If Amanda wanted him, she would have said so. But no, she'd done her best to let him down nice and easy. She liked him, but not enough to see if what he was feeling between them could become something more. Something that at least involved exchanging phone numbers.

Sam grabbed his phone off the nightstand and rolled onto his back. He pulled up Instagram and like a damn fool searched for Amanda McQueen. There were a shocking number of people with that name. Still he spotted Cha-Cha's bright smile in the fifth circular avatar down the list. He clicked on *QueenA* and quickly learned that her social media didn't give away much about her. The photos were mostly artistic shots of various LA streets. Maybe one photo out of every twenty was a picture of Amanda herself, just a close shot on her smiling face. There was one picture of her with her parents on Christmas morning two years before.

Sam was maybe four years deep in her feed when he realized what he was doing. She'd given him the full-blown no-thank-you. He needed to let this, let *her* go. He closed out of her account and braved a look at his DMs. Walls did a good job monitoring them, but Sam liked to look every now and then. He scrolled back to Oscar Sunday and whoa, Walls hadn't been lying. His DMs were filled with messages from all kinds of women. He could have had Walls lock his DMs but the way the messaging system worked he'd also miss sincere messages and tagged posts from fans. He decided it was worth it to take the bad and bizarre with the good.

He scrolled by a message from Dru Anastasia, then scrolled back again. He'd watched her show *Andromeda* with Lilah a few times. He liked the whole space, paranormal aspect of it, but the cast hadn't been enough to keep him interested. Dru was beautiful, though. The message she sent was . . . it was definitely an approach.

> Congrats on your win. You should take me out
> sometime so we can celebrate.
> I think we'd both enjoy it.

She'd added a wink emoji.

The image of trying to "enjoy" a meal with Dru Anastasia flashed through his mind. There was no spark there, only cautious confusion. He closed out of the conversation and moved on to the next message from *BrandonWilliams21*. He'd tagged Sam in a photo of what looked like a school presentation that had a big red A at the top with a scrawled note that said "Good work." Sam smiled as he read the caption.

> I'd never heard of Josiah Williams before my dad
> took me to see *The Sky Beneath Our Feet*. I decided
> to do my term project on Josiah and learned that he's
> on my family tree. Thank you to @TheSamPleasant
> for bringing a member of my family to life.

Sam shared the post on his account and added his own caption, congratulating Brandon on his A and thanking him for tagging him in such a personal post. He may have been nursing a hopeless crush that had already been buried, but at least he'd helped to inspire a high school sophomore. It wasn't what he'd expected from the night, but it was something he could feel good about. With some of the optimism restored, Sam went to sleep.

Chapter 9

It took some doing, but Amanda finally got PJ to stop yelling. The manager of Delightly had rightfully lost his shit, but Amanda was determined to make things right.

When she'd returned from Charming, she'd hoped the week ahead would go smoothly, or as smoothly as they usually went with Dru. She was exhausted, which was usually the case after semi-destination wedding weekends. Even though they'd stayed at a luxury ranch with the best amenities and all the fresh air a girl could handle. Between all the wedding-related activities, Dru's texting drama, and stressing about a barely romantic situation with a certain actor who looked devastatingly handsome in a cowboy hat, she'd barely slept at all.

She'd braced herself for Dru's bad mood when she arrived at her apartment bright and early Monday morning. Amanda knew Dru was under a lot of stress and a lot of pressure. Kaidence had hired Amanda to relieve some of that pressure. Well, a lot of that pressure. Dru relied on her in a lot of ways that had nothing to do with making sure she didn't miss her call times. She'd buoyed Dru in a sense of reality away from the cameras and anytime Amanda went away, Dru seemed to come slightly unglued. She panicked and when Amanda came back to work, she made her pay for it.

Her comments had been a little more cutting than usual, her requests a little more absurd. And that was all after she'd spent a good ten minutes making fun of Amanda's imaginary friends and the crappy wedding she was sure her friend had pieced together for her crappy husband and her crappy guests. 'Cause that was her opinion of Amanda. She didn't actually know anything about her personal life, so she assumed it had to be shameful. Crappy even.

Part of her wanted to tell Dru that she'd actually been at Helene and Ignacio's wedding, the social event of the year. She wanted to casually let it slip that she'd had to work to not be in any of the photos that would be in next week's issue of *People*. She wanted to let it slip that she had a chance to sleep with Sam Pleasant. AGAIN. Instead she'd taken her barbs like she always did, with a nod and a change of subject back to what was really important. Sometimes it worked and sometimes, well, Dru was just committed to being an asshole and didn't let up with her cruelty until she had another distraction.

This week that distraction had come in the form of a botched lunch delivery from Delightly that had sent Dru into a rage spiral the likes of which Amanda hadn't seen in years. It had been the perfect storm of this cannot be happening. On a normal day, Amanda would order Dru's lunch and meet the delivery person by Dru's trailer right before the cast and crew were set to break. This time, though, the delivery had been late and they'd run into her as she was making her way across the lot.

They say in times of stress your senses are heightened and Dru being the stressed-out equivalent of a bloodhound somehow knew Delightly had sent the wrong thing. She'd ordered the carrot soup with a warm quinoa salad. Somehow Dru had clocked the package in the young woman's hand as tomato soup and a sandwich before she'd even handed it over. Amanda watched in slow-motion horror as Dru snatched the bag out of her hand and confirmed that the order was wrong. What came next could only be described as a meltdown. Amanda didn't want to think about the fucked-up things Dru had said over a simple mix-up.

To her credit the delivery person stuck up for herself, explaining that she was just the driver, but that just spurred Dru on. The poor woman was in tears, making a break for her car, way before Dru had run out of steam. She'd pulled out her phone and started to call Delightly, but Amanda had talked her off the ledge, offering to go herself and pick up the right order. Good thing they'd come in separate cars.

But by the time Amanda had arrived at Delightly the damage had been done. PJ had already been briefed on what had gone down by the poor delivery person, who was apparently still crying in the back.

"I cannot apologize enough," Amanda said as she and the manager stood at the end of their vegan pastry display. His face was beet red and every vein above his shoulders was popping out. She had no idea how to fix this.

"You know you're not the problem. It's her! Every time she comes here she's rude."

"I know and I'm sorry."

He reached for a bag on the shelf behind him stamped with the restaurant's signature leaf in the shape of a heart.

"This is it." He handed it over. The correct order.

"PJ—"

Amanda glanced over her shoulder on reflex as the door

to Delightly opened again. The audience for this fiasco didn't need to grow any bigger.

Of course this would be the day for Sam freaking Pleasant to come strolling in. He was with a white man in a very crisp suit and his assistant.

She turned back to PJ, her brain forcing her to deal with the more pressing issue first. "I promise. I will pick up *all* her takeout orders from now on. All of them."

"I'm really sorry. We just can't. In this case the customer was dead wrong. I have to do it. She's banned from dining with us. What am I telling my staff if I let this slide? It goes against everything—"

"I know."

"I'm sorry. If you want to come in and dine with us, you know you're always welcome. But Dru is going to have to purchase her meals elsewhere. I can't ask anyone who works for me to deal with that treatment. And frankly, you shouldn't do it either."

Amanda felt her stomach drop to the floor, as he put his hand on her shoulder and gave it a light squeeze that said, "Look at your life, girl. Look at your choices." PJ was right. She was paid to put up with Dru's abuse, but subjecting the food service staff of the greater Los Angeles area to her behavior was not some right she'd been awarded. Sometimes there were consequences for shitty behavior, and Dru had just lost pretty much the only place in town she actually liked to eat.

"Okay," Amanda said, frustration nearly closing her throat.

PJ nodded, then turned back to the kitchen. The conversation was over. Amanda tucked the food close to her chest, then ducked her head and made for the door. If she moved fast enough there was a pretty good chance Sam wouldn't see her while he was hearing the day's specials. She moved smoothly, quickly, but not quickly enough. Just as she slid by him and his crew, his assistant turned and bumped into her. She stumbled back a step, her ass bumping the corner of a nearby empty table.

"Oh shit. My bad," Sam's assistant said.

"It's okay."

"Hey, it's Cha-Cha."

Sam of course spun around, his eyes wide with disbelief. "Amanda."

"Hey. Nice to see you. I—uh, I have to get going." She took off for the door, but not without feeling the brush of Sam's fingertips on her arm as she rushed by him. He was following her. Maybe if she walked fast enough she could get back to her car and accidentally run him over before she was forced to talk to him. She hurried down the street, and just as she turned the corner where she'd parked her car down a muraled alley, she heard him call after her again.

"Amanda! You dropped your phone!"

She froze, then patted the pocket of her down vest. "Shit." It had definitely slipped out. She headed back just as Sam came around the corner. For some reason the moment she saw him tears sprung to her eyes. She couldn't explain it, but she didn't want her worlds to collide. Not like this.

"What's going on?" he asked, worry creasing his forehead.

"It's nothing."

"It's not nothing. You're crying." Sure enough a few jerk-face tears slid down her cheeks. "Did something happen in there? Do I need to go back and fight a vegan?" His well-intended threat only made her cry harder. She wanted to tell him what had happened, but levels and levels of embarrassment kept her from disclosing the whole truth. Again.

"Some—one of my coworkers came in and they weren't kind to the staff. I was trying to smooth things over so she doesn't become the first person to ever be banned from a vegan breakfast spot."

"Sounds like your coworker is an ass, but why are you crying?"

"Because my coworker is an ass."

"Jesus. Right. Come here." Amanda knew she could keep her distance, but she didn't stop Sam from pulling her into his arms. It was a friendly hug, lacking the heat they'd shared before, which made things so much worse. She couldn't remember the last time she'd had someone really comfort her. She pulled away, suddenly, brushing the tears from her cheeks. "I'm sorry."

"Don't apologize."

"I just—this industry is a lot sometimes. You know?"

"I do. I definitely do."

"I seriously do not know why I'm crying. This isn't even about me," Amanda said, and immediately she knew that was a lie. There had been a month where Dru refused to eat. Anything. Kaidence actually encouraged it. She was impressed with Dru's drastic weight loss, and she was in between shows, so her complete lack of energy didn't seem to matter. Silly Amanda was actually worried about her health. Every day she tried something different. A different restaurant, a different smoothie, a different designer protein bar endorsed by the most trustworthy of housewives.

Nothing worked until she'd tried Delightly. She'd finally gotten back to incorporating a few more places into Dru's diet, but Delightly was her go-to. She didn't want to think about what was going to happen now that she was literally banned from eating there. But none of that was Sam's business and she wasn't going to tell him.

"Delightly is just the only place our whole room agrees on. I've been coming here for years. I'm just upset that she was mean to PJ and his employees."

"Hey, you busy this weekend?"

Amanda felt her eyebrow shoot up. What the hell did this weekend have to do with Dru's tantrum. "No, why?"

"Come out to the ranch."

"What? No. Sam, I—" Surely he couldn't be thinking about sex at a moment like this.

"This isn't about me. Or us. You're clearly stressed. It just so happens I know a guy who can comp your whole stay. Did you even get to see the spa?"

"No."

"You won't even have to see me. I don't *live* at the ranch. You spring yourself from work Friday night and come on down. Enjoy the ranch. Ride a horse, pet a llama or one of our more friendly sheep."

"What about the dogs?" Amanda sniffled. "Can I spend some time with your dogs?"

"Of course. You didn't meet the other two. Hell, if you want, we'll go down to the shelter and pick up a few more. All the dogs you can handle."

Amanda couldn't stop herself from laughing. "I have to think about it."

"Here. Unlock your phone for a second." Amanda unclenched her hand and reached for her phone, which he was still holding. Her fingernails had been digging into her palm so hard she knew her hand would ache when the adrenaline passed. She took her cell and unlocked it with her tear-streaked face before she handed it back to him. His thumbs flew over the screen as he spoke.

"Give it some thought and if you decide you want to come through just text or call me. I'll take care of everything." He handed it back and she stopped herself from immediately texting him so he'd have her number saved. She still wasn't sure if she wanted him to be able to contact her. Her eyes lingered on the freshly saved contact, *TEX*, at the top of the screen.

"You don't have to do this," Amanda said as she glanced up at his handsome face. He was working on the beginnings of a beard. She didn't hate it.

"I want to. I know sad and I know exhausted. You look like you've had enough of both. For real. I won't bother you. I didn't forget what you said. You're not interested. Heard it loud and clear. But . . ." He shrugged, tilting his head to the side. "Come on down. Use as many or as few of the amenities as you want. Eat some bomb-ass food and then battle Sunday night traffic to brave another week with your asshole coworker."

"Shit." She was still holding Dru's now lukewarm carrot soup. "I have to get back." That seemed to be enough to break them both from some spell Amanda didn't realize they were under. She didn't realize how close to each other they still were standing. She didn't realize how badly she still wanted to kiss him, how badly she wished weekends with him could be a reality that wouldn't cost her her job.

"I'll—I gotta go."

"Okay. Hit me up if you change your mind."

"I will. Thanks." Amanda flashed him a weak smile and then turned back to her car. Sam waved at her when she buckled in behind the wheel, then headed back inside toward the restaurant. When she pulled down to the mouth of the alley she checked both ways for traffic. And just before she pulled back out onto the street she could have sworn she'd seen two paparazzi on the opposite corner. She prayed to God that Sam wasn't the one they were looking for.

Sam kept his eyes focused on the mouth of the trail ahead. He'd set out right at sunrise, taking his black mare out to start their day. He thought another long ride with Majesty would help take his mind off everything. Usually the time he spent in the saddle helped clear his head. He could take in the sounds of nature around him, or talk to Majesty about whatever he was thinking. By the time he made it back to the stables Sam would have found some sort of clarity, but today the quiet just gave him more time to overthink and overanalyze. Again and again.

He'd had one hell of a week. Getting kicked to the curb by Amanda. Being offered several roles, each more reductive and stereotypical than the next; more DMs from women like Dru Anastasia, who he had no interest in dating; running into Amanda again. Something about her had him all messed up.

He'd had every intention of leaving her alone like she'd asked. He wasn't going to probe Helene for her number when she got back from her honeymoon. He wasn't even going to ask how she was doing, but when he saw her in Delightly, upset as hell, something in him knew he couldn't just let her walk away without at least checking on her. If she accepted his offer for a weekend on the ranch, he'd continue to keep his word and his distance, unless she changed her mind. He'd do the work of getting over whatever feelings he'd developed for her in the short time they'd known each other, but he realized as he and Majesty had taken their morning stroll that Walls had been onto something.

His breakup with Natalie had been what it was. A necessary end. They weren't in the same place emotionally and it became pretty obvious to him that he didn't want to get to that place with her. Still there may have been something to Walls's suggestion that he'd been moping. Sulking even. Sam was unhappy and unfulfilled. And now it was clear to him love was the thing he was looking for. He'd never admit that out loud, not in those words, but it was the way he felt.

Maybe seeing Zach finally so happy with Evie and seeing just how in love Helene and Ignacio were had something to do with it. He'd been working so hard, he'd pushed his own emotions to the side so he could focus on the emotional needs of the characters he was playing, but clearly his heart was ready to take priority again. He was ready for a boo to call his own. It didn't have to be Amanda McQueen. It couldn't be. She didn't fucking like him. But he had to start opening himself up soon. Maybe ask some people he trusted if they could set him up. He wanted a certain kind of happiness.

Sam dismounted as the barn came into view. He had a call after lunch, but for the most part he'd cleared his day. His brothers and Lilah were working, and Corie and his grandmother were busy helping Evie plan for her and Zach's wedding. He could go back into the city, but after weeks and weeks of award show–related engagements, press, meetings, a wedding, and more press and meetings, he felt like he hadn't had any time to rest at all. Maybe if Amanda didn't come out he'd take advantage of the ranch's amenities himself.

He took his time letting Majesty cool down before he

watered her and removed her tack. He heard Zach's voice as his brother came around the side of the barn.

"'Sup, man. Chris told me you were out here."

"Taking an early break?" It was barely nine thirty.

"Yeah. Jesse just found out one of the vendors is owned by a casual white supremacist so we're terminating the contract. It's been—" Zach sighed before he took off his Stetson and scrubbed his hand over his face. "It's been a fucking morning. I just wanted to come out here and commune with Steve and Bam Bam for a moment." Sam smiled at the way Zach treated his and Evie's horses like they were their children. He could relate as he gently ran his palm down Majesty's side. "What's going on with you? You have a good ride?"

"Ehhh," Sam said, shrugging. "I think I'm ready to start dating again though."

"Does this have anything to do with this VIP package I may or may not be comping this weekend? Miss Leona said you were making eyes at some pretty, curvaceous young thang all through Helene's wedding."

"Yes and no and yes. Amanda is the one I've invited this weekend and she was the one I was making eyes at at the wedding, but she told me she just wanted to be friends. Actually no, she just told me she didn't want to date me."

"So you're letting that go by inviting her to Big Rock for an all-expenses-paid vacay. That's not suspect at all."

Sam laughed at the look of "what the fuck?" on his brother's face. "No. I ran into her when she was having a shitty day and I just thought she should come down here and recharge. I might not even see her."

"That's bullshit, but if that's what you're selling to yourself."

"Nah, man. It's fine, we're just friends."

"When was the last time you invited a girl away for the weekend on Valentine's Day and kept that shit friendly?"

"Valentine's Day?" Sam said, a frown clouding his features. He had no idea what the date was.

"Yeah, pretend you didn't know."

"I didn't." Just then his phone vibrated in his pocket. He pulled it out and looked at the text from his cousin Lilah.

You got pap'd

Sam clicked the link and looked at the story *US Weekly* had run first thing that morning.

SAM PLEASANT, GOOD SAM—ARITAN.

Sam Pleasant retrieves phone for woman who dropped her cellular device outside Delightly in West Hollywood.

There he was in seven or so nearly identical pictures of him jogging after Amanda in front of Delightly. She was in the first and last frames, but you couldn't see her face. That was a relief. He wasn't sure of a lot of things, but he had a feeling Amanda McQueen had no interest in being featured in any celebrity anything.

"Hnng," Sam grunted.

"What is it?" Zach asked.

"Paps found me. I figured they'd be on to me last week if they actually cared."

"Bad or good?"

"Neutral. Anyway—" Just as he went to slip his phone back in his pocket it vibrated again. "Ooh, the phone is hot this morning." A text from a 310 number lit up his screen. He could feel his blood pumping faster as he spied the words Hey, this is Amanda in the preview notification. His thumb flew up the screen so fast he was surprised it didn't go spinning out of his hand. He swallowed, trying to ignore the anticipation that was suddenly heating up his face. So much for moving on.

Hey, it's Amanda.
I hope it's not too early to text you.
I'd like to come Big Rock Ranch
if the invitation is still on the table.

Sam texted back before she could change her mind.

Never too early and the invitation
is definitely on the table.

She responded immediately.

Great. I'll see you Friday night.

He looked up at his brother unable to hide the stupid grin that hit his face.
"The fuck you cheesin' for?" Zach laughed.
"Amanda said yes. She's gonna come out this weekend."
"Wow. You got it bad for this girl, huh?"
"I have no idea what you're talking about."

Chapter 10

"Give me the password one more time," her mother said, yawning. Amanda switched her phone to the other ear and tucked it against her shoulder as she shoved nearly every pair of clean underwear she owned into her weekend bag. She'd texted her mom plenty. Her dad too, but thanks to the time difference and her schedule she hadn't caught her parents on the phone in over two weeks. She was packing to flee the crime scene that had become her life, when her mom sent her a text asking for the password to the Hulu streaming account they shared. Amanda had no clue how she managed, but her mom seemed to log out every time she touched the remote.

"It's just the house number, the landline with an exclamation point at the end. All together." Amanda had set the password one day when she was feeling particularly lonesome. She'd settled on the first phone number and one of the few she still had committed to memory. Thinking of something she and her parents would both remember with ease made her homesick and a little nostalgic. And yet, her mom couldn't remember it for shit. Amanda didn't mind. She welcomed the excuse to be in touch with a part of the world that didn't involve call times and scripts. Especially after the week she'd had, a week she refused to think about now that it was over. It was done. It had happened. She wasn't going to stress herself out by reliving it.

"Okay, let me try that." Her mom recited the password quietly to herself, then let out a little gasp of victory. "I'm in."

"What are you going to watch?"

"This blacksmithing competition show."

"Oh really?" Amanda laughed.

"One of the judges is rather dreamy. I told your father and he got all upset. I told him I was going to get you to introduce me to him if he didn't quit sulking."

"Mom," Amanda laughed. "Please leave your poor husband alone."

"He's mine. I can tease him all I want."

"Relationship goals."

"Damn straight. So you said you're going out?"

"Um, yeah. A friend of mine has—well, his family has a ranch outside of the city and he invited me for the weekend."

"Oh? A friend or a *friend* friend?" Her mom had given up on the dream of planning a wedding years ago, but anytime Amanda mentioned anyone of the opposite sex, her mom starting thinking of good times for them to meet at Kleinfeld's.

"Just a friend, Mom."

"You're going to stay with a friend on Valentine's Day weekend?"

Amanda froze. She knew in the back of her mind the next day was indeed Valentine's Day. Dru had gone on and on about how she and Lacy planned to crash one of their mutual friends' dates. Amanda had shoved that knowledge including the holiday itself to the back of her mind with a subtle roll of her eyes and gone back to setting an appointment to get Dru's apartment cleaned. But now . . . now it still didn't matter. They were just friends, and like Sam said, they didn't actually have to spend any time together if she didn't want to see him. Which she did, but not for Valentine's purposes.

"When I actually get five minutes to date, you'll be the first to know. This weekend is about friendship and relaxation. Nothing else. Where's Dad?" she said, coolly changing the subject.

"He's upstairs, in the room. Playing video games. Some old western thing with cowboys. He's excited because there's a part when you can pet the dog."

"Oh good."

"He stopped playing online. He didn't like the language some of the young people were using."

"Even better. Well, I need to get on the road and I know you want to watch some sexy blacksmiths."

"Sure do, baby girl. Gotta pick out my second husband."

"Do not tell Dad that."

"I will tell him that. He's gotten too comfortable," she joked. If anyone loved the heck out of their wife, it was her dad.

"Mom!" Amanda replied with a sputtering laugh.

They said their love-yous and goodnights and Amanda fought another wave of homesickness and loneliness. She'd seen her parents at Christmas, but she'd only been home for four days. Four days out of the whole year. She knew it had been a mistake and that this year she should ask Dru for more time, a whole week off, but with her shooting schedule and other engagements—no. She refused. She was not going to think about Dru right now.

Right now she was going to grab her toothbrush and make sure she had her silk bonnet and then she was going to hop on the 10 and get the hell out of this town. And maybe in the spring when *Andromeda* wrapped she'd go home again for another visit. She missed her family. She pushed that unique sadness aside with a sigh and finished packing. She doubled-checked that she had her necessities, her phone, extra chargers, and the route to Big Rock Ranch already programmed into her phone.

She grabbed her keys and headed out to her car. Once she was behind the wheel, she loaded up her maps app, then started her favorite eighties pop and R&B playlist. More than two hours of music that would keep her awake and keep her mind off thinking of ways to poison Dru and make it look like an accident, as she drove east toward Charming.

The playlist didn't work, not completely. She listened to her favorite Prince and Janet Jackson tracks over and over and that definitely helped lift her mood, but for some reason she couldn't take her mind off Dru's recent behavior. She knew Dru could be a good person deep down, but for some reason this asshole persona she seemed so committed to just wouldn't let up. She knew she was under pressure and she knew she was still upset about not booking the TV movie project, but Dru needed to channel her emotions better. Maybe after a weekend away Amanda could reset her own feelings about this situation and gently nudge Dru toward greener, more positive pastures—after she found another vegan restaurant that served early breakfast.

Forty-five minutes away from the ranch, she glanced down at her phone and had an odd realization about where she was going and the much needed break she was giving herself. The break Sam had given her. A giddiness flooded through her, a giddiness that made no damn sense. And she suddenly struggled not to lean too hard on the gas. Traffic was moving smoothly. She would make it there with plenty of time to enjoy a bath and some room service before she went to sleep. There was no need to get pulled over for speeding. Still, she wanted to be in Charming now.

When she was twenty minutes away, Amanda grabbed her phone and sent Sam a voice memo so she could keep her eyes on the road.

"'Sup, Tex," she said, trying to sound casual. "Just want to let you know I'm about twenty minutes away. Thanks again for setting this up. Maybe I'll see you around some-time tomorrow."

She hit send, then set her phone back in her cup holder. She was going to make the best of this weekend. She just had to figure out how to spend forty-eight hours at Big Rock Ranch while pretending she had no intention of spending any time with Sam. It wasn't the point of this trip. She needed to rest. She needed to do therapeutic things like taking in the fresh air and petting a horse or two. Maybe she'd even ride a horse. Wouldn't that be something. She was definitely going to sleep in and she wasn't going to spend one minute thinking about if and how Dru was taking care of herself. She had to give herself permission to be off the clock, mentally and emotionally. She'd be back to work soon enough. This weekend was about Amanda and Amanda only.

She passed through the town center of Charming, crossing through the other side to the area populated with horse ranches and produce farms. Soon the ranch came into view, the lights from the main lodge creating a break in a dark expanse of the landscape. Amanda let out a deep breath as she slowed her car and pulled through the large gates, set with a massive *B* and *R* on either side. She'd been there just a week ago, but this time felt different. She knew exactly what the difference was, but she refused to acknowledge it.

She pulled to a stop in the curved driveway of the main lodge and reached for her phone and purse as two young guys, one Asian and one Latinx, approached the car.

The young Asian guy came around the side and opened the driver's-side door for her. Amanda shivered as the cool night air washed over her while she pulled her phone off its charger and shoved it into her purse.

"Evening, Miss McQueen. Welcome to Big Rock Ranch. May I park your car for you?"

"Yes, thank you—Oh my God. I'm sorry. I don't have cash." She'd been in such a hurry, she'd forgotten to stop by the bank or hit up a CVS for some cash back. "Is there an ATM inside?" she asked as she stepped out of the car. She shrugged on her own coat.

"Don't worry about it," he said with a smile.

"Of course I will. I'll make sure I get you guys." Amanda knew they'd probably heard that line plenty of times from cheap guests, but she meant in. She noted the name MATTHEW embroidered into the breast of his jacket before she opened the back door and grabbed her weekend bag and her laptop backpack.

"Can I take your bags for you?" the other young guy with ELI embroidered on his jacket asked as she came around the front of the car.

"I got it, but thank you."

"Sure. Front desk is right through here." He shot Amanda a friendly wink as he opened the manual side of the entrance for her. As she stepped into the comfort of the rustic lobby, the momentary warmth she'd felt from her pleasant interaction with Matthew and Eli dropped to her knees. Sam Pleasant was standing there, leaning against the front desk. Amanda felt herself swallow as she took in the sight of him. How did a man look so good in jeans, a flannel shirt and wool lined canvas jacket? The cowboy hat dangling from his fingers didn't help one bit and neither did the small dog sniffing around at his feet.

He'd been working on a serious five o'clock shadow when she'd run into him earlier in the week. She'd been too upset to process it as something she should add to her Late Night Alone Time files, but now that five o'clock shadow was showing the beginnings of a very nice beard.

Amanda didn't deserve this sort of torture. She had two seconds to figure out how she was going to handle it.

"Hey," Sam said with a bright smile as Amanda crossed the recently polished stone floor.

"Hey. You didn't have to meet me here," she replied, her voice sounding less than calm and cool.

"Of course I did. You're my guest." He stepped closer so they were only a few feet apart, but Amanda could tell he was stopping himself from moving any closer, or even hugging her. She'd drawn her boundaries and he was respecting them, but why did she suddenly regret drawing those lines in the sand? "Good to see you."

"Same," Amanda said, and smiled back at him before she turned to the young Black man behind the desk. His name tag said TANNER. "Hi."

"Welcome to Big Rock Ranch, Miss McQueen. We have suite twenty-four all ready for you."

"Oh no, Sam. I don't need a suite—"

"It's fine," he replied, waving her off.

"We had a last-minute cancellation," Tanner added.

"The Hummingbird cabin popped up, but I figured you didn't want to be out there alone so you're in the suite. You just spread out in that huge bed."

"I guess it won't be all bad," Amanda admitted as she took the keycard from Tanner's outstretched hand.

"You want me to walk down there with you?"

"Ah, sure."

"Tanner, I'm gonna leave Poppy here a minute," he said as he nodded to the small sandy brown dog with a black muzzle sniffing at her sneakers.

"No!" Amanda bit her lips like she could take her sudden and unexpected enthusiasm back. "You—you can bring her." She glanced at Tanner for final approval.

He held up his hands. "He's practically my boss, so that call is between the two of you," he laughed.

"Can I pick her up?" Amanda asked just as the small dog hopped up, resting its front paws on Amanda's thighs. It stretched out its little body and let out the most adorable yawn while looking right up at her.

"Well, I think you have to," Sam said, a smile in his voice. "Here." He slid on his cowboy hat, then took Amanda's bags from her and just as quickly she reached down and scooped the adorable mutt up into the cradle of her arms. The pup immediately started licking the side of her hand.

"Oh my God. You are so cute," she cooed. She glanced back up at Sam. "Actually, you can leave. I have what I need."

"You tell Miss Leona Lovell where her favorite dog is in the morning."

"Okay. Yeah, no."

"Come on. I'll show you to your room."

Amanda thanked Tanner, then followed Sam through the lobby.

"How was the drive?" Sam asked, glancing over his shoulder as they made their way to her room. Amanda had to swallow again. For some dumb reason she really hadn't wanted to see him again, but now that he was here and she wasn't running down the street crying, she was reminded all over again how much she was drawn to him. It helped that she already knew how warm his touch could be, how good of a kisser he was.

"Uh, the drive was fine. There was some traffic getting out of LA, but once I hit the 60 it was pretty smooth sailing."

"Nice." Another knee-melting smile over his shoulder. Finally they arrived at her room and Amanda shifted little Poppy in her arms and used the keycard to open the door. The suite was huge. Way too big for one person. She looked at the large sitting area and the cute desk in the corner. There were double barn doors at the far end of the space, opening to the bedroom where she could see the foot of a massive four-poster bed.

"This is bigger than my place," Amanda said. She set Poppy on the floor, then went toward the bathroom, and sure enough there was a copper-wrapped clawfoot tub big enough for her to do laps in.

"We don't get many cancellations, but lucky for you," Sam said as she stepped back into the sitting room. He set down her bag on the armchair by the TV, then took off his cowboy hat again. She stopped herself from smiling, thinking about who had raised this boy right.

"Well, you should be all set here. Tanner's on until five a.m., if you need anything. Enjoy that bed."

"Actually thought I would take a bath and then pass out, but I'm wide awake."

"Hey, I know it would involve hanging out with me, but if you want you're welcome to come back to my brother's place. My cousins are over there and we were doing a *Friday the Thirteenth* marathon. We were partway through *Jason X* when I left and we were gonna watch *Jason Takes Manhattan* next. You're welcome to join us."

Amanda glanced toward the bed and considered the sleep she could desperately use. And then she thought for a moment if what she really wanted was to be alone. "You sure your family won't mind? I don't want to just bust in on their movie night."

"Nah, it's all good. For real, if you want to come, come. The rest of the dogs are there, hanging out."

"Oh well, why didn't you say that?"

"So you're coming?"

"Yeah, why not." Amanda grabbed her purse and double-checked that she had her keycard. "Lead the way."

"Alright. Let's go, Poppy." He scooped the dog off the floor and tucked her under his arm. Amanda followed as Sam opened the door for her. She stopped before she stepped out into the hall.

"Listen. It's not that I don't want to spend time with you. I just—"

"You don't have to explain. I read my cousin's copy of *He's Just Not That into You* when I was in high school."

"No, Sam," Amanda laughed. "I just didn't expect to see you again. And not so soon. Not under those circumstances. It was a lot to process while trying to be *present* for Helene and Ignacio."

"I get it."

"Sometimes you're—you have no vision for something and then it lands in your lap twice. I was overwhelmed."

"So was I, but I just rolled with it."

"Hmmm," Amanda replied. She could admit to herself that maybe Sam was also handling this wild situation as best he could. Maybe she wasn't the only one feeling a little out of sorts. "Did you know you were inviting me down here for Valentine's Day weekend?" she asked with a smirk.

"When I invited you, no, I didn't, but my brother let me know I was potentially playing myself, but hey, here we are."

"Here we are."

"Pals."

"Pals."

"Who might sleep with each other again."

Amanda rolled her eyes and started walking down the hall, back toward the lobby. "Let's go, Tex."

"After you."

Chapter 11

Amanda watched the road as they made their way back to Sam's brother's house. Absently she made note of every landmark and turn, the changes in fences as they passed different farms and fields. Soon the landscape cleared again and it looked like there were miles and miles of open desert between them and the snowcapped mountains up ahead. The small pup in her arms shifted and rested its head in the crook of her arm. It took all she had not to let out the most ridiculous, contented sigh. She didn't need a spa to relax, just a clear night with a big moon in the sky and the cutest dog ever in her arms.

"She likes you," Sam said, over the low-playing music.

Amanda looked down and scratched the scuff on the back of Poppy's soft head before she glanced over at Sam and flashed him a confident grin.

"What's not to like?"

"You got me there."

"I didn't know cowboys drove luxury sedans," she said, changing the subject. Every moment she spent with Sam Pleasant felt like she was gambling with her self-control. She knew what she'd said and wasn't foolish enough to lie to herself about how pushing Sam away was in direct contradiction to how she was starting to feel about him. But she knew it was less than a good idea to bring attention to the way he looked at her or the fact that they both couldn't seem to stop flirting with each other. The car. The car was a safe subject.

"It's a little cold for us to take the ATVs."

"I'm just messing with you," she replied even though she was trying to marry these two images of Sam Pleasant she had in her head. The cowboy hat and the worn jeans cut quite the figure behind the wheel of a sleek new Tesla.

"My agent told me to stop showing up for meetings in my truck after I started getting real jobs. Also I don't know if you've tried to park an extended cab anywhere in LA but—"

"Actually."

"Oh, word? Actually what?" His warm laugh filled the car.

"Back in my set PA days I drove a ten pass van for, like, three months. Finding places to park that thing was such a pain in the ass."

"So you get it."

"I do."

"I gave my truck to my cousin."

"That's nice of you."

A soft smile touched the corner of his lips, making Amanda think there was more to that story, but she didn't push. "So who am I meeting tonight?"

"I think you met my brother Jesse before the wedding."

"Briefly, yes."

"It's his house we're going to. My brother Zach and his fiancée, Evie, are doing regular date night before date night extreme tomorrow. So they won't be around."

"Okay," Amanda laughed.

"My cousin Lilah will be there. She's the youngest of all the Pleasants. Well, the grandkids. There are four great-grandkids now."

"Oh wow, how many grandkids are there?"

"Fifteen. Lilah's the youngest of eight."

"Double wow."

"Did you just say double wow?"

"Sure did. So your brother and your cousin."

"And my play cousin Corie, she's Miss Leona's personal assistant, but we've known her her whole life so she's family."

"Okay. Got it."

"And Corie's kinda girlfriend, Vega."

"What's the kinda about?"

"They've been doing the will-they won't-they dance for a minute, but they're clearly feeling each other."

"Okay. So siblings, cousins, maybe girlfriend doing the delicate dance." They came to another high fenced property. Amanda could see the lights from some houses off in the distance, but not much else. Sam slowed the car, then flipped his turn signal even though the long desert road was empty. She did love a responsible driver. She glanced up and saw the lone street sign that looked out of place in this very particular way.

Pleasant Lane. Sam turned toward a set of massive gates, then pushed a button up in his visor. The gate slowly opened.

"Oh. So you have your own street. That's cool."

Sam responded with a slight smile as he maneuvered the car up the driveway that seemed a whole mile long. Amanda used Poppy to ground herself in reality as they pulled up to a sprawling cul-de-sac with three large Spanish-style ranch houses. The small dog betrayed her though as soon as they pulled to a stop in the wide driveway of the first house. It started wiggling in her arms, eager to hop out.

"This is where you grew up?" she said. There was no reason for her to be surprised. His grandmother was Hollywood royalty and clearly his brothers weren't doing too bad for themselves either. A beautiful private estate in the middle of nowhere was the least they could do for themselves.

"No," Sam said as they parked next to a shiny black pickup truck. "We moved here after my grandfather passed away. My dad wanted us to be close together so he had Pleasant Lane built." He cut off the car, then turned to her.

"Ready."

"Should I not be?"

"I was saying that more to myself."

"Why's that?"

"I've never brought a girl home after she dumped me."

Amanda leaned back, glaring at him as a smooth, punch-me-in-the-face smile spread out over his mouth. "You know I thought you would be cool about this, but I'll give you that. You get one."

"I'll take it. Thanks." His smile flashed even wider before he opened the door and stepped out of the car. Amanda rolled her eyes, following close behind him as she carried Poppy with her back into the cold night air. She could hear more dogs barking inside, but only for a second. Something or someone suddenly silenced them as she and Sam made their way to the front door. Sam opened the door for her and ushered her into the warmth of the dimly lit entryway, where they were greeted by three more dogs.

"Oh my gosh. Hello." She gently set Poppy down and

then set about petting and patting every dog she could reach.

"Here. Leave your shoes here." He nodded toward a row of boots and sneakers by the front door. Some were close to her size but the rest of them were large enough to row a woman and at least three children to safety. His brother Jesse Pleasant was not a small man.

"Oh sure." She abandoned the puppy parade and toed out of her Converse, setting them beside Sam's worn boots.

"Come on this way," he said, motioning down the hall- way, where she could suddenly hear voices. The dogs pushed their way ahead, guiding them into the large open living room–kitchen area like a welcoming committee. Sam's brother was in the kitchen, digging for something in the large pantry. Three women around her age were sitting on the massive sectional and the love seat that took up most of the living space. There was a TV that had to have been eight feet wide mounted to the wall above a Spanish tile fireplace. The opening credits of *Friday the 13th Part VIII: Jason Takes Manhattan* paused on the screen.

"Finally," the plus-size woman on the love seat groaned as soon as she saw them. The petite woman beside her who appeared to be biracial, Black and Asian, stood, ready to make proper introductions. Another girl who could have been Sam's twin poked her head up from the couch and offered Amanda a kind smile.

"Corie, shut up. Guys, this is my friend Amanda McQueen. This is Vega," he said, motioning toward the biracial woman. She came over and shook Amanda's hand.

"Nice to meet you."

"Likewise."

"And that's my cousin Lilah over there," he said, mo- tioning toward the couch.

"Hi," Lilah said in a quiet, sweet voice as she sat up on the cushions on her knees. She was wearing a pink pajama top that said CHAMPAGNE DREAMS. Amanda had a feeling they would get along.

"The rude mufucka on over there is Corie."

"Amanda, I'm sorry. It's great to meet you. But *you* said you'd be back in five minutes," Corie replied, fixing Sam with a sarcastic grin. Yeah, they were more like siblings than play cousins. Amanda tried her best not to laugh at their back-and-forth.

"Not a damn thing in this whole county is within five minutes of this house," Sam laughed. "I said you guys didn't have to wait."

"Some of us have manners. Nice to see you again, Amanda," Jesse said as he turned around. He had a tub of cheeseballs in his hand.

She smiled back at him even though his expression was blank and impossible to read. That he'd remembered her after their nearly nonexistent interaction the week before shocked her a bit. "Likewise. Thanks for having me in your home."

"Of course. Can I get you something to drink?"

"I'm fine. Thank you though."

"She likes you." He nodded toward her side. Amanda looked down and realized she'd been absently stroking the soft head of the black Lab that had parked itself by her socked feet.

"Feeling's mutual," she replied with a shrug.

"You're a dog person?"

"An *animal* person."

"You'll have to go by the stables tomorrow then. Meet Sam's horse," Jesse suggested.

"I'd be happy to take you," Sam said. And something

warm bloomed in Amanda's chest. This was not the plan. She was supposed to be asleep in a king-size ranch bed. Tomorrow she was supposed to take full advantage of a free trip to the spa, but all she wanted was to spend time with Sam and his horse. And the dogs too.

"I need to use the restroom. Don't start without me," Jesse said as he set the cheeseballs down on the counter.

"Bitch, you had like thirty minutes," Corie said. Amanda managed to hold in her laughter. Lilah covered hers with a pathetic cough.

"Corie, you're free to go back to your house. In Sacramento," Jesse said.

"Just hurry up. It's already late as hell and this is the best one," Corie replied.

"Yeah, yeah. Amanda, please make yourself at home."

"Thank you. I will."

"Come on." Sam nodded across the room and guided her over to the couch with a hand on the small of her back. The dogs followed, gathering at her feet again as soon as she and Sam were comfortable on the couch next to Lilah. Vega made herself comfortable on the love seat next to Corie and then Amanda saw it, what Sam was talking about with their obvious relationship. Corie sat back and pulled Vega's legs across her lap. Amanda quickly shut down all thoughts of her proximity to Sam. How she'd put to bed any chance of simple, casual, familiar touches developing between them.

Not that casual touches, or an under-the-blanket couch snuggle was something she considered having with Sam, but seeing the ease between Vega and Corie brought an odd loneliness back to the surface, that odd tug that had convinced her to sleep with Sam in the first place. She was lonely and worse, she was dying for an affectionate touch.

She'd have to settle for Jason's murderous rampage across the island of Manhattan. She made herself comfortable on the worn leather cushions between Sam and his cousin and did her best to think of anything besides how close their thighs were to touching.

"So how'd you two meet?" Vega asked. "Sam ran out of here so fast we didn't get to ask him follow-up questions."

"Uh, through mutual friends. Helene and Ignacio. After the, um, Oscars, I went to the *Vanity Fair* party with Helene and he wouldn't stop talking to me on the dance floor." After weeks of lying to Dru, it felt weird to tell the truth.

"Typical," Vega teased.

"I'm so happy they got married," Lilah said with a dreamy sigh. "I know you're not supposed to ship real people, but when they were doing press for *Magnet* the fangirl in me prayed that true love would find two people so talented and beautiful."

"They are a great match," Amanda said, laughing about Lilah's earnest declaration. "It's like looking directly at the sun when they are together."

"You're in the industry too?" Vega asked.

"Yeah, she's a writer," Sam said. The touch of pride in his voice turned her stomach. So much for the truth.

"Damn, I was hoping for another ally. I'm a nurse."

"No on-camera work, no horses?" Amanda replied, trying to keep the focus on Vega.

"No. Private-care nurse. Usually for the elderly. I love it, but I'm always looking for someone to relate to when I have no fucking idea what the hell they are all talking about."

"Well, I know jack about running a ranch, so you and I can be clueless there together."

"Deal," Vega laughed.

"What are you working on?" Corie asked.

"Oh, uh. Top-secret thing in development."

"Ah, gotcha."

"It'll be my first writing credit." Amanda hated how smoothly the lie rolled off her tongue. She knew the drill. Knowing her name was enough. All they had to do was a quick search and her profile or lack thereof would pop up in the online movie database. Her first two PA credits were listed, but that was it. She didn't want to lie to Sam or his family, but for now she needed some part of her life that Dru couldn't touch. Luckily, she'd never been added to the call sheet so there wasn't an Internet trail of "Assistant to Ms. Anastasia." Still, work was the last thing she wanted to talk about.

"Lilah, you work at the ranch?" she asked, changing the subject.

"Yeah. I work for Zach. Have you met him?"

"Just for a second last weekend."

"I mean I sort of work for him and Jesse—"

"Not for much longer," Jesse said as he walked back into the room. He flopped his massive weight down into a recliner in the corner that seemed to have been custom-made for his size. The black Lab wandered over and settled under the footrest.

Lilah shrugged, rolling her eyes. "I got promoted."

"You did?" Sam said, surprised.

"Yeah." Another shrug.

"You don't seem so excited," Amanda said.

"Well, I'm getting my own office and everything, but now I have to work downstairs with Delfi. I'm going to miss working upstairs."

"I'll show you the office blueprints later," Sam said,

throwing Amanda a lifeline. She had no clue what Lilah was talking about.

"We ready?" Jesse asked.

"Yeah, let's do this shit." Corie settled farther into the love seat, her hands still draped over Vega's legs. Jesse held up the remote and pressed play. Amanda tried to focus on the most eighties movie opening she'd seen in a long time, but as the ridiculous movie and Corie's hilarious commentary went on she realized the tension she'd spent the whole drive trying to chase away had settled back on her shoulders. She was tight all over and all she could think about was Dru and what mood of hers would be waiting for her when she got home to LA.

"You okay?" Sam asked quietly.

"Yeah, just thinking about work stuff."

"Listen, you're in Charming now, baby. You can leave that all behind."

Amanda couldn't help but laugh. "Thank you," she whispered. "Uh, I've never seen this before. When do they get to Manhattan?"

"You got an hour at least!" Corie yelled across the room.

"Are you serious?" Lilah replied.

"Will you please," Jesse groaned, his tone somehow dry. "I'm trying to watch the best movie ever." Amanda chuckled to herself, but her leg accidentally brushing against Sam's shifted her attention again. A tingle rushed down her thigh and again she was fighting the memory of what it felt like to have Sam's fingers brushing over her bare skin.

"Sorry." She shifted closer to Lilah, putting a little distance between herself and Sam's muscular legs. Those jeans should have been illegal. He didn't say anything, but she heard the small rush of breath leaving his nose as he scooted to the other end of the couch. *Same, bro,* she wanted to joke. The frustration had been building inside her from the moment she saw him in the lobby of the lodge. Normally Amanda was confident in her decisions, but as Lilah offered her a throw blanket from the back of the couch, another twinge of regret hit her. She could think of much better sources of warmth.

It was a little after one a.m. when Jason Voorhees finally met his way overdue end in the sewers under Manhattan. Lilah and Vega passed out halfway into the ridiculous slasher flick. Amanda envied them. Corie and Jesse had jokes for days, but the weight of the week and the long drive had finally caught up with her somewhere around the hour mark where Jason was terrorizing teens on a boat miles away from New York City. All she wanted was to hop a train to Snoozeville. The warm and restless energy emanating from Sam's end of the couch was the only thing keeping her awake. She could sense his every breath, every small shift of his body. Focusing on Jason's rampage was the only thing keeping her from thinking of how differently the night would have gone if she hadn't cut him off so unceremoniously.

Jesse hit stop as the credits rolled and the familiar groans and stretches started around the room. Amanda looked away as Corie leaned over and kissed Vega awake.

Sam eased to the edge of the couch, toying with his cowboy hat perched on his knee before he turned to her. "Ready to head back?" Amanda almost twitched at the raw edge to his voice. Sleepy looked good on him.

"Yeah sure." She stood and shrugged on her coat. "Thanks for having me over," she whispered to Jesse.

"Anytime. Corie, take Lilah with you. She's gonna wake up at four a.m. all confused."

"Copy that. Babe, come on," she said, helping a sleep-walking Vega off the love seat. They all made their way back to the foyer and said their goodnights as they found their shoes. The girls headed in the direction of one of the other houses as Amanda followed Sam back to his Tesla. They were quiet on the way back to the ranch. Amanda attrib-uted it to the quiet beauty of the night. The sky was so clear and the stars so bright she didn't want to interrupt them. Sam didn't seem to mind. He didn't say a word until they pulled to a stop in front of the lodge's front doors. No bellhops at this hour.

Amanda's pulse quickened when Sam turned to her, a gentle, kind smile touching his lips. "I'll walk you in."

"Okay," she managed to squeak out. It was quiet be-tween them again as they made their way through the lobby and the winding hallways back to her room. She dug out her keycard when they finally reached the door, then dug a little deeper for the nerve she needed to say the words that were on the tip of her tongue.

"Hey, Sam?"

"Hey, Amanda."

"Uh, hypothetically, how do you feel about second chances?"

"Well, I would need a hypothetical scenario. What kind of second chances are we hypothetically talking about?"

"Like say a girl, a cute girl much like myself, was a little overwhelmed, by a lot of things, and she thought it would be better to spend time with a cute boy as friends, but then they spent time together as friends and she realized how badly she wanted him to kiss her goodnight. Second chances like that. Hypothetically."

"Hmm, that's tough. If it was a devastatingly handsome man like myself and a woman, one like you, for example."

"Yeah?"

"I'd remind her that I'm a man with feelings too, so while I'd be down for second chances, I don't think I could swing third or fourth."

"Oh no yeah. No, that's totally fair. Hypothetically."

"Come on, Cha-Cha. What's on your mind?"

Amanda felt her cheeks warm at the sound of the silly nickname. "I do like you. I just—just I need to go slow. And yes, I know how that sounds considering we fucked before you knew my name."

"I'm telling you, it's a great story for the grandkids."

"Anyway."

"Listen—"

"Who was your last relationship with?" She instantly regretted it. "Sorry. That was—I don't know what the hell that was."

"It's okay. I was with Natalie Burke and we ended it because things were moving a little too fast for me."

"I've been single for a while and I wasn't expecting to meet anyone, but here we are. And I do like you—"

"We can take it slow."

"Good."

"Do you have any Valentine's Day plans?"

"I really want to meet your horse." She laughed. "I never thought I'd say that."

"I'm going for a ride at seven a.m. if you want to join me."

"I do not," Amanda laughed again.

"How about I text you when we get back and we can meet up for breakfast?"

"That sounds perfect," Amanda said as a yawn broke up the mood. "Sorry."

"Go to sleep." Sam stepped closer, pulling her in tighter with an arm around her waist. There was no elaborate updo and no sparkly jumpsuit, no tux. But there was another quiet hotel hallway and the shadow of a sexy-as-fuck cowboy hat that covered both their faces as he leaned down to kiss her. In the back of her mind, Amanda knew all she had to do was keep Sam Pleasant close to her chest and away from Dru's life-ruining clutches. As he groaned into her mouth she had a feeling that wouldn't be a problem.

Chapter 12

Sam checked the dozen or so photos he'd just taken during their slow morning ride before he glanced over at Evie. She handed Bam Bam's reins to Chris, one of the stable hands, then pulled off her riding helmet. He couldn't ignore the way she lightly touched the well-healed scar on the side of her head. He watched as his brother stepped closer and gently wrapped an arm around her waist.

"You good, Buck?" Zach said before he pressed a light kiss to her neck. His brother had looked at Evie with that same love in his eyes since they were kids. Sam was happy for them, so glad they'd finally come back together and worked things out, even though Evie would always bear the gnarly scar that forced them to confront their drama. Not that they were even officially dating, but he was glad the drama between him and Amanda had been more of a low-key, cautious misunderstanding and nothing that involved a traumatic brain injury.

"Oh yeah. I'm fine." Evie leaned into Zach and kissed him on the mouth.

"Okay if I post some of these?" Sam handed Evie his

phone and waited while she scrolled through the recent images in his camera roll.

"Yeah. Those are great. I'd love to take pictures while we ride, but Bam Bam and I aren't quite there yet," Evie said.

"Yeah. It's a good idea for you to keep your eyes on the trail and both hands on the reigns for now," Zach added. Evie was a more than competent rider, but Zach always put her safety first. Sam didn't blame him.

He took his phone back and just as he went to open Instagram, his phone vibrated in his hand with a text from Amanda.

I can see the barn from here.

A picture popped up and from the looks of things she was about fifty yards away. What kind of gentleman would he be if he didn't go around to meet her?

"Hey. Be right back. Amanda's here."

"Awwww shit," Zach drawled out until Evie slapped his arm.

"Leave him alone. We got Majesty. Go ahead."

"Thanks." He gave his mare a soft pat, then headed around to the front of the stables. Their ride down the trails the whole morning had been exactly what he needed. Peace, relaxation. Some quality time and good laughs with his brother and sister-in-law-to-be, and his horse. He was able to clear his head and just enjoy himself. None of that, the levity or the joy, changed the fact that he'd secretly been waiting for a text from Amanda.

She'd been the last thing on his mind before he'd finally nodded off and the first thing on his mind when he woke up that morning. He'd heard her loud and clear. She needed to take things slow. He wanted to take things slow too. They already knew they were more than capable of burning it up between the sheets, but there was something about her. This warmth and this light that somehow came with this biting humor that Sam couldn't seem to get enough of. Sam wanted to know her and he wanted to introduce her to Majesty.

He came around the side of the stable and there she was, walking down the dirt path. Euca, their Aussie shepherd mix, was trotting beside her.

"'Sup, Tex," Amanda called out.

Sam felt a smile stretching his cheeks out like a fool. He didn't think he'd be this happy to see her, but there he was. Giddy as a motherfucker. "Morning there, young lady!" he called back. "Wasn't sure you'd be up before lunch." Sam walked up the path to meet her. Amanda came closer until just inches were separating them. Sam wanted to kiss her. Just pull her into his arms and kiss the hell out of her, but he wanted the next move to be her call. He knew what he was feeling. The last thing he wanted to do was come on too strong too soon and send her running back to LA before she got a chance to see one of the only horses he knew with a full-on attitude problem.

Her smile matched his for just a moment, before her expression dropped. Her intense gaze ran over his face and for a moment he thought she was about to relay the prophecy of his death. Then suddenly she reached up and lightly drew her finger along the side of his head. His skin instantly heated at her touch.

"You look beautiful in this light, Tex," she said with wistful lilt to her voice. A smile broke out across her face again. "I had a dream I slept all day and then when I finally showed up you said I was too late to see the horses 'cause they'd been shipped overseas for the night."

"I have no idea what that means, but I'm flattered that you were dreaming about me."

"I was dreaming about the horses, Sam. Please," she teased. "I forgot to set an alarm and I think my subconscious was worried I would sleep all day. I woke up. I set an alarm, and here I am." Then all casual and shit, she slid her hand against his. Sam didn't hesitate to lace his fingers with hers. He looked down at their clasped hands and instead of saying something stupid about how well their hands fit together, he focused on Euca. She was patiently waiting for the two of them to follow her on her next adventure.

"These dogs are pretty into you," he said.

Amanda reached down with her other hand and gave Euca a rough scratch behind her floral collar. "She was sitting in the lobby and then followed me out here. I tried to take her back, but the woman at the desk said it was okay if she tagged along."

"It is. You a good trail guide, Euca? Huh?" His dog's response was a sloppy lick to his forearm. "Thanks, girl."

"So you have a horse for me to meet?"

"Bet your boots." Sam turned and started to lead her back to the stables. Euca took point and trotted on ahead. "Her name is Majesty and she's the love of my life."

"How long have you had her?"

"About eight years. My dad actually bought her for my mom, but Majesty and I just clicked."

"So your mom was just shit out of a horse?" Amanda laughed. "What kind of raw deal is that?"

"They moved to Europe so he could film a movie and she's been shopping her face off all around London and

Paris ever since. That former beauty queen is living her very best life. She don't give a fuck about no horse."

"Oh, okay. Well, that doesn't sound so bad. I have a confession to make."

"Spill it, girl."

"I've never ridden a horse before."

He blinked. "You wanna change that?"

Amanda hesitated before she replied, "Not today, but maybe soon."

Sam laughed at the adorable smile on her face. The way her dimples popped was cute as hell. She nudged him back, shoulder to shoulder. "What? So I'm a bit of a coward."

"I didn't say anything."

"I love horses, but I just fear and respect their size and literal horsepower. Also one of my worst fears is getting kicked in the head."

Another burst of laughter erupted from Sam. "I will not let you get kicked in the head."

"Thank you. I'm too pretty to take a horseshoe indent to the face. Plus I love all of my teeth."

"I'll keep you safe. I promise. I do have to warn you though. My horse hates everyone."

Amanda shook her head. "She won't hate me."

"Oh? Feeling confident all of a sudden. I thought you were afraid of horses."

"I'm not afraid of them. I love horses. Like I'm a low-key weirdo horse girl. But there's a difference between dreaming of having your own horse one day and naming her Buttercup and braiding her mane during another horse girl sleepover, and knowing that horses are massive animals that I'm just not sure I would like to climb atop."

"She lets the guests ride her, but she's just not in the

mood for no bullshit. Now, Zach's horse, Steve. That's a horse you bring to a slumber party."

"Really?"

"Oh yeah."

"And his name is Steve?"

"Yes," Sam said, chuckling a bit.

"Steve's gonna love me too."

"He will, but don't get too full of yourself. Zach literally trained him to kiss people on the cheek. Steve's a damn flirt."

"Oh well, then I'll focus on making friends with him."

They came around to the pasture just as Chris was bringing Bam Bam out to join Majesty and Steve during their turnout. He led her over to the fence.

"So the midnight beauty right there is Majesty, the speckled gray fella there is Steve, and black spots there is Bam Bam."

"They are all so beautiful," she said, her voice near a gasp. Sam almost went on telling her about how Bam Bam was their newest addition, but when he looked down he recognized that look of awe on her face. He'd seen it on many a guest's face and felt that special thrill run through him the day his dad handed Majesty over to him. He stood beside her quietly and let her enjoy the moment.

"I wonder what they're thinking," she said quietly.

"Usual horsey thoughts, I'm guessing."

"What exactly is a horsey thought?"

Sam shrugged and played it off like he hadn't wondered about the inner workings of a horse's mind since he was five years old. As if he didn't ask Majesty what she was thinking about at least three times a day.

"I imagine they have great concerns about political matters, both locally and abroad."

"Hmm, yes." He leaned his arms over the railing and continued to watch her as she watched the horses. A few moments later Zach and Evie came out to join them.

"This is my brother Zach and my soon-to-be sister-in-law, Evie Buchanan."

Amanda let out a nervous laugh as she reached forward to shake their hands. "Oh. You're Evie, *Evie*."

"Yes. I am. It's nice to meet you."

"Likewise. I am a huge fan. Like, I'm working really hard not to embarrass myself right now. I didn't really put two and two together when Sam mentioned you two getting married. I didn't realize you were *you*."

"That's actually comforting. I wouldn't want the Pleasant name to eclipse my amazing brand," she said, winking at Zach.

"Not possible, babe. You're too big of a star."

"Okay, okay," Sam cut in before they started making out. Ever since they got back together they'd been attached at the mouth and didn't care what poor fool had to suffer and witness it. "Evie, do you have any tips for a novice rider for getting back in the saddle? Amanda wants to ride but is worried that she'll be decapitated by a renegade hoof to the head," he said.

"I don't want to get kicked in the face. And as you can see, I am very beautiful. We can't let anything happen to my beautiful face," Amanda added, deadpan.

Evie burst out laughing. "No, you're gorgeous and your head belongs on your shoulders. Let's see. I would say it's good to start with getting comfortable around horses. Babe, maybe Steve can come say hi."

Zach pursed his lips and let out two high, quick whistles. Steve lifted his head from whatever he was investigating in the grass and made his way over to the fence. Majesty followed.

"Come here," Zach said to Amanda. "Come step up right here." Sam watched as she made her way over to him and stepped up on the bottom railing of the fence. "Okay. When he comes over here, just hold still. He'll take care of the rest."

"He's not gonna kick me in the face, is he?" Amanda asked.

"You betcha. It's the first trick I taught him. Find the nearest guest and kick them right in the fucking face. Come here, boy. Give Amanda a kiss." Zach gave Steve the cue, a light tap on Amanda's cheek. Sure enough Steve came over and brushed his big horsey lips across her cheek and then gave her a light peck on the forehead. He took a few steps back and waited for his next cue.

Sam reached over and lightly touched her elbow. "You can open your eyes."

She pried them open and smiled. "Can I pet him?"

"Sure. Come here, boy." Steve stepped back over the fence and waited patiently while Amanda stroked the side of his large head.

"Hey, sweet boy. Aren't you the sweetest?" she said quietly, like she only meant for Steve to hear.

"Oh, watch out. Here she comes," Evie said as Majesty nudged her way into the party. Steve backed up, giving her room to shove her face under Amanda's hand.

"I—" Sam started to . . . he didn't know what. Maybe he was trying to save Amanda from Majesty's proven track record of being somewhat of an asshole. But to everyone's surprise all Majesty seemed to want was Amanda's attention.

"Well hello, pretty girl." Amanda lightly stroked her mane. Sam looked over at Evie, who was also watching this exchange in silent awe. Zach just looked confused as hell, his left eyebrow almost touching the brim of his Stetson. The three of them stopped breathing as Majesty came closer and rested her chin on Amanda's shoulder. Amanda leaned into the whole wild spectacle, stroking Majesty's face while she whispered in her ear. After a few long moments, she leaned back and gave Majesty a nod, like whatever business they had with each other was now concluded. Majesty turned and went to sniff around the pasture. Amanda hopped off the fence railing and wiped her hands on her jeans.

"What in hell was that?" Zach laughed.

"Animals just like me," she said with a shrug.

"What did you say to her?" Evie asked.

"I told her that you guys don't appreciate her beauty and see her for what she really is."

"And what's that?" Sam said.

"America's next top model. This horse is all ego. You're a Hollywood man. You should know. You just gotta make her feel appreciated instead of like a problem. Then she'll come around."

"I mean, she has a point," Evie added.

"Maybe I don't need to ride a horse. Maybe I just needed to befriend one and I think Majesty and I are working on something good."

"Well then," Sam said with a chuckle. His laughter died though as soon as Amanda came back to his side and took his hand. The warmth of her fingers sent a tingle up his arms and across his chest. He knew things were fresher than fresh between them, but he also knew how easy it would be for him to be with her like this.

Evie glanced down at their hands, then smiled at Sam.

"Are you joining us for brunch? I've put together a pretty bomb-ass menu."

"Oh, I don't know. Am I?" Amanda asked Sam cautiously.

"You're more than welcome to."

"Oh no, I mean, if you're cooking I don't want to just—"

"I'm already cooking for, like, fifteen if you include what I have to make to get Jesse to four thirty this afternoon," Evie said. "You've met Jesse?"

"I have. And I saw him eat a whole tub of cheeseballs by himself last night."

"See? One more mouth won't matter. Trust me. Plus, Sam gave me his version of how you two got together. I want the deets from *you*, the legit horse whisperer. 'Cause I think you might have literally bewitched him and he just doesn't know it."

"Evie, please," Amanda hissed. "You're spilling all my secrets."

"Oh yeah, you're coming. Let's go." Evie grabbed Zach and they started back toward the lodge. Sam turned to follow but Amanda held him back.

"Are you sure it's okay? I just came down here to sleep mostly. Check out the spa. I do not want to intrude on family time again."

"I promise. It's fine. And Vega will be there too. My grandmother loves a full house," Sam said.

"Right, your grandmother. Thee Leona Lovell. You want me to just walk up into her house, last minute, for a family brunch."

Sam reached down and took both her hands. "I am not saying this as some corny bullshit to convince you to come along just because I want you there. My grandmother is going to love you. There is a chance by the end of the day she may love you more than me."

"Are you the favorite?" she asked with that megawatt smile.

"Depends. I'm my mom's favorite for sure. My grandmother sometimes favors Jesse, but then Lilah moved in, took everyone's fucking shine."

"Poor baby."

"Come on."

"Wait. You also didn't mention that Evie freaking Buchanan was your sister-in-law."

"Soon-to-be, though most everyone here acts like they are already married. I didn't know *to* mention it."

"Are you related to any other super famous, amazing Black women?"

"My mom is a former Miss California, but she won't be at brunch. That's all I got."

Sam laughed as soon as Amanda sucked her teeth. "Let's head back to the house."

She glanced over her shoulder, back toward the pasture. "Wait one sec."

"Sure, what—" He looked over as Bam Bam came over to the fence. Amanda dropped his hand and went back over to greet the young colt.

"Hey, bud. I saw you over there, but I wanted to give you your space. You're special, aren't you? A little shy maybe, but everyone loves you 'cause you're so handsome."

"You should take Bam Bam out on the trails, Amanda. He's been great to ride," Evie called back. Amanda gave him a parting stroke of his nose, then jogged back to catch up with them.

"Maybe if I come back again. Still a little nervous about the whole getting-on-the-horse part."

"After what I just witnessed that makes not a lick of sense, but whatever you want," Evie laughed.

They made their way back to Zach's truck, hand in hand. As they walked Sam wondered whether he should broach the subject of Valentine's Day and see if Amanda wanted to make something official happen between them that night. Like another romp between the sheets or a proper date. Before he could convince himself, his phone vibrated in his pocket.

He pulled it out and frowned at the notification on the screen.

> Dru Anastasia's assistant just tracked me down
> and asked me for your number.

Sam stopped and read the text more closely, just to see if he had read it wrong.

"Everything okay?" Amanda asked.

"Yeah, just a text from my assistant. One second. I just wanna—just wanna handle this so I don't have to think about it for the rest of the weekend." Or ever.

> What did you say?

He knew Walls wouldn't give out his number, but whatever was going on with Dru was starting to look a little suspect.

Walls sent back a screenshot of the conversation.

> Hi, Chris. This is Mandy, Dru's assistant.
> She was hoping she could get Sam's number so
> they could link up.

Hi Mandy. The best way to reach Sam
for professional inquiries would be
through his agent. John Coffey is with TCA
and I'm sure he'd love to chat
with Dru's agent.

I should have been more clear.
I'm so silly.
I meant link up, privately.

What do you want me to say?

Sam did not need this shit right now. He'd just started
on a good path with Amanda again and he didn't need
someone, frankly, as unprofessional as Dru Anastasia messing that up.

Tell her thanks, but no thanks.
Cha-Cha came out and we're gonna give
things a try.

Walls texted back one more time.

"Sam would be flattered, but he's focusing on
his family and career at the time. Best to Dru
with any future love connections." Good? And
tell Cha-Cha I said sup.

Yes, perfect. Hit send. And fuck no.

A laughing smiley and thumbs-up emoji was his final
reply.

It was the right thing to say to Dru, but now Sam felt a

little off about her even having his assistant's information. How the hell did she get Walls's number? Sam shook it off and looked over at Amanda. Her eyebrows lifted and a small smile filled with concern touched the corner of her full lips.

"Okay?"

"Yeah, sorry. Just someone trying to nudge for something they aren't going to get from me. Nothing serious. Let's go." She rubbed the back of his hand as they continued walking, trying to soothe the tension that had suddenly settled on him. Dru shooting her shot shouldn't have bothered him so much. It shouldn't have bothered him at all. Still, it took nearly the length of the property to shake the tone of those texts off so he could focus all his attention back on the ray of sunshine by his side.

Chapter 13

Amanda was doing her best not to sweat or to wallow in the stupid decision not to go back to her room to change. She didn't bring many A-list options, but she should have swapped out her zip-up hoodie for a nicer sweater. Or she should have asked Sam if she had time to run into town to see if she could pick a prom dress to wear to brunch with thee freaking Leona Lovell. The woman was Hollywood royalty. If Amanda's mom knew she was about to set foot in the woman's home she'd have a stroke, resurrect herself, then ask Amanda to ask her for an autograph. Yes, Amanda had been under the same tent with her the week before, but family brunch was different. Family brunch was way different.

On the ride back to Pleasant Lane, she sat in the back seat of Zach's extended crew cab listening to him and Evie tease each other about something funny that had happened with Bam Bam on their ride. Sam showed her the pictures of Evie's horse stopping to befriend a black-tailed jack-rabbit. The whole thing was absolutely adorable, but all Amanda could think about was how she was minutes away from being face-to-face with a true goddess of the stage and screen. Not that Sam wasn't impressive all on his own, but Amanda wasn't starstruck by him. She was just overwhelmed by how bad she wanted to kiss him. Kissing would have to come later. Much later, after she survived her encounter with one of the greatest actors the world had ever known.

They pulled through the grates of the private property and this time, in the clear morning sunlight, Amanda got a better view of the stretch of land that Sam and his family called home. The three Spanish-style houses around the expansive cul-de-sac and a few outbuildings up the side of the lane were way more impressive than the small, two-story Cape Cod she'd grown up in. Though she still missed the tiny attic bedroom she'd made her own.

"First stop. Chez Leona," Zach announced. He pulled his truck to a stop at the center of it all, then glanced over the seat at her and Sam. Sam took her hand just as she caught a glimpse of Euca jumping out of the flatbed behind them.

"Grandma's a little old-school. So I'll walk you in with Evie and introduce—"

"Time out. Is this a *thing* thing?" Evie said, motioning between them.

"Uh, yes? But a fresh thing," Amanda replied, unsure of what Sam had told his brother and future sister-in-law. "A new thing."

Evie waved Amanda off and unbuckled her seat belt. "I'll handle it. Amanda, come in with me and you guys go get cleaned up."

"You sure?" Sam asked, giving Amanda's hand a light squeeze. She appreciated the warm reassurance, but Evie might have been onto something. She responded before Amanda could make up her mind.

"Yes. Your mom raised absolute gentlemen. Don't worry, but if you come in and make it a thing, Miss Leona is gonna make it a thing and you know Corie is gonna make it a thing."

"True," Sam said.

"And I think Amanda would feel more comfortable if it wasn't a thing."

"Say 'thing' again," Zach teased.

Evie rolled her eyes and turned her full attention back to Amanda. "Miss Leona is the best, but I'm just saying if you give her something, she's going to run with it. It's your call."

Amanda glanced between the three of them, then gave Sam's hand a squeeze of her own. "I'll go with Evie. Hopefully, this isn't a total setup."

"You're in good hands," Sam laughed. Amanda kissed him on his scruff-covered cheek, then hopped out of the truck and followed Evie to the front door where Euca was waiting for them.

"Miss Leona is seriously the best. Cool as hell, especially for eighty-two, but Sam is right. She's old-school. Just keep that in mind."

"Got it."

Evie opened the door and let Euca run in ahead of them. As they stepped inside Amanda followed Evie's lead and took off her Converse as Evie toed out of an extremely expensive-looking pair of boots. The entryway had the same style as the entryway of Jesse's house, but this was on a grander scale. A foyer, if you will. Amanda took in the archways and the Spanish tile and she glanced down the hallways that seemingly led to different wings of the house. Off to the right she could hear some Luther Vandross playing.

"Come on this way," Evie said with a bright smile. Amanda let out a deep breath and followed her down the hallway. They stepped into an enormous kitchen, where thee Leona Lovell was swaying in front of a six-burner Viking range singing along to "Never Too Much." Sam's cousin Lilah was sitting at the island with her laptop, wiggling her shoulders along to the beat. She looked up and smiled like she was about to say hello when Evie cut her off.

"Miss Leona! I told you I was cooking!"

The elderly woman didn't even flip her beach-waved blond bob wig in their direction when she replied. "Baby girl, I know you are not yelling at me in my own house. In my own kitchen." She turned to them then, checking in the most hilariously sweet way if Evie had decided to change her tone. Right on cue, Evie's shoulders dropped and she tried again.

"Good morning, Miss Leona. You look so lovely today."

"Much better. Come give me a kiss." Evie did what she was told, crossing the beautiful tile floor before kissing the elderly woman on her cheek.

"I thought I was cooking today. When I suggested a family brunch I didn't mean for you to lift a finger."

"It's my fault," Lilah spoke up. "I mentioned this lemon blueberry crepe tart recipe and before I could stop her, she was gliding outside to get some eggs."

"Glide I did, Miss Lilah," she said, as she swayed a little more, the fabric of her seafoam green tunic swirling around her hips. Amanda wasn't sure what she expected, but she definitely didn't expect Miss Leona Lovell to be so light and fun.

"Did you just get off a horse?" she asked Evie suddenly.

"Yes, ma'am, I did and I am going to shower right now."

"Good. Now who is this?" She waved her spatula in

Amanda's direction. She instantly felt her cheeks warm. *Please let this woman like me*, she thought.

"Geez, I'm so sorry. Miss Leona, this is Sam's friend Amanda. She's visiting the ranch for the weekend. I thought she could join us since we have enough to feed Jesse—"

"Oh, we have enough to feed a small city. Of course you can join us for brunch." She looked over at Amanda before she focused back on the crepe slowly browning in the pan. "We met last week at that lovely wedding."

"Briefly, ma'am. Yes. Yes we did."

"And she watched the worst movie ever with us last night," Lilah added with that same kind smile she'd greeted her with. Amanda already liked her.

"Well, it's nice to see you again. Yvonne, where are my grandsons?"

"They are over at Zach's, showering. Which I am going to do right now. I'll be back in a minute . . . to help you finish preparing this delicious meal." Evie winked at Amanda, then ducked back down the hallway. Amanda knew she was in perfectly good hands, but that didn't help her back away from the edge of a possible freak-out. She was in Leona Lovell's kitchen. In her actual home. How was she supposed to handle that? She realized there was only one thing to do. Get the freak-out out of her system.

"Um, I hope this isn't too much, but I am a huge fan of your work. My mother is even a bigger fan. I had a horrible case of the flu in fifth grade and she let me watch *Glory in the Night* and just—"

Miss Leona glanced over at her. Just the corner of her lip tipped up in the slightest grin, trapping Amanda's voice in her throat. She was not going to cry in the middle of this

woman's kitchen. Miss Leona carefully slid the finished
crepe on top of the small stack she'd started, then set the
pan back on the stove. She turned toward Amanda and, as
if in the most magical slow motion, held open her arms. With
a gracious flick of her wrists and careful nod of "get your
ass over here," she beckoned Amanda into her warm embrace.

"This is like being hugged by Jesus," Amanda whispered. "This is the hug I've been dreaming of my whole
life."

"I find the hugs help calm the excitement," Miss Leona
replied, her voice light and causal. Like she might in fact
be our Lord God herself. Amanda soaked in her grand-
motherly love just long enough for it to seep into her heart.
She took in her light floral perfume and the softness of
her flowing top. Who made thousand-thread-count tops?
She logged it all deep within her mind so she could conjure
it up in her darkest moment. When things got really bad,
she usually turned to her mom, but from now on, she'd
think of the time Leona Lovell took pity on her and gave
her the best hug in the history of hugs.

She took the hint when Miss Leona started to release
her and stepped back out of the elderly woman's personal
space.

"Isn't that better?"

"Much. I still might ask you for an autograph for my
mom before I leave. If that's not too much. I know I am
being rude. I am so sorry."

Miss Leona patted her hand. "Oh, you're fine, baby.
We'll make sure you get that autograph before the day is
over. You want something to drink? Lilah, get her something to drink."

Lilah was already hopping off her seat before Amanda

could make up her mind. "Let's see." She opened the industrial-size fridge, revealing a wide variety of beverages. "What can I get for you?"

"Water is fine."

"And you should try some of the pomegranate punch Lilah made. It is delicious," Miss Leona added.

"And I will also have some of that punch," Amanda added obediently.

Lilah grabbed a fancy glass pitcher out of the fridge, then whispered, "Don't worry. She's my grandma and I still think it's all pretty cool."

Normally Amanda wouldn't have believed her, but it was Leona Lovell. She absolutely did.

Brunch turned into a late lunch, but Amanda didn't care at all. She was just happy to be a part of the gang. She sat at the island with Lilah and helped her pick out some dresses she was shopping for online. When Evie came back, fresh as a daisy and as gorgeous as ever, Amanda got to watch her in action as she and Miss Leona followed through on cooking enough food for a small village and Jesse. Amanda had caught Evie in a few clips of *The Dish* and faithfully followed her on Instagram for years now, but the real thing was impressive as hell.

Sam and Zach joined them and then Corie arrived with Vega soon after. She was still a bit overwhelmed being in Miss Leona's home, but Sam was right. She felt completely comfortable hanging around with him and his family. She insisted on helping Lilah and Zach set the table and when Jesse finally arrived from some meeting in town, they sat down to eat. Amanda found herself between Sam and Vega and directly across from Evie and Zach. Jesse and Miss Leona were at either end of the table.

"So, my grandbabies. And friends. Who has news for me?" Miss Leona said after Jesse delivered the grace.

"Oh, I do," Lilah perked up. "Well, it's not my news, but it's news."

"Go ahead," Miss Leona chuckled.

"Well. You know we do the date auction every year—" She looked Amanda's way. "Jesse and I work with the chamber of commerce to raise money for various things. We helped take over this date auction that raises money for seniors in the area."

"Lilah's been crushing it actually," Jesse said in his strong, deep voice, though he didn't take his eyes off the loaf of French toast piled on his plate. "They already asked her if she could help with some of the summer programming this year."

"I said no, because there is power in no and if I wanted to work full-time for the chamber I would, but that's not my news," Lilah said. "Last year Diana Foster and her friends pooled their money so Diana could bid on Omar Harrison—Amanda, he's a super-hot firefighter, amazing single father. All that. Well, Omar's proposing to her tonight."

"Aww, that's awesome, Li," Evie said.

"That's wonderful news," Miss Leona replied. "Blessings on the happy couple."

"I told him to send us the pictures or video. However they capture the moment. I'm really happy for them. Omar told me his daughter is really excited too. She loves Diana."

"When's this year's auction?" Amanda asked.

"April. It's kind of a spring fling sort of thing. People really seem to enjoy it. And we made a real love connection this time." Lilah was practically glowing. Genuine pride in a job well done. Amanda briefly considered what that would be like before she forced her brain to temporarily erase Dru's existence again.

"I'm trying to get Jesse to enter the auction this time, but he refuses."

Jesse put down his fork and fixed Lilah with a hard stare. Amanda didn't know whether to freeze or hide under the table. She never wanted that look from Jesse Pleasant turned in her direction, but Lilah just glared right back. "And I told Lilah I would do it if she also joins the auction."

"And I. Said. No. I'm not in the mood to date."

"Well, neither am I."

"We got our first review from the *Post*," Evie broke in, grabbing everyone's attention from Lilah and Jesse's back-and-forth. "Didn't love our choice in light fixtures. But the menu was awarded stars all around. The carbonara that Brit helped me perfect was the big hit." Amanda had seen little bits and pieces about Thyme, the restaurant Evie was opening in Manhattan, on her Instagram, but it wasn't open to the public yet and of course, she hadn't been to New York recently. Not without She Who Would Not Be Named.

"That's wonderful, sweetheart. Very proud of you," Miss Leona said.

"Any word on Celia or when the doc will be released?" Vega asked.

"Celia Lamontagne filmed a documentary on Evie's recovery and what it took to get Thyme off the ground," Sam said, filling her in.

"No firm release date yet. We still have more to film, but don't worry, when I know I'll make sure everyone knows," Evie said. "Sam, she told me Larry Johnson asked about you. Did he get in touch with John?"

"Yeah, he did," Sam said, letting out a heavy, frustrated

breath. "I met with him on Tuesday and he had another biopic that would have me cast as the supporting character in my own story. He wasn't the only one though. We got about twenty scripts this week. Which is great. I want those calls. I want those meetings, but I also want to play a leading man or at least an equal man in an ensemble in something with some heft or some humor. I don't want to play a sidekick and I definitely don't want to play a cop."

"Amanda," Jesse suddenly said.

"Yes?"

"You look like you were about to say something."

"Yeah, girl. You have no poker face whatsoever," Corie added.

"Oh," she swallowed. "Sorry."

"Both of you, just chill," Sam warned.

"Seriously. Why are you trying to start stuff with the girl? She's been here a whole hour," Evie laughed.

"Excuse his lack of manners, sweetheart," Miss Leona chimed in. "At my table you are not required to sing or offer a penny for your thoughts for your supper. Or your French toast."

Amanda took a deep breath. "Well, I was hoping to save this conversation for our first—yeah, um, but I would maybe ask Sam to be more specific in what he does want?" She looked over at him cautiously. He looked back at her, waiting for her to go on. "It sounds like you've been doing the appropriate rounds. No harm in hearing people out even if the project isn't right for you, but you are in a position to ask for things. And I'm guessing in a position to pitch some ideas of your own."

"Bloop!" Corie said as she reached for more diced fruit.

"Quiet, you," Sam said with a playful glare, before he turned his attention back to Amanda. "I'm with you. Go on."

"I guess just be super honest with yourself, go for the big asks and if this all goes belly-up and your career is ruined, I heard a rumor that your family owns a ranch. Might make for a softer landing."

"Bloop, bloop, bloop! Girl called the whole family out," Corie laughed.

"No. I just mean you're lucky, right. Having a supportive family is great. My parents have my back and they'll never know how much I appreciate that, but what you guys have here is amazing, from what I've seen so far. If you take big risks and they don't pan out, Big Rock Ranch doesn't seem like a terrible place to start over."

"She's right," Zach said with a shrug.

"I didn't say she was wrong."

"It's not a bad thing," Amanda scrambled to say. She bit her tongue so often with Lady Voldemort, she forgot how freeing it was to speak her mind, but maybe this wasn't the right time or the right place.

"I didn't say it was a bad thing either," Sam replied. His hand slid back over her thigh, giving her an encouraging squeeze. "You're right, I've been . . . rushing. That's the right word. I've been rushing to find the next project because I want to keep up the awards-season momentum, but I don't want to follow up this win with just another project. I want to do something I'm proud of and something I'm excited for."

"You have two brilliant actors, in your grandmother and your father, right under your nose. And all of this to come home to. I say use this time and combined resources and experience to really chase after what you want. Or maybe I'm wrong and I should have just sat here and ate my crepe tart." Amanda dropped her eyes back to her plate and shoved a nice forkful of said tart into her mouth.

She tried not to shiver when Sam leaned over and kissed her on the side of her head. "That was exactly what I needed to hear. Thank you."

"I'm so glad we could do this on Valentine's Day," Miss Leona said as she poured a healthy amount of champagne into her glass. "Get to spend some quality time with my babies and my babies' friends."

Zach went on outlining new plans for the ranch once the weather warmed up again and it seemed like everyone had moved on from Amanda's brash comments. She latched on to the comfort of Sam's strong fingers as they occasionally brushed her thigh throughout the meal. He'd clearly forgiven her, but she hoped she hadn't accidentally gotten herself banned from all future Pleasant family functions. Not that she and Sam were working on a real future or anything. They hadn't even been on a real date, but still. It would be nice to be invited back.

Chapter 14

Lunch went on smoothly after Amanda extracted her whole foot from her mouth. She enjoyed spending time with Sam's family and envied how close they all were. And he was right, well, kinda. She wasn't exactly sure Miss Leona loved her like one of her own after one meal, but she was extremely kind and gracious and made Amanda feel very welcome. By the time Jesse was full and everyone else was well on their way to being drunk on carbohydrates, Amanda felt significantly less awkward.

She sat back, with Sam's arm draped over her shoulders, while Zach and Lilah debated the finer points of LeBron James's shooting average. If his affection toward her made their new situationship a *thing* with his family, they didn't mention it.

"Any hot plans for you tonight, Miss Leona?" Vega teased just before she finished her glass of juice. Jesse made a weird noise at the end of the table. Amanda didn't miss the glance Zach shot in Jesse's direction. Jesse didn't look up, but his jaw clenched. Amanda was dying to know what was happening there, but of course she kept her mouth shut. Sam got her attention with a gentle squeeze to her arm. She turned and met his handsome smile, smiling back at him as a few dozen butterflies fluttered their wings in her stomach. His wink told her he'd let her in on the dirt later.

"I'm going out with Mig and Pam tonight," Miss Leona said.

"Gonna tear the club up?" Corie replied. She stood and started clearing her and Vega's plates.

"You know Mig's granddaughter bought the Gutierrez farm and she set up a wine and cheese tasting for us. I will be skipping most of the cheese and enjoying all of the wine and the conversation."

"Corie, can you get her number for me?" Jesse said. Corie set down the plates by the sink, then pulled out her phone and a moment later Amanda heard a ping from Jesse's end of the table. "Thank you."

"Well, since I guess we're all done here, Corie," Evie said.

"What? I was just putting our plates up."

"Like I said, since we're all done here, I'm really glad we could all do this together and I'm glad Amanda could join us. I don't love all the flying back and forth, but I'm glad we could grab this time together."

"Amen to that." Zach playfully pulled her closer and laid a sloppy kiss on her cheek. Evie nudged him away, but that didn't change the massive smile on her face. They all started helping with the cleanup. After Amanda turned down Miss Leona's seventy-fifth offer to take some leftovers back to the ranch with her, she was starting to feel all the pleasant weight of everything she ate. She tried to hide her yawn, but the yawn won. Sam rubbed a smooth hand down her back as he came around the counter.

"You want to head to the ranch?"

"Yeah. I'm pretty tired. I could use a nap or a massage. Or a nap while I get massaged."

"We can work all of those things out." He turned to his brother.

"What are you two getting into tonight?"

"We're going to Claim Jumpers?" Zach said, sounding unsure.

"The fuck?" Sam laughed, then quickly ducked his head, probably worried his grandmother had heard him swear, but she was busy tinkering with a large iPad on the counter. "That's where you're going on your first Valentine's Day as almost–husband and wife."

"Speak to Evie," Zach replied with a shrug.

"They're doing a nineties high school dance thing. I thought it would be fun. Plus, Brit and Delfi are going," Evie said.

"What are you two doing tonight?" Sam asked Vega. She and Corie were working on loading the dishwasher.

"Uh, we're going on a proper date," Vega said.

"To where?"

"I don't know," Vega replied with a saucy smile. "She said it's a surprise. We're leaving at seven."

"It's freaking Valentine's Day!" Corie said, throwing her wet hands in the air. "I'm not taking my date to a *bar*. I'd ask who raised you bums, but I know Miss Leona, Nana Buck, and your parents aren't to blame for this mess. Tsk."

"You don't have to ask me. It's okay," Lilah said snarkily.

"*Do* you have plans?" Sam asked his cousin.

"You know I don't. It's just nice to be asked. I think I'll help Jesse out with bingo though, since everyone is busy."

"Come to Claim Jumpers. I bet Chris will be there," Evie teased.

"Ugh. No thank you."

Sam turned to Amanda, eyebrow raised. "You wanna go to a cowboy dive bar for the most romantic night of your life?"

"Sure," Amanda laughed. "But is it truly a dive bar, 'cause the nicest thing I brought with me is my comfy cardigan. And by nice, I mean off the Old Navy clearance rack. I don't want to show up and your idea of a dive bar is Hamptons casual."

"Oh no. It's a real shithole," Zach said.

"Try again, young man," Miss Leona called from across the room.

"Yes, ma'am. Sorry. It's a somewhat remodeled dump, but all the locals hang out there. Friends from high school, a lot of our people from the ranch. Cheap drinks and the music *is* usually good."

"You could go in what you have on now and you'd be fine," Evie added. "You guys should come with us."

"You down?" Sam asked.

"Yeah, let's do it."

"Great."

Amanda said her goodbyes, collecting hugs all around except from Jesse, who was still seated at the table doing something on his phone. He did however stand and shake her hand. "Here until tomorrow?" he asked all businesslike.

"Yeah, leaving in the morning so I can beat the traffic back."

He just nodded, then went back to his phone. Amanda had no clue what to make of him. She followed Sam outside and across the cul-de-sac. Only two dogs followed them this time, but they happily trotted back to Miss Leona's when Sam told them to get on.

"So?" Sam said when they got into his Tesla. "That wasn't bad."

"Oh, you missed the part where I basically confessed my undying fangirl love for your grandmother."

"When was that?" Sam said, chuckling a bit.

"When you were in the shower. She handled it well, thank God, but yeah. I was pretty sure I'd blown it right then and there."

"But you didn't. She really likes you."

"Well, I like your whole family. And Vega." She didn't mention how homesick it made her for her parents.

"They all liked you," he insisted. Amanda couldn't help but notice the sudden softness to his voice. She looked up at him through her lashes and fought the urge to sigh at what she saw. Sam Pleasant was looking at her, really looking at her. Not her tits or her ass, which were both amazing, but really looking at her and she couldn't ignore what she saw reflected back at her. Sam liked her. Or he was starting to. She hadn't been on the receiving end of that look in a while, but she knew when it was real. She took his hand and scooted a little closer even though the center console stopped them from getting as close as she wanted.

"I want to apologize for what I said, about your career."

"You kidding? I was serious. That was exactly what I needed to hear. Listen, I talk to Zach about this every day and of course I talk to my grandma and my dad, but they are more on that basic encouragement tip."

"Oh man. That must be awful," Amanda whined before she smiled back at him.

"You know what I mean. Miss Leona is exhausted with Hollywood. She's just chillin' waiting for grandchildren, waiting for *Rory's War* checks to roll in. And my dad—he's great, but he's really focused on his own shit now. And he should be, but you were right. I am in a unique position."

"Listen, it's scary to go for what you want," Amanda said.

"It is." There was more, something just on the tip of his tongue. She could tell, but instead of confessing whatever was on his mind, he turned back to the fancy dashboard and started the car. Amanda took that as her cue to put on her seat belt. Maybe he'd tell her when he was ready. Maybe she'd tell him how much she was starting to like him when things felt a little less scary for her.

They chatted about random bits of nothing as they drove back to the ranch. He told her about the time he tried to sneak into Claim Jumpers as a teen.

"This whole valley knows my whole family and I thought I could just walk in there and order a Tecate."

"What happened?"

"They called my dad and had him come pick me up. He made me sit there while he threw back a good five beers, just chatting it the fuck up with the bartender and the high school football coach. Then he made me drive his drunk ass home. I was *hot*."

"You didn't walk out as soon as you saw the football coach?" Amanda asked as they pulled up to the front of the lodge. Sam stopped just beyond the valet and turned the car off.

"I didn't know it was him. I didn't go to Charming High. I didn't go to high school."

"Oh I'm sorry. I forgot you mentioned you—"

"No, it's fine. I got my GED. But I started doing stunts when I was like twelve and I got cast on *Dude Ranch Summer Camp* when I was fifteen. Anyway I didn't go to Charming High like Zach and Jesse did. There was a different coach when Jesse played. I had no clue who the new guy was. Anyway. I'm legal now and my dad isn't here to stop me."

"Thank God."

"Come on. Let me walk you to your room."

Amanda climbed out of the car and took Sam's hand as he came around and met her at the entrance to the lodge. When they reached her room, she forced herself not to ask him to stay.

"So what time are you picking me up for our super-sexy romantic date tonight?" she said.

"Eight sound good?"

"Eight sounds perfect. I might order a little room service snack before we go. Eight's a little late for me to have dinner."

"Are you kidding? Jesse and I are gonna Greco-Roman wrestle each other for the rest of that corn bread sometime in the next hour. If you're hungry, girl, eat. And if you're still hungry the wings at Claim Jumpers are pretty damn good."

"Oh, this date is gonna involve wings? Cupid knows what I like."

Sam let out the sexiest laugh before he closed the distance between them. Amanda leaned up and pressed her lips to his, sighing into his mouth as his lips parted and his tongue just barely brushed hers. Her body had had the sense to tell her pussy to chill when he was touching her throughout their late brunch, but enough was enough. She felt her body swell with arousal as she pressed closer, running her hands up his strong chest as his hands smoothed their way down to her lower back.

After a few long moments though she forced herself to break their kiss. They couldn't spend the afternoon fucking. Well, they could, but that wasn't what she wanted. Well, it was, but not how she wanted it. She forced her gaze to his plaid shirt. Looking up at those deep brown eyes and that cowboy hat was a little too dangerous. Not that drawing her thumb across his nipple was the safest move either, but that didn't stop her.

"Maybe you can plan to spend the night over here tonight, if you can get away with that. I don't want Miss Leona thinking I'm some kind of hussy."

"Oh, no. Your hussiness needs to be our little secret," Sam said, gripping her ass with both hands. The action spread her ass and her lips apart. She bit her lip to keep from making a noise. She leaned up and kissed him again before she stepped back against the door. Her body missed the heat of him instantly.

"Yeah, stay over tonight. I didn't bring any sexy lingerie, but I have this T-shirt with some Nakia fan art and *Star Wars* pajama pants that will really melt your butter."

"Damn, girl. You know what I like."

"I'll see you at eight."

"Okay." Sam tipped his hat in her direction, then headed back down the hall.

Amanda waited until he turned the corner before she keyed into her room. Inside she collapsed on the bed and buried her face in her pillow. How had this happened? She just wanted to get out of town for a moment. She didn't mean to meet Sam's whole family and she definitely hadn't planned on spending Valentine's Day with him in any sort of a romantical sense.

Amanda rolled over and grabbed her purse. She had to text her mom and let her know that Miss Leona was a living goddess in real life. As soon as her screen lit up she saw several missed texts and calls from Dru.

Call Lux and get me and the girls a table
tonight.

Hello. I know you're out of town but your
phone still works.

Never mind. Lacy took care of it.
You're lucky my mother won't let me fire you
on the weekends. You're fucking worthless.

She looked at the time stamps and the texts were a
whole three minutes apart. She'd just sat down to lunch
when Dru had sent them. The last text came an hour later.

Someone sent me the wrong size.
You can have them.
You're welcome.

There was a picture of brand-new Fenty Pumas, white
with ice blue accents. Amanda was still annoyed with Dru,
but she rarely turned down an opportunity to build her
sneaker collection and she sure as hell wasn't going to turn
down a free pair of almost-three-hundred-dollar shoes. She
took a deep breath and texted Dru back.

Sorry. I was having lunch with family
friends.

I thought you were watching some dumb baby.

Amanda swallowed, her heart pumping hard in her
chest before she remembered Dru hadn't caught her in a
lie. Not yet.

I took the baby to lunch with me.

Whatever. When you get back on Monday just
answer my damn texts.

I will. Have fun at Lux tonight.
I'll be back tomorrow afternoon.

The middle finger emoji Dru sent signified the end of
their conversation.

Amanda tossed her phone on the bed, then went over to
the courtesy phone beside the bed. She pressed zero and
tried not to let the rage stroke she was suppressing shoot
her into another dimension.

"You've reached the front desk at Big Rock Ranch. This
is Christie. How may I help you today?"

"Hi, Christie. This is Amanda McQueen in suite twenty-
four."

"Hello, Ms. McQueen. Are you enjoying your stay?"

"I am. Thank you. Christie, what's the process if I want
to get a massage?"

"Mr. Pleasant already booked a package for you this
afternoon. Whenever you're ready you can head down to
the spa. Or we can have Sven come to your room."

"Oh. Okay then. Um, I'll come down to the spa. I'll be
there in ten minutes?"

"Wonderful. I will let them know you are on your way."

Amanda hung up the phone shocked at how easy that
was. *Everything's easy when you're rich and you literally
own the place*, a voice in the back of her head reminded
her. Not that that was a problem. Sam was a Pleasant. And
the Pleasants owned this ranch and right now, she wasn't
mad at it at all. Amanda took a second to google massage

etiquette because she'd never gotten a real professional massage before, then after she chugged a bottle of the fancy water provided in her room, she moseyed down to the spa to meet Sven. This weekend wasn't going to last forever and she was determined to enjoy every minute of it.

Chapter 15

Sam checked himself in the mirror for the twentieth time. His beard scruff could have used a professional's touch, but he was glad to step away from the clean-cut look he'd been sporting for over a year. He turned around as his brother stepped out of his bedroom. Zach may have resigned himself to the fact that his fiancée wanted to go to a complete dump to celebrate Valentine's Day, but that didn't mean he was going to dress like it. Fresh dark wash designer jeans, crisp shirt and tie, tailored blazer. His cowboy boots clopped against the hardwood floors as he made his way across the room. He slipped his tan Stetson onto his head, then stepped behind Sam to check himself in the entryway mirror.

"I look a'ight?" Sam asked as he moved out of Zach's way. His brother looked him up and down smiling.

"Full bolo, huh?"

Sam looked down and adjusted the silver crest engraved with a wide horseshoe and the *BRR* of the ranch logo. He shrugged. "Eh, why not."

"You look good. And don't worry. She's into you. I saw the way she was looking at you today. Just treat her right."

"That's the plan. Is this all *you* have planned? Hot night at Claim Jumpers?"

"Is this all you have planned?" Zach chuckled.

"She just told me she was interested last night. This is your fiancée, my guy."

"My fiancée has been back and forth between LA, New York, and Paris for the greater part of the last two years, so if she wants to go to Claim Jumpers on Valentine's Day, we're going to Claim Jumpers on Valentine's Day."

"And then?" Sam knew his brother. Ever since he and Evie had gotten together he'd gone out of his way to make every moment of their relationship special. There was no way a trip to Evie's favorite bar was the end of his plans. Zach turned his head and nodded toward his kitchen island. There was an expertly wrapped gift and a bouquet of roses.

"What is it?" Sam asked.

"Tiffany necklace she's been eyeing for a while. Last time I was in the city with her we walked by and she mentioned she'd wanted it for a long time, but she'd been too responsible with her money."

"But now you got money to burn, huh?" Sam laughed.

"You know I'm flush with cash," Zach replied before his expression sobered a bit. He turned back to the mirror so he could give himself one final look. "She didn't have to give me a second chance and she definitely didn't have to agree to marry me. Whatever Buck wants, she gets."

"I get it, I get it. You're in love," Sam chuckled.

"You damn straight! We're spending the night at the Yangs' bed-and-breakfast." Their family friends ran a small produce farm a few miles down the road and offered quaint one-room cabins surrounding their farmhouse, enough to accommodate a half dozen guests. Sam had never spent the night there, but he'd known the Yangs forever and had stopped by on the way home from many a rodeo for donuts and cider. It would be a nice, local place to reconnect away from the ranch and Pleasant Lane. Thoughts of his own sleeping arrangements had him contemplating how Amanda wanted things to go between them after they left the bar.

"You really think Miss Leona is spending a night in with the girls?" he asked.

"Why? What do you know? And if it's some real juicy shit, please don't tell Jesse."

"Yeah, I'm not crazy. She mentioned last weekend that she was seeing someone. She said Jesse scared off the previous guy. You know Mig and them are her ride-or-dies. They'll cover for her."

"Well, good for her." Zach turned around and sighed. "We gotta talk to him."

"Yeah."

"Like, I get it. I don't want to think about our elderly grandmother mugging down either, but she's only getting older and Granddad's been gone for a long time. If she wants a boyfriend, he needs to get out of the way and let the woman live her life. She deserves to be happy."

"Yeah, she does. Even if she just wants to date around for kicks. Jesse doesn't have a say. How's Monday night?"

"Yeah. Let's sit him down."

"Okay. I'm gonna go get Amanda. We'll meet you over there."

"Sounds good."

Sam grabbed his coat and his white Stetson off Zach's coatrack by the door and headed out to his car with Zach close behind him. Zach crossed the cul-de-sac and went to grab Evie from Miss Leona's. Real official date-like.

As he drove back to the ranch Sam wondered if he should make a detour and get Amanda a present. After about ten seconds he decided against it. Not 'cause he didn't want to spoil her, but he was trying to listen. He was trying to pay attention. He'd taken care of her whole weekend at the ranch. The spa package included. She was hesitant to take him up on it and she'd been overwhelmed by their invitation to brunch. A gift on their first date might be a little much. He glanced at the envelope beside him in the passenger seat. It would have to be enough, even if it wasn't from him.

He pulled up to the front of the lodge and parked his car just beyond the valet stand. He grabbed the envelope and stepped back out into the cool night. A sudden thrill rushed through him and settled in his chest as he greeted Naomi at the desk and made his way through the lobby. It had been so long since he'd started something new. Even longer since he'd been excited about someone new.

He'd enjoyed his time with Natalie, but looking back most of that attraction had been based on Natalie's sensuality. It was intoxicating and Sam mistook that for a real connection. It wasn't until she'd dropped the idea of getting married—in front of her parents—before they'd even had a real conversation about their own futures, let alone their future together. Sam knew then that it wasn't in the cards for them.

Things were different with Amanda. There was something about her and it wasn't that she'd somehow won Majesty over with no effort at all. Well, not just that.

Sam arrived at her door, smoothing his shirt and tie before he knocked.

"One second," Amanda called out. A moment later the

door swung open and Amanda stepped forward, a bright smile spreading across her gorgeous face. She was wearing a simple white T-shirt that hugged her large breasts under an open camel-colored cardigan that almost went to the floor. She finished off the look with skintight jeans stretched across her ample thighs and those ice blue Converse. She had on some gloss that made him want to kiss the hell out of her, and her braids were twisted up in a bun on top of her head. She looked great.

"Shit. You look so nice," she said, beaming. Sam's own smile already matched hers. He figured out then exactly what it was. Not just her humor or her sex appeal or the Disney princess way animals gravitated toward her. Or how she didn't realize how rare any of that was. Even some of the kindest, funniest people he'd ever met didn't have that bright energy. Sam couldn't get enough of it and more than that, he wanted to be the one to help refill that well of happiness, whenever she needed him.

He wasn't gonna tell her that shit though. Not yet. He'd learned his lesson and knew what it was like to be on the receiving end of too much, way too soon. He settled for pulling her into a hug.

"So do you. You look gorgeous."

"Nah," Amanda said as she stepped out of his embrace, looking him up and down again. "I mean I look retail supervisor adorable, but I wish I'd packed something *nice* nice. I'm feeling the bolo tie."

"Thanks. It was a gift. Oh, speaking of gifts." Sam handed her the large envelope. "It's from my grandmother." Amanda wasted no time reaching inside. She pulled out two signed headshots from Miss Leona.

"Seriously. My mom is gonna die. I might die too, but

I'll do it privately this time. I've embarrassed myself enough. Let me just put these up and we can go." Sam stepped into her room and she set the pictures on top of her duffel bag on the love seat. She grabbed her purse, then grabbed his hand and pulled him down the hallway.

"Excited?" Sam laughed as he hurried after her.

"Yeah, actually. You were right. I needed this. Also. Oh my God." Amanda stopped and spun around just as they stepped back into the lobby. "That massage was *amazing*."

"Oh yeah?"

"Yes." She spun around and kept walking. Sam sped up so he was right by her side. They both waved goodbye to Naomi, then stepped back out into the night.

"Oh, friggity fuck. Should I get my coat?" Amanda said.

"I can keep you warm. If you'll let me."

"Oh, I'll let you, Tex," she said, winking at him as he opened the passenger-side door for her.

"It'll be plenty warm inside the bar and we don't have to spend any time outside unless you want to."

"I don't want to. Show me this bar."

"Let's do it." Sam slowly pulled to the end of the drive before turning around and driving Amanda into the night.

Sam pushed his way back from the bar with two Dos Equis. Claim Jumpers wasn't packed, but there were plenty of people there for a night made for lovers. Coach Fortner was there too, playing darts at the far end of the bar. Sam skipped that hello. They'd said what's up to Evie and Zach and he'd introduced Amanda to Britany and Delfi, the ranch's executive chef, general manager, and Evie's childhood best friends. They'd offered to pull another table over to turn their double date into a party of six, but he'd shared Amanda with his family all day. He wanted some time alone before she had to go back to Los Angeles and the stress of her job.

They found a two-top opposite the dance floor. Amanda held the table while Sam waited at the bar, accepting a few congratulations on his Oscar win from Brett the bartender and two older white women at the bar he'd never seen before. When he came back Amanda was shimmying her shoulders to the Carrie Underwood blasting through the speakers.

"Ah, thank you," she said, taking the ice-cold beer from his hand.

"You're welcome."

"Let me get a little loose and then I'll put it on you on the dance floor." Sam watched as she took a deep swig of her beer.

"Is that right, Cha-Cha?" Sam asked before he took a sip of his own. He was stopping after one beer so he could drive them home.

"Oh, yes it is. I know what you like. I know you want this bawdy," she said, rolling her shoulders. He tried not to notice the way her tits jiggled, and failed. Now that things were back on and they were moving in the right direction, he was looking forward to picking up where they left off in the bedroom.

"You're right. I'm all about that bawdy, but—"

"Oh, is this our first one-on-one?"

"And then right on to fantasy suites. You've already got a hometown."

Amanda gasped, leaning forward. "You're telling me you watch *The Bachelor*? Please tell me you watch *The Bachelor*."

"Lilah watches *The Bachelor*."

"Are her parents local?" Amanda asked, her brows scrunching together. She was probably wondering why she lived with Miss Leona instead of with her own parents or in her own place.

"Nah. They are up in wine country. My aunt and uncle have a winery up there."

"Oh cool. I like her. She's sweet."

"Yeah, she's a good one." Not that he was gonna put Lilah's business all out there, but he was glad when Amanda seemed to let the subject drop. Lilah still wasn't speaking to her father after he actually tried to arrange a marriage between her and a business partner who was older enough to be her father's college roommate. His uncle Gerald was a good guy, most of the time, but after he raised seven boys, quiet, shy, but smart as hell Lilah confused the fuck out of him.

He didn't understand that she didn't need to be taken care of and he definitely didn't understand that her single status was of her own choosing, not because she wasn't any good at talking to men. Half of Big Rock's single staff members and unfortunately a couple of the married ones were in love with her. Sam knew she'd take the plunge when she was ready. He just didn't know if she'd forgive her dad in time to extend an invite to her parents for Zach and Evie's wedding.

"Anyway, yeah. She's made me watch many an episode of *The Bachelor*."

"And you love it, don't you?" she laughed, taking another sip.

"You know who loves it? Jesse."

"Really?!"

"He pretends he doesn't, but every week he's right in front of the TV with Lilah."

"Jesse's an interesting guy."

"He is, but enough about my family. I want to know more about you, Cha-Cha. We don't have to talk about work, but I want to know everything else."

"I mean, I'll give you the entry-level information. A girl has to have her secrets."

"True, true."

"Let's see. I'm an only child. My parents met when they were, like, eight. Started dating in middle school and have been together ever since. My mom is a nurse at the University of Providence, which I think I mentioned before, and my dad is a facilities manager at the Port of Providence. They are both allergic to dogs, so I don't have to tell you that my childhood was pure misery."

"Oh shit. That's just cruel."

"Isn't it! They used to get so pissed though 'cause I would just bring home random animals and be like, 'What, it's not a dog.'"

"What kind of animals?"

"Oh, anything. Squirrels, raccoons. I trained some of the birds in our neighborhood to bring me random seeds and crap. And of course my crowning achievement, a skunk."

"Nah, you're lying. You didn't skunk whisper a skunk."

"Yes, the hell I did," she laughed. "I tried to convince my mom to let me keep it, but then it was more about convincing my mom not to drop-kick it off our back porch."

"What happened to it?"

"I just let him out the front door. He toddled across the street and promptly sprayed our neighbor's dog."

"Wow."

"Yeah, my mom was like, 'See, that stink would have

been all up in this house.' But I didn't care. Skunky was a true friend. He wouldn't have sprayed me."

"Amazing. Why aren't you, like, a zoologist or something?"

"Tex, if there's anything I love more than playing Russian roulette with your standard case of rabies it's storytelling."

"Yeah?" Sam didn't mean for his voice to have that odd lilt to it, but he felt like Amanda had just let him in on some real personal shit.

"Did you ever watch *Primal Zero*?"

"A bit. My dad was on that show."

"Oh my God! That's right. He was Zork."

"Yep."

"I forgot 'cause—"

"All the makeup."

"Wow. Your family. Anyway. My dad and I used to watch *Primal Zero* all the time and I used to write pages and pages of fanfiction. I finally told my dad about it and he bought me my first computer so I could write and be more organized. He encouraged me to move out here to become a screenwriter."

"And now you're writing on a show. The man knew he was making a wise investment."

Amanda just nodded and let out a sad sigh, as she started picking at the label on her beer.

Sam reached across the table and stoked her hand. She let him, turning her fingers so he could trace the inside of her palm. Her hands were so soft. "If it's not working for you, Cha-Cha, why don't you move on to something else?"

"Because there *is* nothing else at the moment. It was hard enough to get this job. And not all of us have a backup ranch," she said with a wink.

"Fair. That is fair. I'll take that."

"Oh, I know you will. I'm just messin' with you. Look, I know this is part of the game. None of this is actually glamorous. At the end of the day it's a job. Sometimes it's fun and there are cool perks and if you're lucky you get to be a part of something you love and are really proud of, but you know. You can think you're onto something good and still feel unfulfilled."

"If you could do anything, anything. What would it be?"

"Oh man. That's tough. I don't know. I just want to be happy."

"And you're not? Like, with your *life*."

"No. No, I am. I think I just—I can't really wrap my mind around what I really want. I try to picture it and it doesn't seem possible. So all of those dreams and wishes get boiled down to a feeling. Whatever my actual meaning of life turns out to be, I just want to be happy."

"I'm not sure I buy that," Sam said.

"Oh is that right?"

"I don't know. It seems like you know and you're afraid to say it. What did you say earlier? Going after what you want can be scary? What is it you really want?"

"Okay I'll be—I'll keep it one hundred."

"Please," Sam laughed.

"I'm kinda lonely." That confession turned the warmth Sam had been feeling in his chest sour. He curled his fingers gently around hers, like he could will the feeling away. "I knew what I was getting into when I moved out here, but it's been a while and I'm still so homesick."

"Do you think about moving back?"

"No. There's nothing for me back in Rhode Island. I'm homesick for my parents though. I have friends here and you know, Helene. She's an amazing friend. I just didn't think LA would be so lonely. I need a pet skunk."

"If they aren't illegal I'm sure we can find you one."

"I think that's why I've enjoyed this weekend so much. Your family is great and they made me feel so included." She rolled her fingers in his and pulled his hand a little closer. "I know you're not supposed to say stuff like this on a first date, but you should know. I'm crippled with loneliness."

"I know you're joking a little bit, but I think you may be onto something."

"Oh yeah?"

"About LA and the loneliness. Or maybe it's just a millennial midlife crisis, but I think I'm there too. With loneliness. I have a place in Silver Lake, but when I'm not working I'm always here. I miss my family. I really miss my horse."

"It's like you turn a certain age and you think you're supposed to magically become independent in this weird way, but that's not how it works. Anyway, I don't want to feel that loneliness anymore."

Sam raised his beer. "Here's to being a little less lonely." Amanda clinked her beer against his and just as she took down another deep swig, her eyes widened. She slammed her beer down on the table.

"You are more than free to join me, but this song is my freaking jam and I am headed to the dance floor." Sam cocked his head to the side and actually focused on the music coming through the sound system. As soon as he recognized the opening notes to Evelyn "Champagne" King's "Love Come Down," he grabbed Amanda's hand and pulled her to the dance floor.

Chapter 16

Amanda silently kicked herself. She just had to let her honesty pour right out, huh? Who the hell talks about how lonely they are on a first date? She was really enjoying her time with Sam and she had the feeling if things between them continued, those glossy glittery feelings he sparked in her wouldn't go away. Especially if he kept that cowboy hat around. What better way to deaden the vibe between them than to talk about the crippling sadness that came from being thousands of miles away from home while working for someone who was less than a people person. Never mind the fact that she still hadn't been completely honest about what she actually did for work.

A small voice in the back of her head who sounded suspiciously like Helene told her to relax and just be herself. Instead she panicked and dragged Sam to the dance floor. That seemed to do the trick. Zach and Evie joined them, as did Delfi and Britany. Four songs later and she was working on a fine sheen of sweat as Sam moved behind her, his arms draped over her shoulders as they swayed to "Rump Shaker."

"This was a horrible idea," Sam said in her ear. Amanda

bit her lips. She tried her best not to notice the way his dick was grinding against her ass, but it was hard to miss. She spun around and put a little distance between their lower bodies. She grabbed his hands, keeping up to the beat as she two-stepped in front of him.

"Better?" she teased.

"No!"

She tossed her head back, her laughter mixing with the music, just before the song switched to a slow country jam she'd never heard before. That didn't drive her from the dance floor. The opposite. She was impressed with the DJ's work. Instead she stepped into Sam's arms, lacing her fingers behind his neck. She gazed up at him as he tipped the brim of that white cowboy hat back and gazed down at her. She liked what she saw in those brown eyes. A sweet kindness coupled with a searing heat. It was a lot of work to stop herself from kissing him right there in the crowded bar. No one seemed to be paying attention to them, but laying one on him in the middle of the dance floor might change that. She was definitely going to sleep with him before the night was over.

A commotion over by the bar tore her attention away from his handsome face. The bartender was yelling at a blond woman sitting on one of the high leather stools. He reached for her phone, but she snatched it back. Amanda couldn't hear what he was saying beyond a "Now!" that boomed across the room.

"Yikes. Wonder what that's about," Amanda said as she turned back to Sam, but he was still looking toward the bar. She followed his gaze as his eyes shifted to something behind her. Zach and Evie were standing close in a similar embrace, but Zach was also staring daggers at the woman in question.

The bartender waved toward someone by the front entrance, and then a bouncer, who Amanda had thought was just a random patron, came toward the bar. The bartender appeared to be explaining the situation, then pointed over toward the dance floor. Something about his angry gesture made Amanda's chest tighten a bit. Something felt off. The bouncer held his hand out for the phone. The woman refused to hand it over, but it looked like she was showing him something on the screen. That didn't seem to be enough. He motioned to her and her friend and then started urging the two women toward the door.

"I deleted them. Fucking relax," one of the women shouted over the music. Amanda couldn't hear what the bouncer said in response. It seemed like everyone in the place watched as they were escorted out. Sensing the odd shift in mood, the DJ abruptly changed the song, and Amanda absently noted the opening bagpipe screeches of "Jump Around." A few more people rushed to the dance floor and that seemed to break the trance.

"Wonder what that was all about?" Sam said, more to himself. His arms were still wrapped around Amanda's waist even though he'd stopped moving.

"Clownery probably." The sound of her voice seemed to snap him out of it. He looked down at her and smiled.

"Probably," Sam chuckled. "Wanna slow dance to House of Pain?"

"Of course I do."

"Good, 'cause I'm using your body to hide my erection," he joked.

"Oh, then we better stay like this all night."

They went back to swaying to the music, but Amanda couldn't help but notice the bouncer when he came back in the door. This time he stopped and nodded in their direction. She watched as Zach excused himself from Evie. As he walked by he didn't even look at Sam, but he touched him on the shoulder, his cue for Sam to come with him.

"I'll be right back," Sam said, letting her go. A knot rose in Amanda's throat. Two random women getting kicked out of a bar shouldn't have been a big deal. She was sure a few more liquor enthusiasts might be escorted out before they closed for the night. That didn't change the fact that Sam and Zach were suddenly involved.

"You want some water?" Evie shouted over the music, clearly trying to distract her.

"Yeah. I'll come with you." Amanda followed her over to the bar and waited as Evie ordered some waters from the female bartender. Amanda slipped a few singles into the tip jar and waited.

"This happen a lot?" she asked Evie, trying to match Evie's calm demeanor. She didn't seem fazed by this bizarre situation at all.

"I mean more than *never*. I think someone was trying to take pictures of me."

"Oh," Amanda replied. She could feel her expression drop. She hadn't forgotten how famous Evie was, but this seemed like their hometown spot. Didn't seem like it was too much to ask to be left alone. "I'm really sorry."

Evie shrugged. "It comes with the territory. I was just dancing with my man. Now if I was doing lines or something then I might be concerned, but if they just wanted to snap some G-rated content of me at my happiest?" She flashed Amanda a big smile before thanking the bartender for the large plastic cups brimming with ice water in front of them. "But seriously, my therapist would say this falls under 'things outside of my control.' Mac handled it. Zach is willing to handle it further if need be and then we'll get the lawyers involved if it goes that far. I don't want the night to end, so I say we hydrate, then ask the DJ to play some Janet."

"Cheers to that." Amanda took a deep sip, then let out a deep breath. Evie was right. Whatever happened it looked like it was under control now and if Evie could enjoy the rest of the night after having her privacy intruded upon, she could definitely relax and enjoy her night with Sam.

A few moments later he made his way over to the bar. Her skin warmed as his arm slid back around her waist. She turned, just a bit to smile up at him, but her smile faded as soon as she saw the dark look on his face. She moved so she was facing him, putting a hand to his chest.

"What's wrong?"

"They were trying to take pictures of me. Of us."

Amanda felt her stomach drop. Of course someone would take an interest in Sam's social life. Depending on whom they sold them to, they could get a nice little chunk of money for those photos. If she was with Sam— Academy Award winner Samuel Pleasant a whole five minutes after his win—she was running the risk of being photographed with him. She was running the risk of Dru finding out what she was really doing this whole time. She'd run the risk of Dru losing her complete shit and trying to burn her life and her relationship down to the ground with it.

The panic started to set in again. Her stomach felt like it was still somewhere near the floor, and now an odd heat was creeping up her neck and wrapping around her ears. Her flight response was lacing up her sneakers. But her greater instinct to not make matters worse waving its own neon flag forced her to hold still.

Sam was famous and from the looks of things well known by virtue of being a Pleasant long before Oscar nominations had been announced. If fear forced her to walk away now that would be the end for the two of them. She couldn't keep running and hiding.

Would this end horribly? Yes. How could it not? Zach and the proactive bar staff may have thwarted one asshole's efforts tonight, but what about the next time? Sam's career was on the rise and interest in him was only going to grow.

If this was going to end eventually, Amanda refused to be the one to light the fuse. She wanted to enjoy her time with Sam while she still could. She loved the way his fingers felt on her side too much to let fear ruin what could be a perfect Valentine's Day at this perfectly weird bar.

"We're good," Zach said, before he ordered another round for them all.

Sam leaned closer, his eyes scanning her face. She'd made up her mind, but she realized her breathing hadn't returned to normal. "They're gone, but we can leave if you want to."

"No, I—you have more experience with this than I do." She swallowed. "We can do whatever. You wanna stay and rage, we can stay and rage. The DJ hasn't played a single slide yet. Cha-cha or electric."

Sam was quiet for a moment, running his teeth over his bottom lip. Amanda wanted to hug him, then kiss the hell out of him, but she was sure someone else would photograph that. Sam glanced around the room before he took off his cowboy hat and scratched the back of his head. He let out a breath and slid the hat back into place. "Let's get out of here."

"'Kay." They said a quick goodbye to Zach and Evie and waved to Brit and Delfi, who were still fucking shit up on the dance floor.

"Where should we go?" Amanda asked as they pulled out of the dirt parking lot. She wasn't sure if she'd succeeded in keeping her voice light. She didn't want to leave the bar and she definitely didn't want their night to end early just because location number one turned out to be a bust.

Sam let out another deep breath, a little more pained this time, a little more frustrated. He was not okay.

"If there was one place around here. One place you had to show me. Where would that be?"

"We'd need a helicopter," he muttered. Amanda burst out laughing.

"Excuse me, what?"

"I'd show you the whole valley from the air. It's beautiful, but we'd need a helicopter. I'm good, but I'm not gonna charter a helicopter on short notice good."

"So much for the Pleasant name. Can't even get a spontaneous helicopter. What the fuck am I going to tell my family? You made promises, Sam." She smiled wide until he glanced over at her, a smile spreading across his gorgeous face. The smile faded after a moment though and he was quiet. Amanda decided it was a good idea to give him some time just to be in his head. God knew she could use a moment to pull it together after their speedy exodus from the bar.

They drove back to the ranch. Amanda tried not to let disappointment overtake her, but to her surprise Sam drove past the lodge. They drove deeper into the property, up a dirt road, up a slowly rising incline. About halfway up the hill there was a lone cabin. The lights were off, but from one of the windows she could see a fire going in the fireplace. They drove past the cabin and further past a small clearing. The ride continued on and on and seemed to go all the way up the foothills into the mountains. Sam cut the engine, then tilted his head a bit.

"Come on."

Amanda climbed out and followed Sam to the back of the car. They leaned against the trunk and she could immediately see why he'd brought her there. It was butt-ass cold out, but you could see almost the whole ranch from where they stood and what felt like almost every star in the sky along with the enormous waning moon. They stood side by side, only touching arm to arm. For the moment it was enough.

"I don't really have a place," Sam said quietly.

"What do you mean?"

"I don't have a place. Usually when I come back I go to the house and I go to the ranch. I don't, like, go out much and all my childhood spots aren't really private."

"People don't see me," she said suddenly, since they were back to confessing things.

"In what way?"

"People actually don't see me. I mean, it's partly my fault. Well, no, it's entirely my fault. I've made a habit out of being invisible. It didn't occur to me that people would be trying to pap you in your hometown. No one ever cares what I'm doing. Definitely not enough to sneak photos. I'm sorry that happened."

"I didn't expect that either. A lot's changed in the last couple of weeks."

"It's amazing what one statue can do."

"True. Not complaining, but looks like there's some adjusting to do. Just wasn't prepared for it. Wasn't prepared for you either."

Amanda moved off the car and stepped between his legs. Sam didn't hesitate to wrap his arms around her waist. The warmth of his body broke through the cool night air surrounding them. She watched his eyes as they focused on her lips. She couldn't help but think about what it would be like to feel his mouth between her legs.

"So what do we do?" she whispered.

"We try to keep this private until we don't want to keep this private anymore."

"We could do that. It's not hard."

She saw an eyebrow go up under the shadow of his cowboy hat. "It's not?"

"No. Do you even know what Daniel Kaluuya's girlfriend looks like? Mahershala's wife?" Sam paused and she knew he had a vague sense 'cause he'd probably met them at a thing but . . . "See. If you saw them on the street you wouldn't know."

"You have a point. But . . . I don't want to keep this private."

"You know that's enough for right now though, right? Like, it means a lot to me 'cause I know you're serious. I'm not ready to be photographed. I am not a photographed kind of girl. And it's not 'cause I don't think I'm beautiful—"

"Oh, I know. Remember, we spent a good chunk of the morning protecting this beautiful face," Sam laughed.

"It's not a self-esteem thing. It's . . . when something or someone means a lot to me I want to keep it to myself for a while. Just enjoy it for as long as I can. As soon as we are seen together—"

"We belong to the Internet."

"Bitch, we belong to the Internet."

"I get it. I don't want that either."

"Listen, you introduced me to your family, day one. You introduced me to your horse."

"That's huge. You don't even know."

"So, I met your horse. I met your grandma. I'm a little less terrified of your brother Jesse, and Evie, well, she loves me."

"How could she not?"

"My mom can't keep a secret for shit so maybe I won't tell her right away, but as soon as Helene and Ignacio are back from their honeymoon I'll tell Helene. And then maybe we can go double-dating on Ignacio's yacht or, like, go window-shopping for exotic animals and buy the most illegal one. I don't know what rich people do with their free time," she teased.

"We're rich. Not white."

"True. Tex, let's just protect this from the Internet for as long as possible."

"Anything for you, Cha-Cha. Anything you want."

"I want to sleep with you again. And then probably again."

"Oh, we can definitely do that."

"Why don't we head back to my room. Like now. My front is very warm but my butt is freezing."

Amanda felt Sam's hands ease down her hips before he reached around and grabbed her ass in his firm grip. "Better?"

"Much. But we still can't do this outside."

"Okay," Sam laughed. "Let's go."

Chapter 17

Sam pulled back up to the front of the lodge and tried to ignore the clock on his dashboard. Their night wasn't over, but he didn't expect to be back at the ranch just before nine p.m. He needed to turn his mood around and enjoy the time he had left with Amanda before their weekend was over. He glanced through the front doors and caught the shadows of a couple walking through the lobby.

"Head on in. I'll go park."

"I can come with you," Amanda replied, her voice light. Sam could tell she was trying to make him feel better and he really appreciated it. He reached over and took her hand so he could lay a warm kiss on her cold fingers.

"I'd love the company, but in the interest of our collective privacy—"

"Right." Other guests might have seen them together earlier, but things felt different now. Things between them were different and he wasn't coming up just to say goodnight. He wasn't planning on walking back out. "Well, in that case, let me just go freshen up. I've never said that before." She wiggled her eyebrows, so damn proud of herself. Sam chuckled quietly before kissing the back of Amanda's hand one more time.

"Text me when you're feeling fresh enough."

"Oh, I will, baby." She leaned over and kissed him on the cheek, then climbed out of the car. He waited until she was safely inside before he pulled out of the curved drive. He took a U-turn and drove behind the lodge so he could leave his car in Zach's parking space. He took his time walking back to the front, breathing in the night air, wondering where exactly he had gone wrong. The truth was that he'd done the best work of his career and been rewarded for it and as a result he was now a thing. He thought he'd been prepared. He couldn't go anywhere in a hundred-mile radius without someone recognizing him as Jesse Pleasant Sr.'s boy or Zach and Jesse's little brother, but that kind of notoriety had never impacted his love life before. He had never come close to scaring off someone he was starting to care deeply for.

And yeah, even though Amanda had stuck around, handling the whole situation at Claim Jumpers like a champ, he didn't miss the shock and hesitation in her eyes. She was so close to hightailing it back to the city. Things were fresh, but so easy between them. He didn't want to lose her. Not again. All he could do was be cautious and show her that she was his focus now. He stepped into the lobby and greeted the young lady at the front desk with a nod and tip of his hat. He thought about taking a seat in one of the available chairs in front of the central fireplace, but decided against it. Privacy was a firm policy at Big Rock, but at the moment he wasn't in the mood to even risk being recognized. He headed down the hallway toward Amanda's room.

He pulled out his phone as he waited outside her door and thought about braving a look at his social media. He wasn't in the mood for whatever comments were waiting for him on Instagram, but Twitter usually delivered the

appropriate levels of humor at a time like this. Sure
enough the first thing was that photo that was turned
into a meme of Jason Derulo falling backward down the
Met Gala stairs almost ten years ago. JASON DERULO FALLS
DOWN THE STAIRS ON HIS WAY TO VOTE IN THE DEMOCRATIC
PRIMARY. Sam laughed quietly to himself as he ignored the
thousands of tweets hanging out in his mentions and kept
scrolling. A few minutes later a text from Amanda popped
up on his screen.

Okay I'm ready.

I'm right outside your door.

He rolled his shoulder along the wall reaching over to
knock lightly on the door. It cracked open a moment later.
Amanda's smiling face was visible through the small opening. He couldn't help but smile back.

"Hi," she said with a hint of playful seduction in her
voice.

"Hi."

"You wanna come in?"

"Yeah, I'd like that."

"'Kay." She opened the door all the way revealing the
beautiful fact that she was wearing nothing but a white
ranch towel that left almost nothing to the imagination.
Her cleavage spilled out over the edge of the white fabric
that she was holding together with a death grip in her other
hand. Her luscious thighs were on full display, the terry
cloth just barely covering the juncture between her legs.

"Jesus Christ."

"Please come in."

He stepped inside, taking off his Stetson as most of the

blood in his body rushed to his dick. "You could have warned me."

"What do you mean? I thought we decided. We is fucking tonight."

"Oh, we did. I just didn't expect you to already be all butt-booty naked."

"I'm wearing a towel. Gotta leave a little mystery. I took, like, a four-minute shower. I feel like I brought a little bit of Claim Jumpers with me. I wanted to be fresh *fresh* for when I smothered your face with my thighs," she said.

"So you're planning on sitting on my face?" Sam didn't miss the way she was backing toward the bed. He hung his Stetson on the hook on the door, then shrugged out of his jacket.

"I mean I've been thinking about it. Among other things." The smile had slowly disappeared from her face. Her gaze followed his every move as he toed out of his cowboy boots, then went about unbuttoning his shirt. Sam knew that look, pure unadulterated lust, but he'd never seen it on the face of a woman he wanted so badly. When he spoke again he could hear that same level of arousal coming through his own voice.

"What other things? Tell me."

Amanda licked her lips as she leaned against the bedpost. "Well. For starters I think you should come over here and see how wet I am under this towel. I didn't finish drying off all the way." Sam pulled off his button-down and then his undershirt, then crossed the room, crowding right into her personal space. He looked down at the gorgeous brown skin of her shoulders. There was a small bit of lotion that hadn't been properly rubbed. Slowly, he used his thumb to finish the job. Then he moved his hand a little lower, brushing the back of his palm over her tit as he went. He helped himself to the warmth between her thighs as he was greeted instantly by the wetness already coating her slit. Her breath hitched as he pressed his mouth to the curve of her neck.

"You been like this long?" he asked as he used his middle finger to slide between her lips. He found the tiny, hard bud easily, but ignored it to tease her slick entrance instead.

"Uh, since my massage this afternoon."

Sam paused, but didn't take his hand away. "Sven get you worked up like this?"

"No. I was thinking about how nice it would have been if those were your hands all over me. He did an a'ight job." She tilted her head back just a bit so she could look him in the eye. "But I wanted it to be you. I've touched myself a lot, thinking about you."

Sam watched her eyes as he slid one finger inside her slick opening. "And how was it?"

"Never as good as the real thing. I want you to fuck me so bad."

"But?" He leaned down and sucked her bottom lip into his mouth, kissing her deeply. They could get back to their conversation in a moment. "But what?" he said when he finally broke away. Sam nudged her legs farther apart, making room for his whole wrist as he pushed his whole finger deep inside her. She clenched around him, gripping his shoulder with one hand to steady herself. That towel was dangerously close to slipping to the ground.

"But what, Cha-Cha? Tell me," Sam breathed against her fresh-smelling skin.

"I want this to last." She whimpered, thrusting her hips against his palm. He added another finger to the mix, fucking her slowly as she tried to find the rest of her words. "I don't want tonight to end. I'm not ready to go back."

"I can't stop tomorrow from coming, but that doesn't mean we can't do this again, and again."

"Sam," she cried out, her hips working hard against the motion of his fingers. She was wet as hell, soaking his palm with her sweet-smelling juices. He had to taste her and soon.

"Get on the bed," he said. She followed his instructions, shimmying up on the mattress, the perfect height for him to fuck while they both had their feet still on the ground. They'd get to that eventually. Later, when he bent her over and took her from behind so that perfectly fat ass of hers could bounce off his lap. He stepped out of his jeans and his boxers, grabbing the condoms he'd gotten from Zach out of the back pocket. He stroked his erection as she watched him from the bed, still gripping that towel that was barely covering her tits.

He approached the bed and leaned over her as he took the towel from her fingers and parted the fabric, exposing her beautiful body. Sam never had a type, until now. Amanda was his type, every full curve, every stretch mark, mole, beauty mark, every inch of her deep brown skin. He loved the roundness of her belly, her large breasts too big for him to cup in his hand. His mouth watered as he looked at the hard tips of her dark brown nipples, just waiting to be sucked. Reading his mind, she pressed her tits together offering them up to him. He didn't have to think twice. The look in her eyes was enough.

Sam leaned down, sucking one puckered tip into his mouth, before running his tongue over it again and again in lazy circles. His dick ached at that sound she made. A soft hiss and a moan. Desperate pleas for him to keep going. No way she wanted him to stop. He switched to the other breast, before using his hand to push the luscious mounds together a bit more. He opened his mouth, flattening the tip of his tongue so he could worship both of her nipples at the same time. More desperate noises, even louder as she gripped the back of his head, pulling him closer. If Sam died this way, he'd happily welcome his maker in this moment, with his name on Amanda's lips.

He moved to stand off the bed and made quick work of rolling the condom into place. "I'm gonna eat that pussy. Believe me. I just—"

"No. Now. Yeah. I want you now." Amanda slid farther up the bed giving him room to join her, but seemed to suddenly have a change of heart. She hopped to the floor, motioning for him to get on the bed. "I wanna be on top."

"I don't see a downside to this." Sam tried not to bounce onto the bed like an overzealous eight-year-old. He made himself comfortable against the headboard, then held out a hand for her to join him. She came closer to the bed, then seemed to have a change of thought. She hurried across the room, taking her braids down from their high bun as she went, then reached for his Stetson on the hook.

"May I? Or does this violate some sort of cowboy code of hat ethics?"

"You could put on a clown wig and a beret and I wouldn't give a shit. Get over here."

She laughed, delicately placing the hat on her head before hurrying back over to join him. She carefully climbed over his lap, positioning herself exactly where they both wanted her to be. He gripped his dick and placed it right at the entrance of her slick, warm pussy.

"How do I look?" she asked as she teased them both, rubbing herself along the swollen head of his erection.

"I think you need a Stetson of your own. I like it," Sam said with a groan as she sunk down onto him. She took a few inches before sliding back up again. He wasn't packing the longest dick around, but he wasn't ashamed to brag about the thickness of it. It felt amazing, the way she took her time getting used to him, up and down, taking more and more until she'd taken every inch.

She leaned forward, bracing herself with her hands just above his shoulders. "I'm not too proud to admit this." He reached down and gripped her lush hips.

"To admit what, baby?"

"Your dick is amazing. And don't pretend you didn't hear me. I'm not saying it again."

Sam's hips dropped down to the bed as he laughed, losing his rhythm for just a moment. He picked it up again, driving up deep into her sweet, warm cunt. "I only need to hear it once. I'll carry your words with me forever."

He knew she could have continued to clown him all night, but they both gave in to the pleasure between them, shelving the small talk for another time. Sam moved so he was sitting up more against the headboard and pulled her closer, wrapping his arms around her as she continued to grind on his dick. He kept on kissing her, soaking in the way her tongue felt against his, how their bodies moved together, how he also didn't want this night to end.

Amanda pulled back, tipping the hat up so she could rest her forehead against his. "I'm gonna come," she breathed. He opened his eyes to find hers squeezed shut, all her focus on where they were connected. "I'm coming. Oh, fuck. Sam." The sound that came out of her threatened to drive him over the edge, but he held off, gripping her body as she pussy-clenched hard around his cock. After a moment, he took the hat off her and slipped it onto his own head as he rolled them so she was on her back. She let her legs fall open, giving him all the space he needed to fuck her harder, faster. Her hands went up to the headboard, anchoring her against his harsh thrusts.

For some reason the thought of them dancing together popped into his head and Sam came, filling the condom as he slowed then finally ground to a stop on top of her. He caught his breath, then carefully climbed off the bed. He could barely see, but he knew if he didn't get rid of the condom right away, he'd pass out and maybe never move again. He came back from the bathroom and found Amanda on her side with a throw blanket pulled over her. She watched as he came back to the bedroom, a satisfied smile spreading across her face.

"You need to play a cowboy in your next movie. That hat is sexy as fuck."

"Okay. Your turn," Sam said as he reached over and took another bite of the churro and ice cream dessert they'd had sent to the room. After they'd both caught their breath Amanda confessed how hungry she was. She'd been banking on the spread at Claim Jumpers to keep her energy up, but they'd left before she'd gotten to sample the wings. They'd ordered a real dinner and some dessert, then relocated their mostly naked party over to the couch.

"Hmmm. Do you vote?" Amanda asked.

"Yes. I need to be better about local elections because those matter, but yes."

"Okay, same. Your turn?" Amanda took her own spoonful, doing a little dance as she enjoyed the sticky sweetness of the caramel sauce.

"Biggest fear."

"Oh, that's tough. It's somewhere between hurting my

mom's feeling in some horrible way I can't take back and being sex trafficked."

"Same," Sam laughed.

"Really?"

"Yes, my mom or my grandmother. And I feel like there are few things worse than being sex trafficked. Doing life for something I didn't do thanks to lazy crime-scene investigation is up there."

"I thought you were going to say some artsy shit like not living every day to the fullest."

"Nah, doing a bid unjustly in solitary sounds way worse. Not that solitary is ever just."

"Agreed. Okay. I'm coming in hot with this one. Are you ready?"

"I'm ready. Hit me."

"If you could work on any project next, what would it be? This is a safe space. I will not tell your agent or your brothers or whatever. Just you and me. If you could do anything. Tell me."

Sam took a deep breath and tried his hardest to access the truth. There wasn't a clear answer that jumped to the forefront 'cause the truth was he didn't live on Planet Black Actors Get Whatever They Want. He had to learn to manage his dreams a long time ago to stop from crushing his own heart and his passion along with it.

"Tell me. Speak it into existence. What's the project?" Amanda said, urging him on.

"Okay. I'll give you my top three—I should make you sign an NDA."

Amanda laughed, playfully shoving at his knee. "Just tell me."

"Okay. I don't know if you're familiar with Bill Pickett but he was one of the first Black bulldoggers. He paved the way for Black men, and women, to compete in the rodeo. I'd love to do his biopic. I wouldn't have to be in it, but I'd love to produce it."

"Okay. You should definitely be in it. If I had a ton of cash I'd write you a check right now. What else?"

Sam swallowed and dug a little deeper. He hadn't been this honest with anyone other than Zach in a while. "You read comics?"

"I dabble."

"Well, I've heard rumors that they are finally going to move on a *Black Death* movie."

"Sam!" Of course she'd heard of *Black Death*. The comic about the Grim Reaper who inhabited the body of Malcolm Vance, a Black Marine who had nearly died in Vietnam, had been around for decades.

"I'd love to play Malcolm. That shit would be fun as hell."

"Okay, I know we are talking about wildest dreams, but have you told your agent?"

"No."

"Why?"

"'Cause I'd be up against every Black actor in town and a few of the stupid white ones."

"No. Nope. No way. You have to at least float your name. Do not shoot yourself in the foot and keep yourself out of the running." *Black Death* was one of those projects he'd wanted since his grandpa had shown him his tattered copy of issue number one. But Hollywood was struggling to let more than one Black superhero shine. "But we'll come back to that. What's number three?"

"I want to be in a legit rom-com. Or a romantic period drama if I'm really going for it."

Amanda leaned forward, resting her chin on her hands,

on the back of the couch. "You would be an amazing leading man. A perfect Prince Charming."

"I like to think so. Not in a cocky way."

"Why not? Hell, be cocky about it."

"What's your big Hollywood dream?"

"Oh, just tons and tons of weird, sweeping, romantic epics in space. I want everything in space. With kissing. Pirates in space, with kissing. A murder mystery in space, with kissing."

"So you're not just joking about being a big sci-fi nerd, huh?"

"Not even close."

"Do you watch *Banker Down*?"

"Do I watch *Banker Down*? My first spec script was for *Banker Down*!"

"Really?"

"Yeah. When I first moved out here. I was young and fresh and so, so naive. I was like, 'I'll get staffed in no time.' Then reality set its phasers to 'bitch, you thought.'"

Sam burst out laughing. "Can I read it?"

"Ugh. No. It hasn't aged well. It's like season four good when I thought it was season one good."

"I bet it's dope. My buddy and I just started a rewatch before awards season kicked up. I wanna get back to it."

"Oh man," she started, and then yawned. Sam glanced at the clock on the little desk in the corner. It was only eleven, but it had been a long day.

"Should I tuck you in? It's getting late."

"If by tuck me in you mean finger bang me until I fall asleep, then yes."

Sam snorted, then stood to gather everything on the room service platter, glad they'd taken the time they'd needed to talk and connect and refuel. Then he turned back to the bed to get to work.

Chapter 18

Amanda couldn't believe the night they'd spent together and how much sex they'd had.

Well . . . she could believe that part.

The sexual chemistry they'd had since day one was clear from the International Space Station, but Amanda had spent so many nights thinking about what it would be like to be with Sam Pleasant again, what it would be like to kiss him and touch him outside of a one-night after-party situation. And now she knew and she didn't want to let him go. She knew she had to tell him the truth.

She did one more sweep of the room, grabbing her phone charger and stuffing it into her bag. She took out the last twenty she had and left it on the nightstand with a note for housekeeping. She could see why people paid a mint and a couple kidneys for the minimum two-night stay. The Pleasants had something special here with Big Rock Ranch.

"Yup?" she called out in response to a light knock on the door.

"It's me." She heard Sam's perfect voice from out in the hallway.

She hurried across the room and let him in. He'd been

gone for a whole six minutes, but she was happy to see him again. "Hi."

"Hey." He kissed her on the mouth, like he hadn't just kissed her seven minutes ago before he went down to the front desk. He kissed her again once more before he gave her butt a light squeeze. Then he went to the sofa and sat on the arm. He was wearing the same clothes from last night, but he looked sexy as hell. Denim-covered legs, worn boots and all. She couldn't help but picture the alternate universe where he was a rugged farmer and she was his big-breasted wife. Oh, they'd make so many babies to help run that farm. In space.

He took off his hat and slowly rotated it in his hands. "So you're all checked out. You don't even need to bring the keycard back to the desk. Just leave when you're ready." Amanda walked over and stepped between his legs.

"Thank you for a wonderful weekend. I really needed this."

"Oh, my pleasure, ma'am," he said with a wink.

"Um, before I go I have something to tell you and maybe it'll shed a little light on why I was uh—a little skittish at first."

"Sure, what's going on?"

"I'm not a writer. I'm an assistant."

Confusion clouded Sam's expression. Lying to him had been a big mistake. "I—I was embarrassed. It's not an excuse. I should have told you from the beginning, but I just, I never thought we'd end up here. And I never thought I'd like you this much. And also, you're Sam Pleasant."

"Okay," he said slowly.

"I would rather not say who I work for now, for a few reasons, including her privacy, but I do work for an actress.

I understand if that fucks things between us, but I needed to tell you."

Instead of telling her to hit the bricks, never to return, he set down his hat on the couch, then wrapped his strong fingers around her waist and pulled her closer. He rested his chin on her cleavage. Amanda's body reacted immediately. If he didn't cuss her out maybe they could have one more quick round before she had to get back on the road. He didn't say a word though. He just looked up at her, expression open now, like he was waiting for her to go on.

"Helene got me into the party so I could blow off some steam—I don't work for Helene, by the way."

"I know. She would have told me."

"You're right. She would have. Helene doesn't lie about stupid shit, like some people." She laughed ruefully. "Anyway. I just wanted to wear something sparkly and have a good time and then when I saw you again, you being you, I didn't want to tell you I was out grabbing someone's lunch. I know full well how your half live and I know I will never be able to afford real estate there. But I do really like you."

"You know how my grandparents met?" he asked.

Amanda shook her head.

"My grandpa was an assistant. He was the assistant to the head animal wrangler on *Glory in the Night*. He was the guy the horses actually listened to and really loved. Before they were my grandparents they were the only two Black people on a lonely, racist set. He was the only person who would talk to her when the cameras weren't rolling. She was the only person who acknowledged him, but that wasn't the reason why they fell in love."

"If he was wearing a white cowboy hat you don't need to explain any further."

Sam chuckled a little. "Miss Leona saw how patient he

was with the horses and how patient he was with her and she just knew. She could make a life with a man that was patient and kind in the face of all the shit they were dealing with on that set. She was the star and he saw that she needed a friend. He's gone now, but my brothers and I, Lilah and our other million hundred cousins and now four great-grandkids are pretty good proof that their job titles on that set didn't matter one bit. You don't need to be a staff writer. You just need to be yourself."

"Does this mean you want to marry me?"

"No." They both couldn't stop themselves from laughing. "Girl, we just met. I need you to relax."

"Sorry. I don't know what I was thinking. My bad."

"But it does mean that I know what this industry is like and I know that I've found myself in rooms where this bullshit world and this bullshit industry made me feel ashamed for just being myself. I get it."

An uncomfortable heat spread through Amanda's chest as the mere thought of Dru and the rest of her reality outside of this ranch with its amazing spa and delicious desserts suddenly spiked her anxiety. She swallowed and actually struggled against a sudden sting of tears.

"I need this job. I—you know how things are. I have savings, but I do not have financial support from my parents and I'm not in a good enough place to just quit. Plus, there's other stuff at play. Stuff again I'd rather not explain for her privacy." Sam didn't need to know what Dru's mom was like or how Dru basically had no one to be there for her. She could be the biggest of assholes, but she was a person too. Kaidence had hired Amanda and kept her on for so long because she could handle her daughter and treat her with the kindness everyone else in their circles seemed to lack. She wouldn't feel right just leaving her to the wolves.

"Is there any way I can help?" Sam asked.

"I'm sure there is, but no. It wouldn't feel right calling in favors from you. It's more than just a pride thing. I—I need to keep things separate. I don't trust people enough to get me a gig as a solid to you and then not fire me if we split it. I know how jaded that sounds."

"No, it sounds realistic 'cause that's the kind of bullshit industry people do."

"I can smell a real existential crisis coming for my ass any day now, but all of it, it's just really complicated. But I promise from here on out: no more secrets."

"Was this actress the reason why you were crying outside of Delightly that day?"

Amanda hesitated for a moment before she nodded.

"Be real. Is she fucking with you?"

"No. No. She's just a lot and the job is really demanding. You have an assistant."

"Yeah, but I don't think I've made Walls cry in the middle of the street."

"You probably haven't. I really don't want to talk about her."

"Okay. Okay. Come here." Sam stood and pulled her into a proper hug.

She let out a strained breath and squeezed him tighter, burying her face against his shoulder. "I'm sorry."

"Don't be. I'm glad you told me. I don't want you to be embarrassed."

Amanda stepped back, and another stuttered breath managed to escape. "So you want to keep seeing me?"

"Hell yeah. Have you looked at this face in the mirror lately? Girl, you fine. I ain't letting you go."

"I am pretty dope."

He stepped close and cupped her cheeks in his hands, pressing a soft kiss to her lips. Why did she have to go back?

"When can I see you again?" he asked.

"I'm not sure. I'll text you?" She headed over to the bed and closed her bag before checking her purse once more. She had everything. It was time to head back to LA.

"Can't wait. I'll be back in town on Tuesday. So just let me know. I have more meetings."

"I know I have no right to give you career advice right now, but you should talk to your people about *Black Death*. You'd be perfect for it. They should be begging you to meet with them for it. And those checks? Shiiiiiit."

Sam laughed as he scooped his hat off the couch. "You're right. I'll think about it."

"Okay." They met back at the door and Amanda couldn't help but feel like she was leaving a part of herself behind. Boy, she really liked Sam Pleasant. How was she going to survive all week without his sweet breath of fresh air? She leaned up and kissed him twice more.

"I'll text you."

"Not if I text you first."

"Oh, don't threaten me with a good time."

"Go on. Git. I'll wait a few minutes, then circle around to the side exit."

"Oh, this is so scandalous. It's making me so hot, Tex. You don't even know." She kissed him just one more time, then headed out the door. A squeal slipped out of her as he slapped her on the ass as the door closed between them. She thanked the young lady at the front desk as she sent one of the young valets to get her car. As she drove away from the ranch, she tried not to think about how in the world things between her and Sam were supposed to work. She wasn't in a position to quit and even if she was that wouldn't turn her into a Hollywood socialite overnight. They came from two different worlds. He was right, there was nothing to be embarrassed about, but facts was facts. Their lives simply weren't the same.

That didn't change the way she felt about him one bit. It didn't change that she was going to text him as soon as she got home. As she drove through Charming, she promised herself that she wasn't going to run from this. If things ended between them naturally, so be it. But she wasn't going to push him away. Not again. He was too good of a kisser, too easy on the eyes, and brought her too much laughter and joy. She was going to hold on to Sam Pleasant.

At the last stoplight before she turned onto the highway, a text message popped up over her navigation map. She grabbed her phone and clicked over to her conversation with Tex.

There was just a screen grab. It was a cropped screenshot of a conversation with his agent.

Tuesday. I want to talk to you about
Black Death.

Fuck yeah, man. Let's do it.

Amanda wished she had the resources to put herself out there like that. In the meantime though, she was pretty proud of her brave cowboy.

Sam knew he would get shit from his family for strolling back in wearing the same clothes as the night before, but when he walked into Miss Leona's kitchen he realized what he was wearing and what he'd gotten up to was the last thing on anyone's mind. Jesse was straight up pacing back and forth in their grandmother's kitchen. Zach and Evie were standing guard like they were waiting for him to start smashing shit any moment. Lilah was sitting on a stool, just chillin' like Jesse wasn't about to implode.

"Heey, hey," Sam said cautiously. "What's going on?"

"Um—Miss Leona—" Evie started.

"No. Fuck that. What happened?" Sam felt like he was going to throw up.

"No, no, she's okay," Evie rushed to say.

"She didn't come home last night," Zach explained. "And she didn't stay at Mig's."

"Oh shit," Sam whispered. She'd spent the night out with her new mystery man. And Jesse was fucking losing it.

"Yeah," Lilah said before she cringed. She knew too. Of course she did. They all knew the truth before last night. All of them but Jesse.

"She's on her way home now," Evie said.

"And I'm trying to tell our brother here that she is beyond grown, but he doesn't want to listen," Zach said.

"What is there for me to listen to?" Jesse asked. "She lied about where she was going and spent the night out with God knows who. That doesn't bother you?"

"I mean, it does, but I think it bothers us for different reasons," Lilah shot back.

Zach turned to Evie, squeezing her hand. "Babe."

"Yeah." She squeezed his hand back before she left the room.

"Li, can you give us a sec?" Zach said.

Their baby cousin looked back and forth between the three of them, her tongue rolling over her teeth. She hated when people treated her like a child, but that wasn't what was happening here.

"Not trying to pull the grown-folks card on you," Zach said. "Just wanna talk brother to brother. To brother."

"Fine. But Jesse," she said in her soft voice. She hopped off the stool and fixed him with a hard stare. He actually stopped pacing to look at her, even though he was still huffing and puffing. "You really need to back off. If anyone knows how awful it is to have the menfolk in this family butt into your love life, it's me."

"This isn't about her damn love life!" he yelled. Sam couldn't stand when he got like this. He had Senior's hard, authoritative edge, but where their father knew the limits of his temper, Jesse had a point where he couldn't control it. None of the men in their family shouted the way Jesse did. Sam knew where his anger came from, but a lot of time he wished that wasn't the case. Lilah wasn't fazed though. She'd been sick to shit of Pleasant men since she was born. If she could handle her dad and her seven brothers, she could handle all six feet and seven inches of Jesse.

"Whatever. Get all loud all you want. You know Miss Leona. She doesn't care if you live next door. She will kick you right off the lane if you push her too far. Especially if you come at her disrespecting her like this. She is your *grandmother*. She is the matriarch of this family. You need to act like it." Lilah was speaking the whole truth, but Jesse had already tuned her out. Sam could see the vein on the side of his face threatening to burst. Lilah sucked her teeth as she followed after Evie. When they heard a door close down the hall, Zach looked over at Sam. They were going to have this talk with him now.

"Alright. What's going on with you, man?" Sam said.

"Sam, you need to back off," Jesse snarled.

"What the fuck are you talking about? You're the one who's about to Hulk out—" Sam shot back, but Zach cut him off.

"Jesse, you need to relax and talk to us."

No one wanted Zach to bust out the breathing techniques their mom had taught Jesse when he was going through puberty. A growth spurt had tackled his ass at age ten. And by the time he was thirteen he was already. Football and basketball coaches around the state were lined up to get a piece of him, ready to add him to their roster. But Jesse just wanted to bake with Evie and Miss Leona and be left alone.

Kids at school teased him mercilessly for his large, awkward body, and the adults were much worse. People who didn't know him didn't know he was a kid and that made things even harder. Adults who did know him wanted to take advantage of him or make him show off his strength and athletic skill like he was some circus animal. He grew a tough shell quickly, but that didn't stop the pain and confusion from simmering below the surface. There was almost a full year when he barely spoke, only responding to his family when addressed directly.

Something happened when he went away to college and by the time he finished business school and the rest of his peers had caught up with him in physical maturity, he'd seemed to level out, but if people pushed him, that fucking temper. Sometimes you'd see it coming. He'd warn his brothers when they were getting on his nerves. Sometimes, though, the top would just blow right off.

Sam and Zach let out frustrated breaths, both thinking about how they could get through to him before their grandmother came walking in the door.

"You can be concerned about Miss Leona seeing someone new, but you can't stop her from doing it. I want to know why it pisses you off so much," Zach said.

"It's not—" Jesse finally started to unclench. He let out his own breath and tried again. "I know that she doesn't want me in her business, but I am just trying to protect her."

"From what?" Zach asked calmly.

"The guy she's talking to, Frank Chester?"

"Yeah, the organ guy from church. What about him?"

"He was trying to get at the ranch."

"Why didn't you say something?" Zach asked.

"Yeah. I'll fight a Frank Chester," Sam added, making Zach laugh.

"'Cause I took care of it."

"Miss Leona said you scared the shit out of him."

Jesse stopped pacing, then cracked his knuckles. "Literally."

"Oh man!" Zach threw up his hands. Sam winced.

"Okay. I don't want to lose the ranch to some old man who put one over on Miss Leona, but what's Frank Chester, like, seventy-eight?" Zach asked. "You could have given him a heart attack. You can't be rolling up on the elderly like that."

"Whatever, he's fine."

"Okay. So you're trying to protect Miss Leona's wallet and the ranch. Fair. But how do we know this new guy is after her money? He could be a nice dude," Sam said.

"What do you mean 'this guy'? She's out with Frank Chester again."

"Uh right, she is."

"There's someone else?!"

"Jess. Calm down," Zach said, palms up like he could soothe the rage out of him.

"I'm not gonna calm down."

"Fine. Don't. But can you at least go back to your own fucking house? Break some shit over there. Heat the pool and take some laps. Whatever you need to do. But you know damn well Lilah is right. You cannot go off on Miss Leona."

"Fine, whatever. Fuck you two." Jesse stormed toward the door, but Zach grabbed his arm before he could leave the kitchen.

"Nah. Something else is up your ass. Out with it."

"There's nothing up my ass. Senior and Mom are six thousand miles away on a good day. Uncle Gerald is too afraid of Lilah, Uncle Justice just doesn't give a shit. I know Miss Leona is her own woman. I also know she's too sweet and too kind and eighty-two fucking years old. If someone in our family let Corie have her way, she'd be setting Miss Leona up with a different dude every week. Do you know the STI rates among the elderly?"

"Okay. I do and no, I don't want to think about that. But I don't know why you think Evie and I don't care—"

"Or that I don't either," Sam said, offended as hell. He loved his grandmother and it was fucked up for Jesse to imply otherwise.

"I cut back at the ranch so I could be present and shit, for Evie and the family. I'm here, man, and I care about Miss Leona too."

"Yeah, I know. Let me go." Jesse stormed out of the kitchen and down the hall, slamming the front door behind him. Zach scrubbed his beard as Sam leaned against the counter.

"He needs to go to therapy," Sam said. "That was fucking wild."

"I know," Zach sighed. "Should we call Senior?"

"Maybe. Mom will just calm him down, but Miss Leona and Senior are the only ones who really get through to him. Evie used to but—"

"She's Team Zach now. The traitor."

"You noticed that too?"

"She used to be his homie. Now she's my woman, with, like, no time for him to adjust."

The ten years Evie and Zach were on the outs she'd kept in touch with Sam and Jesse, but she really talked to Jesse to the point where she'd made him her ultimate emergency contact. It was her connection to Jesse that had brought her back into their lives when she'd lost her memory. Jesse was glad to have her back in his life as a friend, but her love for Zach had taken the lead in the saddle. There was no conversation to be had about it. It was what it was.

"Can we sign him up for a class or something?" Sam said. He wasn't trying to be funny, but Zach laughed anyway. "I'm serious. Does he have any friends outside of the ranch and the senior center? Is his whole world the ranch and the old people?"

"Fuck. I think so. Jesus, maybe I haven't been present."

"You just got Evie back. You guys are opening the restaurant and shooting a documentary. It's all right for you guys to take this time just for the two of you."

"And now you have Amanda? She okay after last night?"

"She's great! Just left."

"She's a good girl, man. Evie loves her. Majesty loves her too! That's a damn miracle."

"Yeah, she's what's up."

"You go change and shower, 'cause you look like you just rolled back over here."

"Yeah. Let me go to do so."

"I'll call Senior."

"Sounds good."

Sam headed out to get cleaned up, still thinking of what he could do to help his brother. Maybe he could invite him up to LA just to get a break from Charming. Or maybe they could go to Vegas or something. Just to get him out of town. Whatever it was, it was clear Jesse needed something. Sam just wasn't sure what.

Chapter 19

Amanda rolled onto her back, trying not to giggle. She'd only meant to text Sam, but when he replied asking if he could say good night over the phone she couldn't think of a reason why not. As soon as the word *TEX* lit up her phone screen, she knew it wasn't going to be a quick call. She'd only been away from Big Rock Ranch for eight hours or so, but the thought of talking to Sam again made her giddy. As soon as she heard his voice, the soft, smooth "Hey, Cha-Cha" rolling off his tongue made her whole body tingle. Dru had a packed week and Amanda needed all her sleep so she could keep up with Dru's schedule and her attitude.

She double-checked the clock and did the math on how long she had. Twenty more minutes. Twenty more minutes before she had to brush her teeth and wash her face and get ready for bed. A tiny voice in the back of her head screamed, *FUCK THAT. You kinda have a boyfriend now. You stay up all night and tell this boy how much you like seeing him naked.* She wouldn't, but man, was the thought tempting.

"I don't believe you," Amanda said, trying to catch her breath. She'd never been the giggling type. Until now.

"Why would I lie? Damn Cha-Cha. I thought I was among friends. You telling me I can't confess my darkest secrets to you anymore?"

"No! Of course you can. Teeexxx," she laughed. "Listen. When it comes to *Banker Down* I don't play around. I just can't believe you spent all afternoon reading *Banker* fic. I have to stay away from it. I'll go down a rabbit hole and a week later I'll wake up screaming about how Jens and Calloum should have gotten together way sooner."

"They're together. It's legit. It's canon. I'm still pissed they killed Banker III."

"Thank you! She was the best. They seemed to learn their lesson about fridging, but I maintain that they need to resurrect her pure soap opera style. You don't get Angella Weller to slum it on your cable sci-fi show and then kill her off right after she meets the love of her life."

"You know it was her decision, right?" Sam laughed a little more.

"No. I know. She got cast in the *Flight* remake and made, like, a bajillion dollars, but I still hate the way they did it."

"She could still come back and do guest spots. No fictional death needs to be forever."

"Amen to that shit." Amanda sighed and reached for her stuffed Pluto plush under her pillow. "I'm glad you called. It's nice to hear your voice."

"Couldn't agree more. I love the sound of my voice."

"Ha. Ha."

"You know I'm playin'. I do have bad news though. Well, good news and bad news."

"What's that? Gimme ya news."

"I won't be able to see you this weekend."

"So you were just using me, huh? I let you catch a glimpse of this beautiful, beautiful face. I let you touch this sweet, sweet ass, sample of this prime pussy, and you're just going to leave me. I won't be ignored, Samuel."

She smiled as Sam's laughter came through the phone. "Are you sure you don't want to be an actor?"

"God no. I hate cameras, but what's up?"

"My brother Jesse. He's going through some shit so I figured he and I could get out of town. We're going to Bali for a few days."

"Oh, just to Bali."

"Wanted to take him to a different time zone so he wouldn't be thinking about the ranch, and he loves to swim."

"I'm trying to picture him doing a lazy backstroke."

"Oh, that mufucka can swim. He won't touch a horse, but if you challenge him to a fifty-meter breaststroke he'll grab his goggles and tell you not to be late."

"That's amazing. I love it. Brother time in Bali sounds like fun." Another sigh escaped. Part of her was still in disbelief at how easy it was to talk to Sam. How well they got along and how she was truly disappointed that seeing him on Friday wasn't going to happen. The other part was the disbelief that she had a kinda boyfriend to miss at all. "Well, do you want to hang out when you get back?"

"For sure. And that way I can give you something back."

"What's that?"

"Housekeeping found a *Sailor Moon* shirt under the bed. Plus my assistant still has your makeup bag from the night at the W."

"Oh my God! Thank you so much. Thank your assistant

and housekeeping! I haven't fully unpacked yet." She'd put her things like her toothbrush back in her bathroom, but her dirty clothes were still in her bag on the floor. She'd be responsible about them in the morning. She didn't have time now. She was too busy talking to her kinda boyfriend. "Was that the good news?"

"I have a concrete reason to see you again. I have to get this stuff to you. It's my chivalrous duty. As your man."

Amanda rolled her bottom lip between her teeth as her heart bloomed with warm sparkles and unicorn tears. Things were moving so fast, but hearing those words from him? It was exactly what she wanted. "Are you my man now?" she asked quietly.

"I want to be," he said, his voice filled with soft sincerity.

"I do like that idea. I just don't want you bragging to all of your friends."

"Listen. When I get back I'll talk to my team. I'm gonna make sure you keep your privacy as much as possible."

"I mean, I'll enjoy that while it lasts, but we know that won't work."

"Will you let me try?"

"Of course. And I'll do my best too. I—yeah." Amanda checked the clock on her nightstand. She had six more minutes. "If you change your mind—"

"About what?"

"About being my boyfriend."

"I don't think that's gonna happen, but if for some crazy-ass reason I do—"

"I want a letter. Like a dramatic-as-fuck handwritten letter. I want to feel it, hold it in my hand as I sit on Venice Beach, while tourists complain about the homeless problem while doing nothing to fund housing initiatives in their own communities. I want to hold that letter in my hand

and weep before I cast the biodegradable paper into the ocean as a way to start the grieving process of getting over you."

"Cha-Cha," Sam laughed. "You are extra as fuck."

"I'm sorry. I keep most of this bottled in. You're letting the real freak in me out."

"I'm here for it and I can see the writer in you now. That was some batshit poetry."

Amanda wasn't quite sure which part it was, but something he said brought her right back to reality. Suddenly she was thee Samuel Pleasant's girlfriend and that sure as hell didn't change the fact that she had to be up at the ass crack of dawn to wait on thee Dru Anastasia.

"When are you leaving for Bali?"

"Tuesday. After my meetings. I'll be in town but—"

"I'll be at work."

"Look, I know what you said, and I'll wait until you're ready to tell me who you work for. But when you're ready to quit, I can help you."

Amanda's throat felt like it was closing as tears threatened to rise in her eyes. She didn't know what was wrong with her. He was just being kind, but maybe it was the mere offer, a way out of a situation that still felt extremely impossible and yet necessary at the same time, something about it in that moment was a little too much. Because she knew he meant it. Amanda had met so many shitty, dishonest, manipulative people since moving to California. But Sam Pleasant wasn't one of them. Still she was too scared to believe the full truth of what it meant to have someone like that in her life.

"I appreciate that, Tex. And I will let you know. On both counts."

"Oh, there was another thing."

"Yeah?"

"Can you send me your *Banker Down* script?"

"Absolutely not."

"Why?"

"'Cause it's ass-trash garbage in a garbage boot."

"The fuck is a garbage boot?" Sam laughed.

"Not sure, but the answer is no."

"Please. I've read all the good fic I can find and something tells me you captured Banker VIII's likeness perfectly."

"Damn," Amanda said under her breath. "Fine. Only because if you understand the fine complexities of Banker VIII's relationship—"

"With his uncle—"

"Then you'll understand why he can't bring himself to tell Munico how he really feels."

"Whenever they pull the plug they better get them together. They've been dragging that relationship out forever. People are getting pissed."

"Me. I'm people. I will riot. Okay. I'll send it to you. Text me your email address."

"I will."

"I should go. I turn into a pumpkin at, like, nine on Sunday nights. I need my beauty rest."

"'Kay."

"We'll talk soon?"

"I'll text you tomorrow."

"'Kay. Night, Tex."

"Goodnight, Amanda."

"Night." She ended the call before she let out a high-pitched moan. He was trying to kill her. She was sure of it. She went about her bedtime routine, and when she was done wrapping her braids, there was a text from Sam with his email address and a picture of Majesty headbutting Bam Bam. She loved that asshole horse.

Amanda pulled out her personal laptop and found the file buried in her online drive. She'd go back to it every now and then, think of revising it and resubmitting it for a writers' program, but the time never seemed right. She went in and added a footer to let Sam know she meant business: *If you are reading this, Samuel Pleasant cannot be trusted. Run.*

Amanda set Gus's food on the ground, then rinsed off her hands. She looked around the kitchen. Everything was put away and the cleaning service would be by the following afternoon to dust and shine the whole apartment when they were on set. She checked the fridge one more time for the premade breakfast kits she'd found Dru that cost a small fortune. Dru had complained at first, but it turned out she liked them. Win, win.

"Okay, Dru. I'm gonna head home," Amanda called out. "I'm gonna go." Dru was in the other room watching some weird dating show on Netflix. Their day hadn't been half bad. Dru behaved herself on set and she'd gotten a call for a different made-for-TV romance. Travis Cooper was already signed on to play the male lead. Most women in their age bracket had at least a little bit of a thing for him since middle school, so she had that to look forward to. Amanda missed Sam like crazy, but at least Dru wasn't making things worse.

Amanda grabbed her phone off the counter and stuck it in her back pocket. When she went to grab her bag she gasped, scared shitless at Dru's sudden appearance by the coffeemaker she never used.

"Jesus Christ. You scared me. I'm heading out. I'll see you in the morning?"

Dru didn't say anything. She just shook her head, then tilted it a little to the left.

"What?" Amanda asked.

"There's no fucking way."

"What are you talking about?"

Dru's eyes narrowed as she came into the kitchen. "Turn around."

"Why, what is it?" Amanda spun around. "Is there something on my back?"

"Beyond a little extra padding? No." Amanda rolled her eyes at her horrible fat joke. "That's not what I was looking at."

"What is it?"

"Oh, nothing. Just you. Hanging out with Sam Pleasant." Amanda's whole body went cold. "What?"

Dru strolled over and shoved her phone in Amanda's face. "You little fucking liar," she said with a smirk. Amanda looked at the screen. Dru was on some gossip site and sure enough there was a picture of her and Sam on the dance floor at Claim Jumpers. Her back was to the camera, but Sam's face and that unmistakable cowboy hat were in clear view. You could see Zach and his own tan Stetson just off to their left. There was a small circular picture inset of the larger photo that showed a magnified image, making it clear those were Sam's pearly whites flashing in the middle of that dive bar. Apparently that woman had managed to hide one photo from the bouncer's view. Or maybe someone else had taken it.

Either way it was definitely on CelebGossip Central.com. Amanda scrolled to the bottom of the article, skimming for certain details. It named the bar, went into detail about what

Sam was wearing, it even mentioned that Evie Buchanan and her beau, Zach Pleasant, were also two-stepping the night away. Amanda was cited as an unnamed friend. Unnamed friend. She could handle that. But the speck of anonymity still couldn't stop her from nearly shaking. This was not good.

She swallowed and handed Dru back her phone. "Sam Pleasant went to a bar with friends. What does that have to do with me?"

"How stupid do you think I am? Your hair is up the exact same way and you are wearing that same cheap sweater." She plucked at the fabric covering Amanda's shoulder. "They haven't figured out who you are. They don't give a fuck who random hangers-on are, but I need to know. How the hell do you know Sam Pleasant? Why the hell were you keeping this from me, and when the fuck are you going to introduce me to him so we can start our A-list baby-making empire?"

"Excuse me? What?"

"How do you know him?"

"I don't. That's not me!" Amanda sensed she was caught, but she didn't care. Everything was all so new. She wasn't ready to let Dru have a single piece of it, especially when Sam was halfway across the planet with his phone on Do Not Disturb.

"Mandy. Please. I look at that big dome and those discount braids every day. I know what you look like from that angle. I know it's you. I know you lied about taking care of your friend's baby this weekend 'cause you were somehow hanging out with Sam in his hometown. You have an in and I want that in too."

The odd smile on Dru's face let Amanda know that Dru wasn't angry for being kept in the dark. The opposite. She was very pleased. Pleased with herself for figuring it out and pleased with herself for having trapped Amanda in a corner.

"I seriously have no idea what you're talking about. Also, you're the famous one between the two of us. If you want to meet Sam Pleasant, ask some other famous person to introduce you."

The expression on Dru's face dropped, like maybe she'd tried that already and it hadn't worked. She shook the moment off and kept pressing.

"Are you saying this isn't you?" Dru swiped her finger across her phone screen again and brought up one of Helene and Ignacio's wedding photos. In the foreground the bride and groom were in each other's arms. In the background were Amanda and Sam. Amanda had seen all the photos that had been published in *People* magazine and this wasn't one of them. She'd been very careful to keep an eye on their professional photographer, careful to practically run from the man anytime she saw him coming. Someone else had taken this photo and apparently posted it.

"How—"

"You seriously think I'm stupid. This is easy Internet Stalking 101. Some dingus violated what one would think was an ironclad pre-wedding NDA and posted it on their Instagram. When I saw the pictures at the bar I knew that updo looked familiar to me. I did a little digging and I remembered I'd seen something in the background of one of Helene Sawyer's wedding photos. And there you are. Slow dancing with Sam. Color me impressed. I didn't think you'd be able to even speak to a guy like that. Let alone dance with him."

In this photo, even though the resolution wasn't great, even Amanda could tell it was definitely her. The shape of her face, her round cheeks and full lips, even her smile. It was undeniable. She was caught.

"Anyway, I'm gonna go." Amanda tried to step around Dru, but Dru stuck out her arm, blocking her way. She wondered if Dru could really fight, 'cause she considered knocking her on her ass right then and there.

"Let's try this again. You work for me and since you've been lying to me about hanging out with him you're gonna make it up to me. You're gonna introduce me to Sam Pleasant. You're gonna introduce me to his brothers and his amazing grandmother. Then you're gonna convince him that he and I would be perfect together. You're gonna get him to ask me out."

The thought of Dru and Sam anywhere near each other drove bile to the top of her throat. The thought of Sam being with her, touching her, calling Dru his girlfriend. That was too much.

"The Pleasants are exactly what I need to shoot my career to the next level. Sam can get me real roles. Not this TV shit. Not to mention what rubbing elbows with Leona Lovell will do. Seriously, Mandy. Why didn't you think of this sooner? You had the golden goose all along."

Something in Amanda's brain snapped, a hot rage flashing over her skin, warming her face and scoring the tips of her ears. She felt the words rushing to the tip of her tongue. She knew she was making a mistake but she couldn't stop herself.

"No."

"No what?" Dru took a step back.

"No. I won't introduce you to Sam or any other member of the Pleasant family. You are the last thing he's looking for in a partner and I would never let you near him just so you could use him."

"Feeling protective, are we?" she said, mocking her. "Will you lighten up? This is how this Hollywood shit works. You think people get together 'cause they really care about each other?"

"Um, yeah."

"And how would you know? I bet you're still a virgin." Dru really needed to lay off the junior high–level insults, but it didn't matter. Amanda wasn't giving her a single thing she wanted.

"I know because I know what Sam is looking for and it's not you."

"I—" Dru stared at her, looking at her face very carefully. Amanda could hear her own teeth grinding with rage. "No way. No. Are you dating Sam Pleasant?"

Amanda swallowed again, forcing herself not to blurt out the truth. She owed herself, *and Sam*, better than for Dru to be the first person they told outside of his family.

"You're serious? You're Sam Pleasant's girlfriend. Sam Pleasant, one of these hottest guys on Earth, is dating you. Like on purpose, not to fulfill some sick promise to a witch."

"Yes and you don't have to say shit like that to me."

"Oh yes. I do. How long has this been going on? And how dare you hold out on me?" A look of disgust swept over Dru's features as she suddenly looked Amanda up and down. "You haven't had sex with him, have you?"

Amanda ground her teeth together, refusing to answer again. "That is none of your business."

"Oh my—what the fuck?" Dru let out a screech of laughter. "Okay. Okay. If he'll fuck you, I'm sure he'll fuck me. Hell. I don't see why he wouldn't marry me. At least he could take me places and not die of embarrassment. But

I'm not sure if I want your sloppy seconds. Yuck." Dru shook her body with a dramatic shudder.

"Are you done?"

"Oh no. I'm just—"

"I don't care. I quit." Amanda grabbed her purse and stormed to the door.

"Oh, you adorable dumbass. You really think this is going to work out. Guys like him sleep with girls like you behind closed doors all the time. What, you think he's going to marry you or something?"

"Who knows, but he's not going to be anywhere near you," she called back over her shoulder.

"Okay, Amanda." Dru laughed. "Have a nice life, boo-boo. I'll have a new assistant by noon tomorrow. When he's finished with you, you'll have no man. And no job. Good luck!"

Amanda walked even faster, wishing she could slam Dru's soft-close door behind her.

Chapter 20

Amanda squeezed her eyes closed. The sun had been up for hours. And so had she. On her way home, she'd been such a nervous wreck, actually shaking as she tried to drive back down the hill to her place, that she'd pulled over and called her mom. It took some work to get the words out through her hysterics, but she'd told her mom everything that had happened. She'd had to go back to several different beginnings, just to answer her mom's questions.

The fact that she'd been keeping so much about Dru and the way she acted from her parents for so many years just made things worse. Her parents had no idea Dru was such a dick. They had a sense that she was somewhat of a diva, but Amanda had never let on how many times Dru had made her cry. How many times she'd put her in the middle of horrible situations with her cruel behavior. She'd never told them just how trapped she felt.

Her mom managed to talk her down enough so she could drive home, but as soon as she stepped inside her little bungalow, she paused and looked around, thinking of the day she'd moved in, sure it would be temporary because one day she'd be a television writer and she'd be able to own a place that actually faced the street and how that definitely wasn't going to happen. She'd be lucky if she could afford to keep this place for the rest of the year. Silly dreams like affordable, curbside housing and a job she enjoyed were so far out of her reach. When the weight of that pathetic feeling crashed down on her it brought the tears back with it.

She'd spent most of the night crying, but when she'd dozed off, she'd had horrible dreams about screaming matches with a certain television actress and working her old high school job inside a Circuit City. Her eyes hurt like hell and she'd need at least a gallon of water to replenish all the tears she'd shed. It would probably help soothe her throat after all the loud out-and-out sobbing she'd done before a pounding headache begged her to calm down, at least a little so she could sleep.

Deep down she knew her position with Dru hadn't been sustainable. There were people who stayed on as lifelong assistants, but they worked for people who were kind and paid them enough to do crazy stuff like get married and have children of their own. Dru didn't want Amanda to have a future. Dru didn't even want Amanda to have friends, or the slightest shred of happiness. Still she never expected their end to go down the way it had. She never expected to quit in such a spectacularly stupid fashion. No, she'd been right to quit. The things Dru had said, the things Dru wanted from Sam and his family, there was no way Amanda could sit by and encourage that to happen. She sure as hell wasn't going to hand her own boyfriend off to another woman like a used baseball glove.

The screwed-up things Dru had said to her about how ridiculous she was to think that Sam would really be with her, out in the open, loving—or at least liking—her for the world to see, had hurt. It hurt a lot. She knew then that while Dru was in part a result of shitty parenting, Dru was an adult now and Dru made a lot of adult decisions to treat others like shit. Sticking by her signaled that Amanda was willing to overlook her behavior. No, it was an affirmation that she supported her behavior. The way Dru spoke to her wasn't shocking. It was textbook Dru Anastasia.

Over time she'd actually gotten worse. She'd been a brat when Amanda started working for her. She'd escalated to full on dickhead and Amanda couldn't stick around and cheer her on. She tried to picture what it would be like to show up to work day after day with Dru knowing that she and Sam were an item. Dru would do her best to continue to torture her about the impossibility of them as a couple. The impossibility of Sam seeing her as not only an equal, but an object of his affection and desire.

She was right to quit, but maybe she should have given her two weeks' notice. Maybe a month so she could at least start looking for another job. And at least part of Dru's parting prophecy was true. She was out of work. And worse, she couldn't get in touch with Sam. A fight with her former employer wasn't reason enough to put in a 9-1-1 call to Bali, but still. She wanted to tell him what had happened. She wanted to let him know that Dru was now one of the handful of people who knew about them.

Dru wasn't exactly a gossip. She was more of a shit talker who only talked shit when it was to her own personal benefit. Would the news that her former personal assistant was dating Sam Pleasant somehow be to Dru's advantage? Amanda wasn't sure. She could anticipate Dru's needs and her moods, but the inner workings of her brain were still very confusing and unsettling to her. Also, fuck Dru.

Amanda rolled over again and buried her face in her pillow. She'd forgotten to wrap her braids and her scalp was starting to hurt from the tight bun fighting to stay twirled up on the top of her head. She had to get out of bed. Her mom was right. Things would be okay. And if things weren't okay, then she would move home. She was lucky to have parents who loved her so much, parents who would support whatever decision she made next. Hopefully, her next move wouldn't be so impulsive.

The sound of her phone ringing had Amanda peeling her face off her pillow. It was her mom's ringtone.

"Hey, Mom," she answered. Her voice sounded like she'd swallowed sandpaper.

"Just taking a quick break. I wanted to check on my baby girl."

"I'm okay. Thank you. I'm still in bed."

"That's okay. You get your rest. You've been working hard."

"Well, I have all the free time in the world now," she said with a mirthless laugh.

"I talked to your dad. You can come home if you need to."

"Thanks, Mom," Amanda replied, her voice cracking. She loved them so much, but she didn't want to go home. Her whole life felt so unfinished. Going home meant giving up. Giving up on Sam and giving up on her dreams. She swallowed and stopped herself from another crying jag. She didn't have enough water in her body to support one anyway. "I'm going to take a hot shower and then try and come up with a plan."

"You know you can do this. You're a McQueen. You can do anything."

In theory, her mom was right, but she wasn't back to that level of hopeful determination quite yet. She heard a beep in her ear and when she glanced at her phone, she saw Helene's name lighting up her screen.

"You have to go?" her mom asked.

"It's my friend. I think she's back from her honeymoon."

"Go talk to her."

"'Kay. I'll call you later." Amanda switched over just before it went to voicemail. "He—"

"Oh my God. Sorry, I know you're at work. But have you been online yet?"

"Well, no. I'm not at work. I quit."

"What?! What do you mean you quit?"

"What's going on online?"

"Oh fuck," Helene said. The sound of her voice had Amanda's blood pressure ratcheting up. She let out a shuddered breath as a text message alert pinged in her ear. She glanced at the screen and saw a text from a high school friend named Sarah. Before she could bring it back up to her ear, three more alerts cycled up at the top of her display.

"What is going on?"

"I'm guessing you didn't approve a source close to you to go public with your relationship with Sam? Do you have a relationship with Sam?"

Amanda swallowed, closing her eyes. "No. And yes. What the hell is going on?"

"I'm sending you a link." A second later a text with a TMZ link popped up on her screen. She ignored the now ten different alerts in her message box and went right to Helene's text. She skipped the headline in the thumbnail, trying to convince herself that the words SAM PLEASANT IS OFF THE MARKET. OSCAR WINNER IS SINGLE NO MORE were nothing to be worried about. Amanda clicked on the link and did her best to keep from passing out as a picture of her and Sam dancing at Claim Jumpers filled the screen below the headline. Inset in the bottom corner was a selfie from Amanda's Instagram. Her personal Instagram where she'd amassed a whole two hundred and ten followers, mostly friends from college and her early years in production.

The room started spinning as she tried to make sense of the words below the photos.

> Sources close to the couple say Pleasant's girlfriend is a former personal assistant. The two have been spotted around Hollywood in recent weeks and spent Valentine's weekend in Sam's hometown of Charming, California.

Sure enough there was a picture below of the two of them talking at the *Vanity Fair* party where they'd met and another photo of them talking on the street outside of Delightly a few days before she'd gone back to the ranch. Amanda's face was in shadow, but with context it was clear it was her with Sam. She scrolled back up to the top and the time stamp on the article was only thirty minutes ago. Whatever damage had been done was only going to get much worse.

"Helene," Amanda choked out.

"Where are you?"

"I'm—I'm at home. Please tell me you're back."

"Yeah, we're on our way to the house right now. Okay. I need you to do two things. Set all of your social media to private. All of it. Even your Twitter even though you never use it. Lock down everything."

"'Kay."

"Then come over to Ignacio's place. Our place."

"Okay. Okay. Hele—"

"Don't worry. We're gonna sort this shit out. Just come over."

"Okay." Helene ended the call before she could panic anymore. Amanda's hands were trembling when she switched over to Instagram. Thirty-four minutes and she already had six hundred more followers. She sent her account to private. Then deactivated her Twitter. She didn't even bother with the forty-step process to delete her Facebook. She quickly changed into presentable clothing, then sped across town to Ignacio's house in Silver Lake.

All the drive did was ratchet her nerves up from a solid twelve to a very uncomfortable sixteen and a half. She needed to get in touch with Sam and she needed to figure out a way to murder Dru while making it very clear to the courts that her homicide was completely justifiable. Apparently, Dru *had* decided ratting Amanda out would help her career. Who else would leak those photos in such a spectacularly invasive way?

Ignacio's housekeeper, Meryl, buzzed her through the massive iron gates that led to the obnoxiously steep driveway that brought you up to their house. Helene was waiting for her in the ridiculous fourteen-foot doorway. She was wearing this effortless yellow maxi dress that made her dark brown skin glow. Amanda had to stop herself from flinging herself into a sobbing heap in Helene's arms, but as soon as she got out of her car, Helene looked at her, her head inclined in that way that was pure love and concern. Tears started flowing down her face. She stepped into Helene's arms and wept.

"Don't worry. We'll find out who we have to kill and

then we'll make it look like a very intentional message to anyone who thinks about fucking with you again."

Amanda stepped back, wiping her face. "It was Dru. I know it."

"Oh, I'm gonna fuck that bitch up. Come inside."

"How do you look even better than when you left? You look amazing," Amanda said as they walked into the immaculately decorated 1920s Art Deco style home. She'd been to Helene's apartment plenty of times, but only once to Ignacio's house, which they were now sharing. Award-winning directors sure knew how to live.

"Sun-kissed and dicked down. Girl. Honeymoon of a lifetime."

"Where's Ignacio?"

"He's on the phone. He's coming down in a sec. Come on."

Amanda followed her deeper into the house to the kitchen. For some reason she couldn't help but think of the welcoming warmth that filled Miss Leona's kitchen. Her heart clenched on itself again. Somehow she's felt like she'd betrayed his whole family.

She took a seat that Helene offered in the breakfast nook tucked against a large bay window that looked out over the backyard. Helene grabbed them some fancy boxed water Amanda had a seen at a few charity events, then sat opposite in her own chair.

"Okay. Tell me literally everything. Last I knew you basically told him to kick rocks at our reception and now you're a couple."

"Yeah, about that." Amanda rehashed everything from the moment they met again in front of Delightly to the night before when Dru had essentially forced her to defend Sam's honor and their new relationship. "He's back from

Bali on Sunday, but I can't wait that long to talk to him. It's the middle of the night there."

"And you know for sure Dru did this?" Helene asked as Ignacio came into the room, his light brown skin also a bit darker due to their tropical honeymoon getaway. He greeted them both with kisses on the cheek and then settled in in his silent, supportive observer way that made him both an amazing friend and filmmaker.

"I mean, I don't think anyone in his family would do this. They aren't this bored or petty. And Sam would have told me."

"He would have. He's not about this life. Not like this," Helene asserted. "And no one at the ranch?"

"I mean, it's possible—" Amanda's phone chimed in her purse. She looked down at it, her eyes springing wide. "That's Dru's alert tone."

"Answer it," Ignacio said, his voice deadly. Amanda appreciated that he was ready to fight Dru on her behalf. She pulled out her phone and looked at the text message.

See you locked your Instagram. Smart.
I wouldn't check Twitter if I were you.
A lot of people are wondering the same thing
I am. How someone so underwhelming could
land Sam Pleasant. Somehow makes him seem
less attractive. Weird. Anyway. Thanks for
saving me from his horrible taste in literally
everything. Byeeeeeeee!

Amanda slid her phone across the table so Helene and Ignacio could read it. She shouldn't have been shocked by the painful way Dru had just implicated herself, but the dig about her impacting Sam's appeal had really stung.

She could only imagine what people were saying about her and Sam. What they were saying about her. Amanda knew exactly how cruel people could be online, especially over something that shouldn't matter like someone's looks. She knew she was beautiful and she loved every inch of her curvy body, but that didn't matter to avatared masses who'd already decided the types of faces, bodies, and skin tones that were acceptable in certain circles. She knew all kinds of people pictured Sam with someone more like Helene. Hell, someone more like Dru. Not a plus-sized, now unemployed nobody.

"Oh, okay. So she wants to fight. Cool," Helene said as she handed the phone to her husband.

"I'm trying really hard not to be sick right now. Like, I had this feeling in the back of my mind that Dru was going to be the one to ruin this—"

"She hasn't ruined anything yet. Did she make your day very unpleasant? Yes, okay. This sucks. But we're not letting this bitch-ass bitch *ruin* anything. You have to talk to Sam."

"I know. I—I don't know how he's going to react though. I mean, we talked about this. Specifically this. I practically begged him to keep this under wraps and then someone on *my* end of things blows it up to the whole universe. How am I going to explain this to him? How am I going to explain this to his family? Jesus. His grandmother!" The Pleasants were *not* a tabloid bunch.

"No. No. Your end nothing," Helene cut in. "Dru didn't have to do this. She could have been happy for you. Even if she were jealous, which she clearly fucking is, she should have taken a deep breath and let you live your life. Also if she was into Sam she would want him to be happy and if he's happy with you—"

"Yeah, that's not Dru. She is the misery who wants all the company. This is why I didn't tell her you and I were friends. Can you imagine how she would have tried to use that to her advantage? You and Ignacio."

"I can't be bought or used," Ignacio said with a playful scoff that made Amanda finally laugh.

"Okay. So fuck Dru," Helene went on. "You don't work for her anymore. She can eat all the dicks. Let's talk full damage control. Does she have anything else she can use to hurt you? Does she have any of your things?"

"No. I purposely made myself as bland and boring in her presence as possible and you see how she reacted when things changed. Jesus," Amanda sighed, the tears rushing back to her eyes. She took a sip of water and tried not to let the tears win. "I need to talk to Sam, like, soon, and I have to find another job. Like now." She took her phone back and like a complete fool opened her Twitter. Even with her account locked, her mentions had exploded. She quickly scrolled and stopped when she actually saw a picture of Sam coupled with a Bossip headline.

"Oh my God. This is so bad."

"Give me your phone." Helene took the device and set it over on the kitchen island.

"Twitter is eating me alive. I wish I could be above all this, but I can't."

"Amanda, stop. You're human and this sucks. Forget all the people who want to tell me, every damn day, that I'm not half Mexican because I don't look it. If you want I can show you all the awful things people said about me when we announced our engagement. Some woman sent Ignacio pictures of her nieces from Guatemala begging him to consider a woman from his home country instead of me.

Then some ashy-ass dude actually said I was erasing the progress of the entire race for not marrying a Black man."

"If I'd known I contained so much power," Ignacio said, shrugging. "Everyone is going to have their opinion, but it's what you and Sam want that matters. What can we do?"

"Yeah. We can reach out to *People* and at least ask them to do something." Helene picked up her own phone. "My girl over there loves positive spin and a fresh love story. I am not above calling in favors."

"Just let me curl up in a ball and die."

"No can do. Let us help you."

Amanda ran her hands over her face and cupped her chin. She loved Helene so much and she never wanted to make her think that their friendship was about anything other than how well they got along and how much Amanda enjoyed her bright, loving company. "This is plenty. Just letting me come over. I mean, you guys just got back from your honeymoon and I just busted up into your house with my drama. Let me get out of your hair." She'd started to stand up when Helen fixed her with a look that could burn a hole in the detailed crown molding high above their heads.

"Where do you have to be?"

"Nowhere. I'm just all up in your—"

"Nah, park it."

"Helene."

"I'm serious. Stay as long as you like. This one might be itching to get back to work, but I'm off the hook for at least another week. You sit here with me and watch awful TV and eat amazing food and figure out how to stop me from driving over to Dru's house right now so I can throw her off her balcony."

"She doesn't have a balcony."

"Shame." Helene reached across the table and took her hand. "Let me help you. What do you want? What do you need? Tell us and we'll see what we can do. What's the point of friends with connections and more money than the pope if they can't help you out?"

"I mean, friendship is the point," Amanda said as Helene immediately rolled her eyes. She knew she wasn't going to slink back to her hole of sadness and eventual poverty, not right away. Helene wouldn't let her, not without a fight and what some might consider out-and-out nagging. She looked at her amazing friend and her equally amazing husband.

"Just give me a moment. I'm not programmed to prioritize my needs."

"Oh girl, that's my specialty. Come on. Let's get selfish," Helene said with a wink.

Amanda smiled back at her as a wave of sadness washed over her. The truth was, she knew exactly what she needed. "I need Sam. I need to talk to him."

Chapter 21

Sam came back from the bathroom to see his phone screen shining in the dark. He'd changed the Do Not Disturb settings on his phone as soon as he and Jesse had landed in Bali. He knew he'd miss Amanda like crazy, but even with his international cellular plan he couldn't spend his whole vacation with his brother texting his new girlfriend. But as he crossed the expanse of their private beachside bungalow something told him whoever was blowing up his phone wasn't reaching out with a calm, friendly hey-how-ya-doing.

He scooped his phone up and saw the text from Walls.

Sorry to bug you, man. But you need to see this.
They are destroying your girl online.

Sam clicked through to the article Walls had sent him, his blood boiling as he saw the headline. He clicked back to his messages and saw similar texts from Corie and Lilah with the same article and more from Bossip and TMZ. There was another text from Zach just saying to call him when he could. He had a feeling what it was about.

He called Walls.

"What the fuck is going on?"

"No clue. I just got off the phone with Corie. They are trying to keep Miss Leona from seeing it for now. What's the play? What do you want me to do? You want me to call Coffey?"

"No. He won't care about this. I mean, he will, but he trusts me. He won't freak out unless I freak out."

"Are you freaking out?"

"Not sure yet. I need to talk to Amanda."

"You sure? Looks like her people leaked this."

"What people? She's—" He almost let slip that she wasn't a writer, but a personal assistant, but he knew she still felt embarrassed about her job even though there was nothing to be embarrassed about. "She doesn't have people. This isn't her style of bullshit."

"Well, someone leaked it. What do you want me to do? What's the next move?" Walls asked just as Sam heard the door to Jesse's side of the bungalow open. His brother ambled in, half asleep, scrubbing his hand over his face, then sat down on the edge of Sam's bed. He had his own phone in his hand.

"Nothing. Don't do anything yet. I need to talk to Amanda. If I know her the way I think I do she had nothing to do with this. She doesn't want this kind of attention or this kind of heat."

"Alright. I'm turning off the comments on your Instagram."

"God, please. Thanks, man."

"No problem. Call me back."

Sam ended the call, then turned on the bedside lamp. Jesse looked up at him, squinting. "Lilah and Corie called me and told me to wake you up. You should call your girl." This vacation had done wonders for Jesse's temperament, but he knew what his brother wasn't saying. *Talk to Amanda and get to the bottom of this before I start making calls.* Jesse didn't play when it came to anyone in their family. If he thought for one second that Amanda was trying to hurt or use Sam, he'd do his best to make sure she never came near him again. Sam appreciated it, but he knew there was no way she did this.

He switched over to her contact, smashing his thumb on the little phone icon. The line rang twice before she picked up.

"Sam," she said, her voice breaking into a sob. "I'm so sorry."

He hated that she was upset, but the sound of her voice took some of the pressure off his chest. "Cha-Cha, don't cry. Tell me what happened."

"You saw everything?"

"I saw the TMZ post. I'm guessing there's more." He glanced over at Jesse, who seemed to be going through Twitter.

"Same stuff on different sites. Dru did this."

"Dru who?"

"Anastasia. I work, well, I worked for Dru Anastasia. She's—"

"A huge asshole!" he heard someone say in the background.

"I'm with Helene and Ignacio."

"Oh, good. I—okay. Tell me what's going on." Sam listened as Amanda filled him in. She told him everything. How Dru had spotted her in the CelebGossipCentral photos and then tried to force her to hand Sam and his grandmother up to Dru on a silver platter. She showed him the texts that made it pretty obvious that Dru had been the one to contact TMZ and connect all the dots between the truth and the little information on the other gossip site.

"Then I fucked up and told her you and I were together. I know I shouldn't have said anything. And I definitely shouldn't have quit. I just—"

"Wait, wait, wait. Dru Anastasia. She's been trying to get at me for weeks."

"Ugh. She mentioned thinking you were attractive, but I didn't think she'd make a move."

"Baby. She did more than make a move. Hold on." Sam went back to his text chat with Walls and scrolled up until he'd found the screenshot he'd sent him the same day he and Amanda decided to give things another try. He forwarded it to her. "Look at the name in the text. You were with me when she sent that text. She was pretending to be *you*."

"Oh my fucking God. She knows I hate the name Mandy too."

"Do I get to kill her now?" he heard Helene say.

Sam went on with a humorless chuckle. "I just ignored it 'cause I thought she was just some random person trying to get at me."

"This is all my fault," Amanda replied. "I should have told you I was her assistant. If I had been honest with you from the beginning this never would have happened."

"I'm not sure I believe that. Doesn't sound like subtle or chill are her thing."

"When you put it like that," Amanda said before she let out a defeated sigh. A different kind of pain bloomed in Sam's chest. This whole situation was beyond fucked up, but in that moment all he wanted was to be back in Los Angeles, holding Amanda in his arms. She had Helene and Ignacio, but he wanted to be there for her, with her as they sorted this out.

"I'm coming back." He looked over at his brother, who nodded in agreement.

"No, Sam. Don't. This is awful, but it's not life-or-death. You do not need to rush back across the globe for this. Stay and enjoy your time with Jesse."

"Nah, he's with me on this."

"He's awake too?"

"The Pleasant brothers move as a unit. A G Unit, if you will."

Sam smiled as Amanda finally laughed a bit. "That was a terrible joke, but okay. Tell him I'm sorry. Tell your whole family. I didn't want this. For you, for me—"

"Baby, I know. No one is blaming you. I'm blaming fucking Dru. Just stay offline and try and lay low for a bit. Maybe don't go out shopping with Helene."

"I won't," Amanda laughed again. "I promise."

Sam assured her he'd keep her updated on his travel plans and then they reluctantly ended the call. Sam tossed his phone on the bed beside his brother and ran his hands over his du-rag. What a fucking mess.

"I'm sorry, man," he said to Jesse.

"It's okay. I got the break I needed. And you're not gonna enjoy yourself, sitting here stressing about her. We're not getting a flight anywhere until the morning, though."

"Yeah, I know." He wanted to get back, but it wasn't even four a.m. yet and they were looking at no less than twenty-five straight hours of travel before they were back in California. He wasn't going anywhere in a hurry.

Jesse stood and clapped him on the shoulder with his massive palm. "Tell Walls silence is the plan for now and let John know what's up just so he doesn't panic."

"Okay," Sam said, trying to organize his thoughts, beyond the image of Amanda's smile he often brought to mind.

"You're really into her?" Jesse asked.

"Yeah, I am. It's still new but—" Sam swallowed not shocked by what he was feeling now that he knew Amanda was okay. "I'm falling in love with her."

"I could hear it in your voice."

Sam watched his brother as he went back to his room, feeling like there was something he should say. "You'll get there one day," he called after him.

"I doubt it, but thanks for keeping hope alive," Jesse said, before the door separating their rooms snicked closed behind him.

Sam got back in bed and shot John a quick email, letting him know that he and Amanda were in fact a thing, but no comment was the stance for now. Not a minute later his phone vibrated with his agent's response.

Sounds good. Hope to meet her sometime. Looks like a sweet girl. We'll talk when you're back.

With that he felt like he should have some peace of mind, but he stared up at the ceiling, his mind scrolling through that TMZ article over and over again. He'd never been an object of gossip before. Not like this. Now he knew that he hated it and he hated it even more for Amanda.

He'd wanted to be an actor since he was a kid. He knew the shitty parts of fame that came along with it and he knew the Oscar win and the press surrounding it would put him out there in ways no one in his family but his grandmother had experienced. He was still processing the exposure and what it meant for himself and his career, what parts to skip over and ignore and what moments to embrace and put toward his personal growth.

He'd been working toward this and been trained for this for years and for him it was still a mindfuck. Amanda wanted none of it, but she wanted him and if he was going to be the right man for her, he had to do everything in his power to protect her.

Amanda had no idea how long thirty-six hours was until she spent twenty-four of those hours being part of the entertainment news cycle. She'd spent most of the day with Helene while Ignacio went out to a last-minute meeting at the studio, but when he came back she figured she'd imposed on the newlyweds' hospitality enough. Helene made her promise she'd call or come back over if she changed her mind. She almost made her promise to take her up on her offer for any and all assistance, both personally and professionally.

She'd spent most of the night ignoring texts and then flat-out blocking numbers. When Dru made a point to send her screenshots of several of Twitter's cruelest tweets regarding her physical appearance and clear gold-digging status, she decided it was time to block Dru's number. She'd ordered takeout she knew she shouldn't spend money on, then after checking in with her mom, she'd made a nice blanket fort for herself and cried herself to sleep.

In the morning, though, she felt oddly revived. Rage energized her and helped her realize that Dru might be an unbelievable asshole, but it had forced her to do the thing she should have done long ago.

She pulled up her spec script for *Banker Down*. It was old, several seasons old, but there was good stuff there. Her parents and her hometown were waiting for her and while she was still a whole day away from getting to see Sam, she was certain of one thing: She wasn't ready to give up on her professional dreams just yet. For the rest of the day she binged the pilot of every sci-fi, fantasy, thriller, and paranormal show she could find online, and then that night, after another overpriced delivery, she started writing.

Amanda followed Sam's directions and pulled into the guest space under his condo. She entered the code at the elevator up to his place. They'd been in touch as he traveled back to the States, then back to California, and decided it would be best for them to meet at his place. The closet Amanda called home wasn't suitable for guests, and if this conversation got even more sad and depressing, they didn't need the audience of Sam's family checking in on them at the ranch. If he decided to cut her loose she'd send them all an apology for getting Sam mixed up with Dru's dramatic shit. She knew he didn't blame her, but she knew how this all looked from the outside and as far as they knew the one common denominator was her.

When the elevator chimed, announcing she'd arrived at his floor, it struck her just how completely wrung out she felt. When she wasn't crying, she was writing, and when she wasn't writing, she was stressing herself to the point of exhaustion trying to imagine how this conversation with Sam was going to go. After the initial panic, reality settled in. If she and Sam decided to stay together, large-scale public scrutiny would be a part of her life. She was strong, but she didn't know if she was that strong.

She didn't know how to feel when she saw him leaning against his doorway. She swallowed and matched the hesitant smile that stretched across his face as she made her way down the hall. The last few days made it pretty clear, but the emotions warring in her were proof that life wasn't fair. She walked up to him, forcing her hands to stay by her sides.

"Good to see you, Cha-Cha."

"Likewise, Tex."

"Come on in."

"Thanks." Amanda slipped by him as he held the door open for her. She couldn't help but brush his bicep as she went by. He followed, letting the door close behind them. She looked around, thinking of how modern and sterile white this place was compared to his grandmother's palatial home. It made sense for a young, single guy who had suddenly added a lot more zeroes to his checks. But it wasn't Sam. The white paint and the gray furniture lacked his warmth. The black-and-white art on his walls, while gorgeous, lacked his joy. No wonder he went back to Charming every chance he got.

"You're not here much, are you?" she asked as she turned to face him. She instantly forgot her own question when she saw the look on his face. It was close to the same look he gave her when he saw her standing in the middle of that hotel room in nothing but a towel. This time though, there was something more behind it. More heat. More care. More need. She was powerless against that look.

"I am here to have a very important, very adult conversation about our future, our mutual expectations, how I can issue a formal apology to your family, especially your grandmother, but right now all I can think about is the way you're looking at me and how much I missed you and how a good, dirty make out session that leads to the bedroom is what I really need," she blurted out.

"You don't owe my family an apology. They aren't upset with you. We should definitely talk about our expectations and our future. I'm hoping that conversation involves whether you wanna have kids and where you think is the best place to honeymoon."

Amanda laughed *and* kinda hoped he was only joking a little.

"We can definitely move things to my bedroom, but I wanna check in with you first. Are you okay?"

"No," she said honestly. "Are you? Your privacy was violated by a madwoman with an unearned grudge."

Sam chuckled a bit, then held out his hand as he nodded toward the gray sectional in the middle of the living room. "Come sit down." Amanda joined him on the couch, resisting the urge to climb into his lap so she could soak up all his warmth and maybe kiss him a little.

"Helene said the same thing, that I didn't do anything wrong, but I shouldn't have told Dru about us. When she asked, actually, when she demanded that I set you two up, I saw red. Literal red. I had no idea what jealousy meant until that moment."

"Oh yeah?"

"Yeah. I just—I still can't decide what hurts more. That I care what strangers are saying about me or the fact that I actually trusted Dru. I knew what she was like, but something in my head made me think I was somehow exempt from her poison. It was too much to think of her trying to use me to spread that shit. She had no idea how much I care about you. And this might sound how it's going to sound, but I hated the idea of her hurting you, but I also hated the idea that she thought she was good for you. Like she's what you need."

"I appreciate that, Cha-Cha, but what about what you need?"

"Well. For now I need a job. Helene said she would

make up a job for me and put me on her and Ignacio's in-house staff payroll for a year."

"That sounds great."

"It was very kind of her, but I can't do that."

"Why not?"

"'Cause I don't want it to impact our friendship. What if I—"

"What? What if you take advantage of Helene's kindness? Try and sleep with Ignacio? Sell stories about them to the tabloids?"

"Yeah, you know me."

"Exactly. You wouldn't do that to Helene 'cause you're actually a good person and you're a good friend. Someone tried to hurt you and me, and you didn't try and scramble and point fingers, you're sitting here thinking about my family and how they are handling this. You're not Dru. You're the most beautiful woman in the world—"

"Don't tell Twitter that."

"Actually . . ."

"Actually what?" Amanda asked as Sam pulled his phone out of his back pocket.

"I have a little something to show you. While Twitter is a garbage heap of a garbage fire, I found that you and I have a solid number of people who support our undeniable love." Sam made a dramatic show of clearing his throat. "'Starting the Protect Amanda McQueen at All Cost prayer circle. Who's with me?' There are four hundred responses, about ninety-eight percent positive."

"What about the other two percent."

"Bots. Russian bots. I'm sure of it, but wait. There's more. 'Wow. I didn't know who Sam Pleasant was until about twenty minutes ago, but he's fine and he clearly has taste.' There's a picture of us both. Several people agree with this assessment. There are more tweets about you crushing people with your ample thighs, but some of them were a little much and then I started getting jealous."

"That's so sweet," Amanda laughed.

"Oh, there's more. 'Um, Amanda McQueen is stunning. Can you say cheekbones? Yas, bitch. Get your man.' There are a lot of tweets making it clear that I am the type of man people think you should have."

"I guess the Internet isn't all bad."

"It's not." He took a deep breath. "This is life now, Cha-Cha. For all of us. People have their opinions and twenty-four hours to just spew them out into the ether, but that doesn't change the way I feel about you and I hope it doesn't change the way you feel about me."

"It does though."

Sam's eyebrows shot up as his chest sank. "Oh yeah? Okay."

"This all felt too good to be true from the very beginning. A nobody assistant dating an Oscar winner—"

"Nah, that's not gonna work."

"Oh."

"You're more than just your job. We're not going to sit here and act like you're less-than 'cause your career isn't going the way you thought it would. Remember when we were sitting at my grandmother's table and you were telling me how lucky I am to take risks because I have this amazing safety net?"

"Yeah?"

"Well, you know what I'm looking at right now? The catch of the day."

"What?" Amanda burst out laughing. "That doesn't make one damn lick of sense."

"I know. It sounded way better in my head. I know you

don't want to lean on me and Helene, but I'm saying this right now, not as the man who is going to dick up and down as soon as we finish this conversation, but as someone who genuinely cares about you as a friend and respects you as a writer. And . . . I read your *Banker Down* spec."

"Oh God."

"Nah, oh God. It was good! And I'm saying that as a huge fan of the show and someone who reads a lot of scripts. It's damn good. So, Ms. McQueen. You have this net. You have the support. What are your dreams and how do we help you achieve them?"

Amanda took a deep breath and looked back at Sam's painfully handsome face. They'd already shared so much in such a short time. She could be honest with him. She could tell him what was really in her heart and at the top of her career bucketlist.

"I want to show-run a sci-fi series with no less than four seasons on HBO and figure out who we need to bribe to make sure it's an Emmy winner, every time."

"Four seasons on HBO and an Emmys sweep. Got it. What else?" Sam asked.

"Well, I think I need to work something out with Helene's glam squad. If I'm gonna be photographed with you I need a perfect five minutes face." Amanda paused for a moment before she reached over and took Sam's hand. She missed his smooth skin and his warm touch. She didn't want to go any longer without either in her life. "I don't want to hide anymore. Not behind Dru, not behind any job or this notion that there is no part of any spotlight for me. I have no desire to be out in front, but I want to be with you. By your side."

"I want all of that for you. I want to help make it happen if you'll let me."

Amanda couldn't speak. She'd had her parents and Helene, but it was really something to have Sam on her side. A nod of agreement would have to do. Sam moved closer, pushing his leg under hers on the couch. Amanda almost gasped as his warm fingers spread out over her thigh. She couldn't wait any longer. She leaned forward and brushed her lips against his, then again and once more until he kissed her back. His arm came around her waist and Amanda let herself lean back against the cushion, far enough for Sam to climb over her. She sighed into his mouth as he settled his weight between her hips, letting her feel every inch of his growing erection against the fabric of her jeans. Amanda broke the kiss before her body took over and she started rubbing herself along his length in a shameless display of the need fighting to get out.

She looked at him, drawing her fingers over his lightly stubbled cheek.

"Where's your cowboy hat?"

"Out at the ranch. Attracts a little too much attention on Sunset."

"That's a shame. I like you in that hat. You should keep a spare here. Warm up this place a bit."

"I think we need to get you a proper hat. Shade those beautiful eyes from the blaring sun."

"I'll need a different hat for every day," she said, biting her lip.

"A different hat for every day of the week. With boots to match," Sam replied with a smile and she knew this was it for her. It was too early to say the words out loud, but she'd found her man and she wasn't going to let him go.

Epilogue

Amanda let out several quick breaths and fought the urge to fiddle with her gown. She'd survived the hard part. She'd survived the short walk from the hotel to the luxury SUV that would take them the short drive to the Met. And the hardest part, the red carpet.

It had taken a lot of doing, but between Sam, Miss Leona, and Helene calling in a biblical amount of favors Amanda had been outfitted with a once-in-a-lifetime ensemble. A flowing gown made of royal blue, bright red, and sunny yellow, complete with a gem-encrusted cape with a train that felt three blocks long. She'd ditched that heavy-ass garment as soon as possible, but from the moment she'd taken Sam's hand and stepped down from the high luxury car, she knew they'd both pulled it off. A handsome prince with his own waist-length red cape, and Amanda, his Snow White.

Her glam squad had finished the look with a full Fenty face, complete with blood red lipstick and false eyelashes that practically brushed her forehead. Her phone was tucked in an apple-shaped clutch covered in bright red Swarovski crystals. Daryl, Miss Leona's wig technician, had crafted a bob lace front of beautiful white ringlets instead of Snow White's signature soft black curls and installed the unit with such precision that when Amanda finally looked in the mirror, she had to remind herself shocking bright white hair wasn't naturally growing from her head. The red bow in her hair was lined with wire to keep its arches and knot in perfect place.

"True Love" was the theme and Sam had always planned on going as a Disney prince in search of his princess. When Evie pointed out that Sam's look was actually for Prince Florian and not Prince Charming, their decision was made for them. Besides, sending Amanda as a plus-size Cinderella felt a little too on the nose.

She'd listened to every single one of Helene's tips, not smiling as she turned this way and that to be photographed as Sam and their handlers helped her and her mile-long cape up the red carpet and up the Met stairs. She snuck a look at her phone just as they sat down to dinner and finally felt her natural smile spread across her face as no fewer than four celebrity sites had already named her and Sam the best dressed of the evening.

The last few months had been an absolute whirlwind. She and Sam had holed up in his condo for two days before they both had to get back to work. The studio was interested in Sam's interest in *Black Death,* and Amanda?

She had to get back to her writing. She'd talked things out with Helene and instead of putting her on a fake payroll, the two of them had started working on a new pilot together. Female bounty hunters falling in love and fighting their way through space. Ignacio had loved Amanda's initial pitch and he'd decided to option the idea, giving her the funds she needed to stay afloat and keep her place for the time being. Anytime she was having any hesitations about accepting their support neither of them would let a second pass without reminding her they hadn't gotten to where they were without help. It was best to just embrace it and chase her dreams with all her heart.

When Helene was due back to set for her next shoot, Miss Leona had stepped up and gotten Amanda an invite to the *Rory's War* writers' room. For the last two weeks she'd been shadowing the showrunner's assistant. It was a medical drama, not science fiction, but it was a primetime show on a major network, with an A-list cast and a massive budget. She knew enough about set life from working with Dru, but things were so different on this side of the process. She'd already learned so much and every night she found herself aching to get back to her own writing, just imagining what it would be like to see her own characters playing out her stories on the screen.

And then there was Sam. And a special horse named Majesty. They'd spent every weekend they could at the ranch, and eventually Amanda started to ride the beautiful black horse. She wouldn't say she was an expert, but each time she felt more and more comfortable in the saddle. She loved taking morning rides with Sam, following him down the easy trails as he led them on Bam Bam. She didn't realize how quiet and peaceful Charming could be. How much of a relief it was to have that time together to just unplug and take in the scenery. They talked endlessly about work, new shows and books they wanted to share with each other. Sam was teaching her all kinds of stuff about the ranch, his former life in the rodeo, and, of course, horses. He'd read all her scripts, giving her amazing feedback, encouraging her to keep going and keep producing her best work.

After they'd officially stepped out for a double lunch date

with Helene and Ignacio, holding hands as they entered the fancy lunch spot in Santa Monica, there had been another wave of Internet attention, but this time Amanda was prepared for it. Mostly she knew to ignore it. It didn't stop the random asshole from leaving a cruel comment here or sending a mean tweet there, but none of that mattered, because she still had her parents' unconditional love. And Sam and the whole Pleasant family had her back. It was still a shock to see her picture with the occasional headline. But that shock couldn't come close to the pure rush of happiness she felt whenever she was in Sam's arms.

She'd found herself a damn good boyfriend.

She blew out another short breath, then looked over to catch Sam looking at her with that gorgeous smile. He leaned over and whispered in her ear.

"How are you holding up, Cha-Cha?"

"Good," she replied, matching his grin.

"Did I mention how beautiful you look right now?"

"Oh, I know I look good, Tex." She glanced at his lips, wishing she could kiss him, but she didn't want to flirt with the idea of smearing her lipstick all over him. He looked down at her lips in kind, sliding his hand across her satin-covered thigh.

"Later, baby. I promise. I'll make it worth your wait."

"Oh, I know you will," she whispered back.

"McQueen?" Amanda looked up as Helene nodded toward the entrance to the ballroom. "Ladies?"

"Oh yeah. I'll come with." She squeezed Sam's hand before she stood up. "I'll be right back."

They made their way across the dining room to the ladies' restroom just as a wave of people emptied out of the space. They'd probably just missed some great restroom gossip. Amanda gathered up her dress and successfully used the facilities before she stepped back out to the sinks to wash her hands and check that her makeup was still in place.

Amanda reached under her gown for one quick adjustment of her Spanx, turning as she heard a woman farther down the sinks gasp. She looked up and saw Rina, one of her favorite pop singers, standing by the hand dryers gawking at Amanda's feet.

"Oh my God. Are you wearing cowboy boots?"

"Yeah," Amanda laughed. The gown and the cape were so long and her boobs were pushed so high up to her chin, she figured she was owed one bit of comfort for the evening. She'd gone back to one of Sam's favorite suppliers, the Country General Store in the valley, and picked out a comfortable hand-stitched pair in ice blue. They fit like a dream. While other women were ready to ditch their heels, her feet were the last thing she'd been thinking about.

"Fucking amazing," Rina replied.

"I'm digging the nun getup, but I'm a little lost on the theme." Amanda had seen Rina and Kata, the other half of their pop duo, making the rounds earlier in their matching embroidered habits.

"There's no greater love than my love for the Lord," Rina said, clasping a rosary in her hands as she bowed her head deeply.

"Amazing and kinda blasphemous. I'm here for it."

"Thank you. You seriously look amazing. And those titties! They are sitting, girl."

Amanda looked down at her cleavage, which had attracted a lot of attention during the night. She didn't mind though 'cause she was mostly focused on the look of lust in Sam's eyes whenever he glanced her way. She knew she was in for a *great* time as soon as they got back to the hotel. She stuck a finger between her breasts, giving them a little jiggle. "I should have hidden some snacks in there."

"Ugh, for real. All this damn fabric and I forgot to line the pockets with candy or a turkey sandwich. We're getting pizza as soon as this thing is over. Whatever they are about to feed us will not be enough."

"So are we!" Helene yelled from the stall.

"Love it. See you back out there," Rina said with a smile before she twirled around and headed for the door. She stopped short just as she almost bumped into the next woman entering the restroom. Amanda tensed as Dru walked past Rina without a hint of an excuse-me. Dru almost skidded to a halt as soon as she saw Amanda. She was wearing a skintight, knee length leather dress with a red heart stitched over her chest. Her hair was pulled back in a severe braid that was draped over her shoulder. She looked amazing if not uncomfortable as hell. Amanda almost wondered how she was going to hike the full-body condom up so she could use the bathroom.

A moment of tense silence filled the air and the distance between them. Amanda knew what was coming. A rude comment about her weight or her dress or her hair. How silly she and Sam looked? How foolish? Who did they think they were? But just as Dru fixed her mouth to spew her venom, a toilet flushed and then another. Amanda realized she simply couldn't hear her over the layered sounds of rushing water.

"Girl," Helene said as she stepped out of the stall. "Empire waist everything. This dress is comfortable as fuck." She and Ignacio had come as Romeo and Juliet, and Helene looked beyond stunning in her light, flowy gown that did amazing things for her breasts. She stepped to the sink doing a double take as she spotted Dru still seething near the door. Helene scoffed and went back to washing her hands. She dried them, then turned to Amanda as more women filtered in and out of the room.

"Ready?"

"Yup."

They pushed past Dru and out the door without a word or another look in her direction. They eventually made their way back to their seats, but not before Helene graciously introduced Amanda to a number of friends and VIPs she had yet to meet. It took some getting used to, hearing Helene introduce her as an up-and-coming screenwriter, but she forced herself to smile and accept her kind words, dressing for the job she wanted, taking on the title with pride, if not a bit of terror. She'd get there one day. She could do it.

Sam stood and pulled out her chair for her, helping her get her gown back under the table. "All good?" he asked, gently running his fingers over the back of her neck once she was settled in. Yeah, she was definitely going to put it on him the first chance she got.

"Never better."

Don't miss Zach and Evie's story in

A COWBOY TO REMEMBER

Available now
And keep an eye out for

JESSE'S STORY

Coming soon
From Rebekah Weatherspoon
And Kensington Books

Connect with

Visit us online at
KensingtonBooks.com
to read more from your favorite authors, see books
by series, view reading group guides, and more.

for sneak peeks, chances to win books and prize packs,
and to share your thoughts with other readers.

facebook.com/kensingtonpublishing
twitter.com/kensingtonbooks

Tell us what you think!

To share your thoughts, submit a review,
or sign up for our eNewsletters, please visit:
KensingtonBooks.com/TellUs.